Garters and Spurs

DeLORAS SCOTT

Harlequin Books

TORONTO • NEW YORK • LONDON
AMSTERDAM • PARIS • SYDNEY • HAMBURG
STOCKHOLM • ATHENS • TOKYO • MILAN
MADRID • WARSAW • BUDAPEST • AUCKLAND

Harlequin Historicals first edition July 1993

ISBN 0-373-28779-8

GARTERS AND SPURS

"For someone your size, you certainly don't make any bones about tangling with a rattlesnake, do you, Miss Carter?"

For the first time, Sara realized she just might be in deep trouble. The civilized mask Fargo had worn since she'd first met him had been peeled away by his anger, leaving deadly eyes and a hard, cold mouth. "Then you'll fight him?"

"I'll fight him. But if you're ever inclined to bargain with my life again, check with me first."

"There won't be a next time," Sara retorted. "If there is, I'll ask. That is, if you still have a life to bargain with."

Fargo hooked his arm over the saddle horn. "You know, Miss Carter, I sincerely hope the other ladies in Tombstone are less sassy than you."

"I'm sure they are," Sara replied sweetly. "But they're not nearly as interesting."

Dear Reader,

Welcome to another great month of Harlequin Historicals. These four selections are guaranteed to add spice to your summer reading list.

Garters and Spurs, from popular author DeLoras Scott, is the tale of Fargo Tanner and his search for the man who killed his brother. But when clues lead him to lovely Sara Carter, Fargo finds himself doubting his intentions.

In the last installment of the TEXAS series, Ruth Langan tells the story of *Texas Hero* Thad Conway, an ex-gunslinger who just wants to run his own ranch—alone. But prim schoolmarm Caroline Adams is determined to change his mind.

When impoverished Sir Giles of Rathborne hatches a scheme to enrich his coffers in *The Cygnet* by Marianne Willman, he turns a young bandit into a missing heiress and falls under her spell.

As a secondary character in *Sweet Seduction,* the first book in the NORTH POINT series, Barbara Johnson was a woman of exceptional courage and depth. Now, in *Sweet Sensations,* author Julie Tetel gives Barbara her own story in which she enters into a bargain with a mysterious drifter in order to keep her family safe.

July also marks the release of our Western short-story collection—*Untamed—Maverick Hearts* with stories by Heather Graham Pozzessere, Joan Johnston and Patricia Potter. Whether you like reading on the beach or by the pool, Harlequin Historicals offers four great books each month to be enjoyed all year round!

Sincerely,

Tracy Farrell
Senior Editor

Books by DeLoras Scott

Harlequin Historicals

Bittersweet #12
Fire and Ice #42
The Miss and the Maverick #52
Rogue's Honor #123
Springtown #151
Garters and Spurs #179

Harlequin Books

Historical Christmas Stories 1991
"Fortune's Gift"

DeLORAS SCOTT

was raised in Sutter's Mill, California—an area steeped in history. At one time it was gold country, and the legacy of wagon trains, cowboys and miners has remained. It's no wonder she enjoys writing about a chapter of history referred to as the Old West.

Prologue

The Arizona Territory, 1875

Sara Carter lay on her back in the hayloft, inhaling the sweet, musty aromas and studying the cobwebs in the rafters. A smile tickled the corners of her mouth as she mused over her craftiness at getting out of her chores. A feat she was seldom fortunate enough to accomplish. But as luck would have it, her mother thought she was at the corral helping her father and brothers with the wild mustangs they'd brought in a week ago, and her father would be too busy to give it any thought.

Thinking about her two older sisters, Megan and Joan, Sara giggled softly. Though still morning, the weather was already indicating another unbearably hot day. She could easily picture the sweat accumulating beneath their sunbonnets and the damp streaks on their faded work dresses as they hoed the garden behind the house. They deserved it. They were always making remarks about how she acted more like a boy than a girl. Sara assured herself that they were just jealous because she was the prettiest of the lot. And though they considered her skinny and the baby of the family at fourteen, she could still ride and shoot better than either of them. It was an accomplishment she was quite proud of, even if they weren't.

Hearing the thud of horses' hooves striking the ground, Sara wondered who the unexpected visitors were. Maybe it was the cavalry, checking to be sure all was well. Or, better yet, Apaches. They had always fascinated her.

Curiosity getting the better of her, Sara sat up and peeked through a crack between the wooden slats of the barn. Squinting into the bright sunlight, she could barely make out four riders, cast in dark silhouettes and headed for the house. She saw her mother step through the doorway to greet the visitors, the hot breeze causing her flaming red hair to blow into her face.

Sara plopped back down. The men had probably come to purchase cattle. Having lost interest, she scooted her slender body around in the loose hay until she was comfortable again, paying scant attention to her long skirt, which was now scandalously hiked up well past the buttoned tops of her shoes. Satisfied, she closed her eyes, ready to take a long nap.

The sound of her mother's shrill screams and shots being fired jerked Sara straight up. Again she peeked out the crack. She could see only two of the strangers. As before, it was difficult to get a good look. In shock, her heart pounding against her breast, Sara watched a big, laughing man drag her screaming mother from the porch.

"Why you fightin' me, woman?" Sara heard him say. Then he laughed. "I'm better than that Injun you bed."

He threw the small woman to the ground; his harsh laughter rang in Sara's ears. As she anxiously waited for her father and brothers to come to the rescue, she began striking her fist against the wall, ignoring the splinters and the pain. Then she remembered the shots. Had the two other men killed her father and brothers?

Sara sucked in her breath when she saw Meg suddenly run around the side of the house, carrying a shotgun. Not bothering to take aim, Meg pulled the trigger and missed. Before she could take off running, the other man grabbed her around the waist and threw her close to where their mother lay. Tears ran down Sara's cheeks as she watched the men eagerly rip away her mother's and sister's clothing. Oh, please, God, she silently prayed, make Papa and the boys safe. Make them come help.

The missing scavengers suddenly returned, laughing and ready to partake of the entertainment. For the first time, Sara got a good look at one of them.

As if in a bad dream, Joan appeared in the doorway with a pistol, her face twisted with hate. But before she could pull the trigger, one of the men drew and shot first.

Sara's body was shaking so badly she could barely manage to get her hand to her mouth and smother her screams. She didn't want to watch what was happening to her mother and sisters, but she couldn't close her ears to their pathetic whimpers.

"Hell, Dodd," croaked the lanky man who had murdered Jane, "how many more bitches are there?"

The big one called Dodd climbed off Sara's mother, and another man took his place. "I heard tell there was four women and three men."

"We done took care of the men."

Sara now knew there would be no salvation.

"Then that leaves one female still unaccounted for." Dodd pulled up his pants and looked down at Meg. "Search the damn house." He kicked the other man off Meg and took his place.

The killer went inside. Minutes later he came back out. "Ain't no one there. I'll check the barn. Where are you, little girl?" he called in a singsong voice as he moved forward. "I got somethin' for you."

Sara squeezed her eyes shut and scooted away from the wall, her hand still clamped over her mouth to prevent any sound from escaping. She curled into a ball. She couldn't stop shaking, and though the screams had stopped coming from her loved ones, the sound continued to ring in her ears.

"I'm coming to get you."

Sara's eyes flew open when she heard the voice from below. She had to do something! Anything! She had to help her mother and sister. Still terrified, she forced herself to her feet. Taking one slow step at a time, she made her way to the edge of the loft and cautiously looked down. The spindly man was almost directly below her, drinking from a whiskey bottle. Frantically, she glanced around the loft until she spied the pitchfork several feet away. She stepped back and out of sight. With a sinking heart, she watched the dirt and hay filter through the cracks between the floor boards underfoot.

"So that's where you are," the man said in that sickening singsong voice. "Get ready, 'cause I'm aimin' to join you."

Sara heard glass crash. He must have tossed the whiskey bottle aside. Knowing he couldn't see her, she grabbed the pitchfork. As he moved toward the ladder, so did she. Her fear had somehow turned to cold hatred and a need for revenge. She was standing only a foot from the top of the ladder when she heard him start his climb. Holding the pitchfork in readiness, she waited. As soon as his head popped up, Sara brought the pitchfork forward with all her might, embedding the long, sharp tines deep in his pockmarked face and neck. Even as he fell, she was already starting to climb down.

The moment Sara's feet touched the hard earth, she looked about, desperately searching for something she could use to protect her family from the invading vermin. Her gaze suddenly came to rest on a rifle leaning against a bale of hay. The man she'd just killed must have left it there. She snatched it up and checked to make sure it was loaded.

Sara left the barn, holding the rifle at her side. As soon as she saw the men, she began pumping the lever and pulling the trigger. The men were taken off guard. She killed two of them, and wounded the third, but he managed to get onto his horse and ride away. He was the leader of the group, the big one named Dodd, whose face would forever be embedded in her mind.

Though everything had happened in a relatively short period of time, to Sara it had seemed like a lifetime.

Chapter One

Southern Texas, 1881

Thomas Logan Tanner owned an empire with enough cattle, land and money to earn any man's respect. Even at fifty-five, he was someone no man dared cross—until now. A deep, unfamiliar anguish sliced through him like a hot blade. He raised a big, gnarled fist and brought it down hard on an end table. The Mexican pot sitting on top of it fell and shattered, breaking the silence.

"Coop said you wanted to see me."

Startled, Tom jerked around and stared at the man who had entered the room. Seeing the cold, uncaring expression on his son's face was all it took for Tom to regain his composure and hide the deep hurt he was feeling. Every time he looked at Fargo, it was as if he'd stepped back in time. Fargo was the spitting image of him nearly thirty years ago. "Where the hell have you been? In town with some whore? It's been over three hours since I sent Coop to find you."

Their cobalt-blue eyes locked in a silent battle of wills.

"What do you want, Pa?" Fargo finally asked, refusing to answer the questions. "I got things to do."

"Jude's been murdered. Not that you probably give a damn. You always were a cold, unfeeling bastard."

Fargo's cocked smile didn't reach his eyes. "And you were a good teacher. How did my younger brother manage to get himself killed?" He pulled paper and a cloth tobacco pouch from his shirt pocket, then proceeded to roll a cigarette.

"I got a telegram from some sheriff in New Mexico saying Jude was brought in with a reward on his head. I say it's a lie, and someone murdered him. Get your gear together. I want you headed that way first thing in the morning."

"You shouldn't have sent Jude away, Pa," Fargo stated matter-of-factly.

"What the hell do you know? I had to get him away for a spell. You think I'd let a son of mine go to jail because of a little shootin' spree? If Jude is dead, I want you to find the man that did it and put the varmint six feet underground. The Tanners have always taken care of their own."

"I don't need to be reminded. In case you've forgotten, I'm a Tanner, too."

"If by some chance they got the wrong man and your brother is alive, bring him back. The marshall came by the other day to say he agrees with me that Jude was only actin' in self-defense."

Fargo, who had started to leave, turned in the doorway. "How much did that cost you? Better yet, if I do bring Jude back, how long do you plan to keep getting him out of trouble?"

"You got a short memory, boy. He hasn't done anything you didn't do when you were younger."

Fargo moved back into the room. "Oh, no. Don't try taking credit for something that didn't happen. You were never a father to me after Jude was born, and you know it." Fargo gave his father a contemptuous smile. "I took care of myself, and I sure as hell didn't have a wet nurse always getting me out of trouble."

"Get out of here. And don't come back until you've taken care of the man responsible or you've brought Jude back home alive. I don't care how long it takes."

Fargo turned and walked out of the room, leaving Tom with a strange sense of foreboding.

"Fargo?" Tom called. He received no reply. He could hear the heels of his son's boots striking hardwood steps as he ascended the wide staircase.

Weighed down with worry, Tom collapsed on the sofa. Suddenly he felt very old. What would he have said if Fargo had come back into the room? That the pain of having lost his favorite son seemed unbearable? Not hardly. Fargo would have looked on it as a sign of weakness. Tom wondered if Fargo knew of Jude's jealousy. Fargo had the strength and the looks, as well as the charm. A charm that he could lay on as thick as molasses when he saw fit. But behind all that was a heart of steel. If Fargo didn't like someone, he'd as soon shoot him as look at him. And he'd done it on more than one occasion. But Tom still hoped that, with age, Fargo would mellow and become more forgiving.

He ran his fingers through his gray-streaked hair. He and Fargo didn't share a closeness. Tom knew he hadn't done right by Fargo, but it wasn't anything he could change now. If something happened to Fargo, everything he'd accomplished would have no meaning. At least Fargo wasn't a fool. He had brains and knew how to use them. He was also the fastest draw Tom had ever seen. No question about it, Fargo was the best man to take care of the job at hand.

Tom leaned his head back and tried to relax. Everything would turn out all right. All his worrying was for nothing. The sheriff in New Mexico had to have made a mistake.

Las Cruces, New Mexico

More than one person stared openly at the stranger riding into town. The men took note of the hard set of his jaw, his cold eyes, and his handy revolver. The women thought him strikingly handsome and delightfully dangerous.

The stranger brought his horse to a halt in front of the sheriff's office, then dismounted with the litheness of one accustomed to being in the saddle. His spurs jingled as he walked through the open doorway.

"Howdy, mister. What can I do for you?" the man behind the desk asked, his tin badge proclaiming his profession.

"Came to claim Jude Tanner's body."

Sheriff Grogan's hand settled on the butt of his gun as he studied the tall intruder casting a shadow over him and his desk. His steely eyes alone were enough to make Grogan wary, and his dusty clothes and hat made it clear he'd traveled a considerable distance. "You related?"

"Name's Fargo Tanner. I'm his brother."

"How come you don't look alike?" When he received no reply, Grogan continued. "Come to take him home?"

"I want to see him first."

"I couldn't believe it when I read that telegram telling me not to have him buried." Again he waited for some kind of explanation, but Fargo Tanner was as tight-mouthed as all hell. Grogan relaxed his grip on his gun.

"Ol' Doc Bunker did a good embalming job. Your brother's at the mortician's place, straight down the road."

"Who shot him in the back?"

"In the back? He got shot right between the eyes."

"Jude was too fast a draw. He must have been waylaid."

"I didn't ask the bounty hunter any questions when he brought him in."

"What bounty hunter?"

"It's legal." He opened the drawer of the scarred desk, pulled out a poster and tossed it on top. "Look here. Five-hundred-dollar reward, dead or alive."

Fargo ignored the piece of paper. "Has the bounty hunter already picked up the reward?"

"Yep."

"What's his name, and where can I find him?"

The sheriff leaned back in his chair and propped the heel of his boots on the desk. "Well, now, that might be hard to say. He calls himself Hawk, and he keeps his identity a secret."

Fargo's lips curled into a half grin as he reached in his vest pocket, pulled out a ten dollar gold piece, and dropped it onto the desk. "Surely there must be something you've forgotten."

"Maybe there is at that." Grogan's feet hit the floor with a thud, and he snatched up the payment. Grogan bit the coin to make sure it was real. "But not much more. He wears his hat low to hide his eyes, and the bandanna over his nose covers the rest of his face. But there's a couple of ways you can spot him. He rides a mighty fine paint horse and has a mean dog that I swear's the size of a colt. Got a dark muzzle, a long tail, and he's doe-colored." He shook his head. "Never saw anything like him. I asked Hawk where he got the mutt, and he said the dog was a Dane.

Well, let me tell you, he didn't pull anything over my eyes. I knew he hadn't told the truth. Whoever heard of such a critter?''

"Does Hawk live in these parts?"

Sheriff Grogan rubbed his chin. "Maybe..."

Fargo dropped another gold piece onto the desk.

"But I don't think so. He's gotten himself quite a reputation. I've heard he's delivered outlaws to as far as Texas, and that he never fails to get his man. Always brings his captives in at night. Makes it harder to be seen, I reckon."

"He keeps busy," Fargo said. "Either that, or his reputation exceeds his ability."

The sheriff shrugged his shoulders. "Like I said, he's good. Real good. He's brought in some mighty tough men. 'Course, he's got that damn dog to help."

"Were they all dead?"

"I don't know. Why you askin'?"

"It makes sense. If they're dead, they can't identify him. Did you ever stop to think he could also have a bounty on his head?"

"Nope, I reckon I didn't." The sheriff leaned forward. "Rumor says if you want to get in touch with him, look toward Tombstone."

Fargo nodded and left. After seeing Jude's body, he sent a telegram to his father. He'd decided to have his brother buried until he could be taken home—after his murderer received his just reward.

A short time later, Sheriff Grogan stood in the doorway of his small office and watched Fargo Tanner ride out of town. Grogan never had cared for bounty hunters, and Tanner looked as if he could be a mean son of a bitch. If I'm lucky, Grogan thought, Hawk and Tanner will end up killing each other. Good riddance to both of them. He spit tobacco juice at a beetle moving along the ground, then grinned. He'd hit him dead center.

Grogan turned and went back to his desk. It didn't bother him in the least that he'd lied about Hawk. There wouldn't be money jingling in his pocket right now if he'd told Tanner he'd never heard of the bounty hunter before, and had only seen him that one time. Hell, the kid was thickheaded. He'd actually refused the reward money. Grogan had pocketed the tidy sum himself—a fact that he didn't want discovered. He chuckled at how well everything had turned out. The only reason he'd known to send Tanner to Tombstone was 'cause Hawk had said something about Tombstone to that dog as they took off. Once again, it had paid to keep his ears open.

The Arizona Territory

Fargo slowly worked his way around the large crowd of people gathered at the Schieffelin Hall ball. The affair was to celebrate the near completion of the magnificent building being built to honor Ed Schieffelin, the man who'd discovered silver back in '77. Because of that strike, the town of Tombstone had grown up out of nothing. Tombstone. A town so notorious that people back East even knew about it. But what Fargo wanted had nothing to do with Schieffelin or the town.

The center of the large room had been designated as the dancing area; hence, the crowd lingered around the outer edges. The men were dressed in fine suits, and the women who weren't talking or dancing seemed to be parading about, showing off their fancy gowns. The windows were open, but because of the lack of a breeze, the ladies' perfumes left a heady odor in the air.

Fargo had deliberately arrived late so that no one would notice him. Apparently not a wise move. The dance floor had become increasingly more crowded, and, because of the shifting bodies, his search had become an impossible task. So he'd finally picked a wall near the entrance, where he stood watching and waiting.

After he'd first arrived in Tombstone, Fargo had quickly learned of an Irishwoman by the name of Nellie Cashman. He'd heard she owned a hotel that catered to miners, and that she stayed well informed about most things going on in town. So Fargo had set about developing a friendship—not an unpleasant task, since Nellie had turned out to be a very beautiful lady.

Unfortunately, Nellie had never heard of any man called Hawk. However, she did know Sara Carter, a woman rancher who owned a dog that fit the description he'd given. She was apparently a fine, upstanding member of the community, and Nellie doubted that she would have any reason to associate with bounty hunters.

It was Nellie who had told him about the Schieffelin soiree and suggested he go, because Sara Carter was sure to be there. Fargo grinned, remembering how he'd hightailed it to Sam'l Black's Tailor Shop to get properly outfitted. His plan was simple: get Miss Carter outside, throw her on his horse, take her out in the middle of nowhere, and make her tell him who Hawk was and where he could be found. Certainly not the noble way of handling things, but what constituted a noble deed? He'd come to find the man who had shot Jude. The sooner he'd taken care of that, the sooner he could take his brother home.

Four men with well-groomed dark hair and full mustaches strolled into the room, drawing Fargo's attention, and apparently everyone else's, too, because the hall became momentarily hushed. Whispering ensued as heads turned away. Curious, Fargo looked at the older gentleman standing beside him. "Excuse me, sir, but who are those men?"

The man curled his lip. "You must be new in town. Those are the Earp brothers. Virgil, Wyatt and Morgan. The one on the end, to your right, is Doc Holliday."

"Which one's wearing the badge?"

"That's Virgil. He's the marshall. They're a bad lot, but the finer people of the town tolerate them."

"Why is that?"

"I'd hate to think what this town would be like without them. Since Virgil took over, the cowboys have learned to be on their best behavior. 'Course, the Earps collect ten percent on all the gambling in town, so they make sure everything runs as smooth as possible. I think Virgil overstepped his bounds, though, when he passed a law that says whores have to buy a license. I don't think I need tell you who pockets the money."

Fargo's interest now centered on the woman gracefully moving toward the Earps. She fit the description Nellie had given him, but he needed to be sure. "Who's the lady?" he asked, nodding his head in the woman's direction.

"That's Sara Carter. She's got a fine ranch between here and Elgin."

"Seems strange she would be on friendly terms with the likes of those men," Fargo said.

"Oh, Sara's friendly with everyone, and you'll never find a finer lady. As pretty as she is, it's hard to believe no man has gotten her to the altar. Now if I were a few years younger..." The man scratched his head. "Say, my name's...."

Fargo didn't hear the rest. He'd already moved away to get a better look at Miss Carter. She continued to move in the opposite direction. From what he could see, she certainly wasn't the prettiest female he'd ever laid eyes on. She looked of a matronly sort, with her auburn hair pulled tight into a bun on top of her head. Friendly or not, why would she want to join a group of men whose reputations had spread all the way to Texas?

As Fargo weaved his way toward the notorious gunfighters, he began to get a better look at Miss Carter. A woman far too thin for his taste. And, though her apricot-silk gown draped loosely across the bodice, it failed to hide her lack of a full, ripe bosom. He preferred a woman with plenty of meat on her bones. A woman he didn't have to worry about not being able to handle a night of unrestrained passion. He chuckled. Miss Carter looked like the type who would pass out cold if a man so much as touched her.

Fargo managed to position himself behind and a little to the left of Doc Holliday. Now he could look directly at his objective. Miss Carter proved to be considerably younger than he'd thought. She glided to a stop in front of the men, her lips already spread into a smile. It was a vivacious smile that carried total amusement with it, and completely transformed her looks. Large, warm green eyes fringed with thick dark lashes dominated her face. She had high, delicate cheekbones, a straight, almost perky nose and full lips. Though too thin, and definitely lacking in desirable female attributes, Sara Carter had a face few men would be apt to forget. She was indeed a rare beauty.

Without warning, Sara Carter suddenly shifted her gaze from the gunfighter dressed in black to Fargo. Fargo nodded, but she offered no sign of acknowledgment. Not even a long eyelash fluttered. After a brief study of him, she returned her attention to her friend. A moment later she was led onto the dance floor by Doc Holliday. And the older gentleman had told him she was friendly with every-

one? Fargo shook his head in amusement. Apparently her
friendliness didn't extend to strangers, he mused.

The gunslingers left some fifteen minutes later, and the
hostile attitude of the crowd seemed to dissipate. Fargo
grinned inwardly. He had a sneaky hunch the boys enjoyed stirring up trouble, which was probably the only
reason they'd arrived in the first place. And Miss Carter
probably felt the same way. That would explain her grin
when she'd first approached the small group.

For an hour, Fargo moved about the hall, keeping a low
profile. He talked to men about local outlaws and bounty
hunters, but he didn't get the answers he wanted. During
the time he spent socializing, he also kept an eye on the
auburn-haired woman, who continued to enjoy herself on
the dance floor.

As he finished off a cup of watered-down punch, Fargo
contemplated his position. When he'd left Texas, he hadn't
planned on being gone but three months. Now he was
having second thoughts. It hadn't occurred to him that the
man he'd be looking for might keep his identity a secret.
It now looked as if locating him would prove to be more
difficult than he'd anticipated. And his original plan, to
ride off with Sara Carter and scare the hell out of her, carried little weight. She had too many friends. Fargo released a sigh of resignation. Miss Carter appeared to be his
only possible source of information. If he played his cards
right, maybe she'd invite him to the Bar C Ranch. He
wanted to see her dog.

Sara stood off to the side with her two closest friends,
discussing the man who had been watching her the greater
part of the evening. A prickling sensation on the back of
her neck had alerted her to his scrutiny. She'd first noticed the gentleman while she was talking to Doc Holli-

day. Even then, she'd felt a strong sense of wariness. Now he just stood off to the side, blatantly watching her, looking as if he were in deep thought.

"This whole thing is unnerving," Sara commented. "If the biddies about wouldn't condemn me, I'd go over and find out why he keeps staring at me."

"How could you even consider such a thing, Sara?" Rose Halverson exclaimed. "No lady of quality would be about to do such a thing."

"I wonder who he is?" the young widow Penelope Stewart crooned. "If I had seen him around town, I would have remembered. I think you should be flattered, Sara. He's obviously attracted to you. Just look at those shoulders.... Though I must admit he looks a bit lanky. Maybe it's the suit he's wearing. I wonder if he's Spanish."

"He's too tall," Sara countered. "I've never liked tall men. I'm constantly having to crane my neck to see their faces."

"He looks like the brooding type to me," Rose added. She flipped her fan open and began waving it in front of her face. "And dangerous. He's not the sort of man you should be around, Sara."

"Really, Rose, you sound like some old married woman. That's exactly what makes him so exciting," Penelope persisted.

"I *am* a married woman, Penelope," Rose reminded the widow. "Cyrus may not be dashing or dangerous, but at least I know he'll come home every night."

Penelope's full lips spread into a wide smile. "I do believe all of our questions are about to be answered, ladies. The *dangerous Spaniard* is headed in our direction."

Sara looked up and watched the man approaching from the other side of the hall. He had a certain grace to his stride, which, for some unknown reason, reminded her of a black swan. Contrary to what Penelope had said, in her estimation he wasn't handsome, at least not in a pretty sense, like some of the men she knew. On the other hand, he wasn't a man that women would fail to notice. He absolutely reeked of masculinity. She liked his thick black hair, which had been properly trimmed, but, then again, she'd always been more attracted to dark men than light. He wore a white, crisply starched shirt, and his black vest, trousers and waistcoat were impeccable.

As if he could read her thoughts, his eyes suddenly locked with hers and Sara felt as if she'd been submerged in liquid silver. Even though he was still halfway across the room, the heat that he emanated was unbelievable. It would be very easy to fall prey to those smoldering eyes and fine masculine looks. As he drew closer, he flashed a dazzling smile that took Sara completely off guard. My Lord, she thought, with all that charm, the man could probably coax blood from a stone! When he stopped in front of her, Sara couldn't think of a thing to say.

"Excuse my boldness, Miss Carter, but would you allow me the pleasure of a dance? The name's Fargo Tan—Tucker, and I'm new in town."

Sara's sixth sense told her to refuse. But the attraction she felt could not be denied. "Thank you, Mr. Tucker. The least I can do is welcome a stranger to Tombstone." She felt his broad grin all the way to her toes.

He offered his arm, then led her onto the dance floor. From a distance, his eyes had appeared to be black. Instead, they were a deep blue. And he definitely wasn't Spanish. His dark skin came from having spent many hours in the sun. "How long have you been in town, Mr. Tucker?" *Why do I sound so calm?*

"I just rode in a couple of days ago. Nellie Cashman suggested I attend. She thought it would be an excellent opportunity for me to meet ranchers."

"Oh? And have you?"

"No."

"Are you one of Nellie's boarders?" Sara asked as she was pulled into a pair of strong arms and skillfully guided in time to the music.

"No, I'm staying at the San Jose House. We just happened to meet one day and became friends."

"How did you know my name?" *He even smelled good.*

"I asked."

"I'm flattered."

Fargo chuckled. "I guess I've really made a fool of myself. I saw you and the other women talking about me."

"I apologize for our rude manners. Actually, we were debating about why you've been staring at me all evening."

"I'm the one who should be apologizing. I do believe you've mesmerized me with your beauty."

Sara was taken aback by the statement. It seemed such an intimate thing to say, considering they had just met. "That's quite a compliment."

"I've been standing around trying to get up the nerve to ask you to dance. I figured that since we hadn't been properly introduced, you'd turn me down."

"Believe me, it's a pleasure to dance with a gentleman who knows how to keep his feet moving in time with the music. What brought you to Tombstone, Mr. Tucker?"

"Cattle. I own a big spread in Texas, and I'm checking out the possibility of starting another one in this area. I plan on making comparisons of the quality of beef the area is producing. Tomorrow I'm riding out to see Ed Harris."

"I know Ed well. I also know he wants to sell his spread. Are you thinking about buying it?"

"I want to look at some of the other ranches before making my decision."

Sara knew Ed needed the money badly. Between the border gangs, the Mexicans and the Chiricahua, he'd lost about everything he owned that stood on four legs, and he couldn't afford to hire hands. Ed and his family were good people, so Sara decided to try to give them a hand with the sale. Besides, it would also give her a chance to see Mr. Tucker again. "There are some very prosperous ranches around, including mine."

Never missing a step, Fargo leaned back and looked down at the petite woman. "Surely you're teasing me?" he asked with the proper inflection of surprise. "You're so young, I assumed you still live with your family. I can't even picture a lady like you riding a horse across the range. No, I think a carriage would be more your style."

Sara laughed. "I'm not that young, and women out here learn to ride at an early age. My parents are dead, and I can assure you I'm equally capable of running a ranch. You know, it isn't just the land you have to consider."

"Are you referring to the breed of cattle?"

Sara decided the warning she had been about to give might scare him off. She settled for a milder approach. "This is open range, and a man has to know how to protect his land and stock. Why don't you come to the Bar C Wednesday morning? My cattle boss can show you around. You might even consider staying for supper to sample the end result."

Fargo smiled. "I'll be looking forward to it."

So will I, Sara thought.

The music stopped, and Fargo led Sara back to her friends. After introductions were made, Fargo excused himself and left the hall. He'd accomplished what he'd set out to do.

Penelope rolled her eyes. "I don't believe it. He's even better looking up close."

"Why had he been staring at you, Sara?" Rose asked.

"He said he was admiring my beauty."

The corners of Penelope's penetrating eyes crinkled with delight. "Rose, is it possible a man has just stepped into our Sara's life?"

Sara shook her head in denial. "Don't look so concerned, Rose. He isn't the type of man I'm attracted to. Too tall. However, there's nothing dangerous about him. As a matter of fact, I do believe he's shy."

Both women looked at Sara as if she'd lost her mind.

"Sara," Penelope whispered, "you *can't* be that naive!"

Chapter Two

Sara let the horse continue to move the buggy at a leisurely pace as they traveled down the long stretch of dirt road that crossed the wide, rolling valley. What with the surrounding mountains, she felt as if she were the only being on earth. The rooster tail of flying dust kicked up by the buggy wheels was the only thing to herald her existence. Ahead were the Whetstone Mountains, full of caves, hidden springs and rattlesnakes. Sara knew from experience that when cattle got lost in those mountains it was often years before they were seen again. When found, they were walleyed from having gone so long without seeing a human being.

Because of the varying shapes of the mountains, the Apache had a name for each one. But ever since childhood she had applied her own names. One she called Prayer Mountain because it reminded her of two monks with their heads bowed in prayer, and another she called Camelback because it looked like a camel's back.

Sara unbuttoned the top three buttons of her yellow town suit, welcoming the feel of the slight breeze against her bare skin. As always, she felt a fierce sense of pride as she looked out across the miles of land covered with grass, mesquite, low bush, scatterings of elm and clusters of salt

cedar that, when in bloom, reminded her of pink cobwebs. This was her land, stretching from the San Pedro
River to the Whetstones. Though she had enjoyed her
week in Tombstone, knowing she would soon be home
made her feel good, as always. For six years she'd fought
and worked as hard as any man, and now she had a cattle
ranch even her father would have been proud of. Of
course, discovering a silver mine on the land had helped.
But none of it had come easy. Now she and her sister Megan were wealthy enough to enjoy the comforts that labor
had produced.

But there were always concerns lurking in the back of
her mind. What would happen if or when the Apache
leader, Azul, died? Or what if the renegade Geronimo and
his followers decided to attack the ranch? Because of her
orders not to fire on an Apache, her family and men were
vulnerable. Too vulnerable. And though she'd met many
fine Apache, there were always those she'd rather stay
away from—just as with white people. And then there were
the Clantons, who were always looking to grab some free
cattle. Beef brought a good price in Mexico, and there were
no questions asked about where the cattle came from.

Sara suddenly brought the horse to a halt. Up ahead, a
small band of mounted Apache had blocked the road.
Worried that they might be unfriendly, she tightened her
fingers on the revolver hidden in the folds of her skirt. As
soon as she saw Azul sitting quietly among them, she relaxed. To Sara, the man's lined face seemed a contradic-
tion to his alert black eyes. His age was undeterminable,
but he had to be well along in years. A colorful cotton
headband circled his forehead, and, like the younger
braves, he wore a faded shirt, pants and knee-high moc-
casins.

Sara flicked the reins to move her horse forward. She knew Azul to be wise but wily—very little escaped his attention. He also had the unnerving habit of appearing seemingly out of nowhere.

As the buggy drew closer to the small group, Sara's horse began tossing his head and snorting. Realizing that the gelding was ready to bolt, she tightened her grip on the reins. But one of the braves grabbed the harness, preventing the horse from going anywhere.

"Welcome, Azul." Sara greeted in his native tongue, for the man spoke little English.

"Greetings, Hair of Fire. It has been many moons."

"Too many, my friend. Are your people doing well?"

"Not as long as Mexico pays a bounty for our scalps and the white eyes send us to the San Carlos Reservation," Azul said. "The mountains are our home, not the desert."

"If the Chiricahua are hungry, you know my cattle are yours."

"It is not enough."

"What more can I do?" Sara asked.

"You can do nothing." Azul looked up at the clear blue sky. "The days pass quickly now, and the time soon approaches when I will join my ancestors."

Sara doubted that; she suspected it was a ploy for sympathy.

"I am glad I shall not live to see the People forced to obey the white man's law, while they take our land away from us."

A movement behind him caught Sara's eye. One of the braves held a rope. The other end was knotted to the wrists of a white man. The man looked as if he'd seen death a dozen times. He was hunched over, and she couldn't see his face, but she could see his filthy, torn and bloodied clothing, his hair—so matted with dirt it looked gray—and the many lacerations on his limbs. She found it hard to believe he could still stand. Seeing him sway on his feet, Sara wondered how long he'd been forced to follow the Indians on foot. Though tall and strongly built, he wouldn't last much longer if he didn't get help. "I'll take the injured man," Sara stated. She knew her chances of getting him were slim, but she had to try.

Azul raised his weathered hand, and the brave in the back moved his pony forward. The staggering captive was barely able to follow. As the brave came to a halt next to Azul, he gave a hard yank on the rope, causing the stranger to lose his footing. Just before he toppled facedown onto the ground, he looked up. Sara gasped in dismay. It was the man she'd met at the Schieffelin Hall dance. Fargo Tucker. And to add to his already precarious situation, he had the shaft of a broken arrow sticking out of his back. Sara tried to hide her shock, but she knew her face had already mirrored her feelings.

"You know this one?" Azul asked suspiciously.

Sara tried to make her face as stoic as his. "Yes."

"Does he work for you?"

"No. Why would you ask?"

"He was sneaking up on my braves as they killed one of your cattle."

Sara shoved her straw hat back so that she could look him straight in the eye. "Then the question is an unnecessary one. You know I've instructed my men to let you have what you and your people want. We have an understanding, and I would personally shoot any man who disobeyed that order."

Satisfied, Azul nodded and started to turn his pony away.

"Wait!"

Azul looked back around.

"Are you going to give me the man?" Sara asked.

"He is mine!" the brave, who had Fargo in tow, declared. "You cannot cheat me of what I have planned for this one. I, Ocha, would question if Hair of Fire now wants to join the other white-eyes against us."

Sara had heard of this man's hotheaded ways from other braves who occasionally stopped at the hacienda for food or drink. The deep-chested, narrow-eyed warrior stood well over six feet tall. "He is new in the territory, and unaware of our agreement," Sara replied.

"Ocha is right," another brave called out. "Kill this one and there will be fewer of them to trouble us!"

"I asked him to the ranch," Sara persisted. "I am the one at fault, for I should have told him of our agreement. I won't let it happen again." Sara quickly glanced around at the angry faces. Her plea had gained her nothing. "I heard Ocha was a mighty brave. Not one who walks with his tail between his legs."

Ocha's broad chest swelled with indignation. "You make a challenge for one who is half-dead. How do I know *he* won't be the one to run with his tail between his legs?

"Hair of Fire would challenge Ocha?" Although Azul questioned her, his words were more of a warning.

"I challenge Ocha to fight his captive when the white man is healed and healthy."

"Why would I agree to such a foolish thing?" Ocha barked out. "He would not give me the same honor. He is already mine to do with as I choose."

Sara knew she had no business pursuing this, but she couldn't bear the thought of what would happen to Tucker if Ocha left with him. She heard Fargo groan. "If he doesn't meet you, I'll take his place."

The other braves broke out laughing and pointed their fingers at Ocha.

"Fight a woman?" they asked in unison.

"Why not? Your words have no meaning. The Apache have many powerful female warriors."

"Powerful, yes," Ocha said. "You are weak. I take my prisoner and go!"

"Are you too cowardly to fight him?"

"I fear no man!" Furious, Ocha threw down the rope as a declaration of war. "On the day of the second full moon, we fight to the death. If he is not here, one of your people will take his place."

"But that doesn't give him much time to—"

"Any Apache would be ready by then. The white-eyes are weak. The second full moon!" Ocha kicked his pony and rode off in a cloud of dust.

"I do not think Hair of Fire wise," Azul stated. "The white man is already at the door of his ancestors. Why have you done this?"

Sara realized she didn't have an answer. She knew better than to interfere in such matters, and Ocha felt perfectly justified in taking the life of one who wouldn't hesitate to do the same. "I'm doing what I think is right" was the best reply she could give. Azul nodded, and for a brief moment she thought she saw a sadness in his eyes before he turned his pony away. The others followed.

After securing the reins, Sara leapt from the buggy and ran to the still figure on the ground. Paying no heed to the dirt or blood that collected on her yellow skirt, she squatted and felt for a pulse. It was weak, but he wasn't dead. Sara stood and looked around, trying to decide what to do. She had no way of getting the big man into the buggy. The Apache wouldn't help; they'd already melted into the underbrush, leaving no indication they'd ever been there.

Her mind made up, Sara hurried back to her horse and unbuckled the harness. Fortunately, they were less than a mile from the hacienda. She gave the horse a hard whack on the rear, and he took off down the road, headed for home.

Having no idea how long the wait would be, Sara snatched the water canteen from the buggy and hurried back to Tucker. Now all she could do was wait for some-one to come after her.

In less than an hour, Sara spied what she'd been watch-ing for. Dust rising into the air. Her men were on their way. A few minutes later, she could clearly see them coming up the road.

"Are you all right?" Will Langdon asked. The cattle boss slid from the saddle before his mount came to a halt. He looked at Fargo. "What happened?"

"An Apache got him." Sara stood and tried to dust off the back of her skirt. The men were hitching a horse to the buggy.

"What was he doing on Bar C land?"

"This is Fargo Tucker. I met him in Tombstone. I'll ex-plain later. We have to get him to Carla. Will, this man has to live because if he doesn't, you're going to be in serious trouble."

"Why me?" Will asked as the other hands placed Fargo on the buggy seat.

Sara ignored Will's question. "One of you'll have to get in, too, so he won't fall out," she ordered.

"Sara," Will persisted, "what does all this have to do with me?"

"I'll explain later." Sara climbed up onto the seat be-side Fargo. One of her men sat on the other side of him. "Will, just pray he lives."

* * *

By the time Will and Sam had Fargo lying facedown on
the kitchen table, Sara and Carla, the chubby Indian
housekeeper, had already gathered what they hoped would
save Fargo Tucker's life. That was something Sara had
begun to think wouldn't happen. He already looked ready
to be buried on Boot Hill.

As Carla cut Fargo's bloodied shirt with a sharp knife,
Sara kept impatiently brushing away the persistent strands
of auburn hair that continued to fall in her face. Carla
carefully worked the material away from the wound.

"This one has the gods on his side," Carla stated in her
broken English. She moved her dark, stubby fingers
around the wound. "The arrow won't leave no damage.
The feathered end is broken off. We have to push the arrowhead through the front of his shoulder, then pull it out.
The blood will start flowing again."

A shudder worked its way down the length of Sara's
body, but she wasn't about to question the housekeeper's
decision. Carla's doctoring had saved more than one ranch
hand's limb—and more than one ranch hand's life.

"I have leaves soaking." Carla pointed to a bowl. "As
soon as the arrow is removed, we'll plug the hole with the
leaves. Once that's taken care of, we'll see to the rest of his
wounds."

"What can I do to help?" Sara asked.

"For now, we must get his shirt off."

"Will, Sam," Sara called to the two men, who were
standing next to the wall, "sit him up so we can get his shirt
off and drive the arrow out the front."

"Damn," Sam muttered as soon as they had him
propped up into a sitting position. "They must have beat
the sh—" He had forgotten there was a lady in the room.
"If he lives, he's gonna have some nasty-lookin' black

eyes, and from the way that blood is dried around his nose, I'd say it's broken.''

The women pulled off Fargo's shirt.

"And look at his sides," Sam continued. "I'd be surprised if he don't have some broken ribs to boot. But them Injuns made real sure he'd stay alive till they finished what they'd started. If he lives, he's gonna be laid up for some time.''

"We can see for ourselves, Sam," Will snapped out at him.

Carla took hold of the stub of the shaft sticking out his back. As if someone had turned on a switch, Fargo came to—with a vengeance. Though he was delirious, it quickly became evident that Will and Sam weren't going to be able to keep him on the table. Sara moved forward to add her strength, but backed off when Tucker delivered a smashing blow to Sam's jaw. "Do something!" Sara yelled to no one in particular.

"Like what?" Will asked, just before receiving a fist in the stomach. He wrapped his arms around his gut and doubled over.

As quickly as he'd gained consciousness, Fargo suddenly collapsed onto his back, out cold, and the movement shoved the arrowhead out the front of his body. Everyone stood staring in disbelief, while at the same time not wanting to get too close, in case the big man came to again.

"I'll be damned," Will muttered in amazement. "He did the job for us!" He reached a hand out to Sam to help him up off the floor.

"Is it safe?" Sam questioned as he rubbed his sore jaw.

"He's spent his strength," Will said with little conviction.

"I'd hate to have that feller mad at me." Sam remained at a safe distance. "Maybe we should get more men in here, just to be sure he don't give us no more trouble."

"He'll be out a long time," Carla stated. "One of you pull the arrow out the rest of way so we can get him patched up."

By the time Fargo had been bandaged and tucked in bed, his body already felt hot to the touch. Sara turned a deaf ear to Will's insistence that it wouldn't be proper for her to be in the same room with a naked man. Will ended up being ordered out of the house.

Not bothering to change their soiled dresses, Sara and Carla remained at Fargo's bedside the rest of the day and all that night, fighting his high fever. They regularly applied damp cloths to his forehead, and forced between his lips a liquid mixture that Carla had concocted. At times it took both of them, and a few men to boot, to keep the delirious man down. He mumbled, cursed and thrashed around in the bed, and one time he would have succeeded in ripping away his bandages had he not passed out.

The few words Sara understood of Fargo's ramblings apparently had something to do with a tanner and the Triple T ranch. Whatever the problem, Fargo's anger was apparent. What with Fargo's name being Tucker, she deduced that the Triple T could be the ranch he'd mentioned owning in Texas. And perhaps the tanner worked on the ranch.

By the afternoon of the second day, an exhausted Fargo lay quietly in the big bed, his face damp with perspiration.

"Carla," Sara said as she placed her hands on her sides and stretched, "it looks like he's going to be quiet for a while. I'm going to bathe, take a nap and put on some clean clothes. If you need help, call Sam. He's sleeping next door, in the other bedroom.''

The chubby woman nodded. "This one should be quiet for some time now. Once the fever has passed, he'll rest peacefully."

"I can't understand how he's managed to toss and turn for so many hours. He looked ready for a coffin when I brought him here. One would think he's been fighting the devil himself."

"The man has powerful medicine."

"After I take my nap, I'll return so you can get your sleep. We're both worn out." Sara yawned as she left the room.

Something wet lapping at his face brought Fargo slowly out of his deep fog. He finally managed to break through and open his eyes. He couldn't believe what he saw. It had to be a dream! The monster had a massive head, and its tongue—

"Phew!" a soft voice whispered. "What are you doing in there? You come out immediately!"

The beast turned and trotted to the woman standing in the doorway. It finally occurred to Fargo that the beast might be a dog.

Pretending to be asleep, Fargo stole quick glances out of his eyes that were nearly swollen shut. A woman wearing a blue muslin dress quietly stepped inside. Only a small candle lit the room, and he couldn't be sure of the color of her hair. Possibly dark brown, maybe even black. She was a pretty thing, with a pleasing figure. She stood on tiptoe to get a better look at him, but refused to come any closer. Then woman and animal disappeared, and he didn't get a second look.

Fargo reached up to rub his eyes, but a sharp, slicing pain in his shoulder deterred any further movement. His body ached worse than if he'd ridden a bronco for a week. Indians! Now he remembered. He'd been attacked by Indians. Had they put him in a tepee? His head began to swim. Had he really seen a beauty and a beast? Couldn't have been a dog. Who would name a dog Phew? Had those damn Indians given him peyote? He closed his eyes and drifted off into a dreamless sleep.

Sara sat on the rocking chair at Fargo's bedside, trying to make herself comfortable. Since late yesterday, his fever had come and gone. She wiped her hands on her course cotton skirt, her gaze coming to rest on Fargo's tousled black hair and the dark stubble on his face. How could it become so thick in such a short time? He looked somewhat better now that he'd been cleaned up, but not much. The bruises on his face and body varied from pink to purple to dark blue. She still found it strange that the only deep cut on his face was over his left eyebrow. Carla had had to stitch it shut. Still, even with all that, plus being haggard and drawn, he had a good face, with long, thick lashes and a strong jawline.

Sara straightened in the chair.

Actually, it was a devastating face. Devastating because of the effect it had on women. Even Penelope and Rose had felt the effect. Of course, Rose, being conscious of her married status, had taken longer to admit it. Ignoring the bandaged shoulder, Sara let her gaze drift down his strong neck and forearms, which, even at rest, clearly showed their corded muscles. The mat of short black hair on his chest tapered down to a narrow— Sara pursed her lips. The bed sheet had put a halt to her perusal. After all his tossing and turning, even Carla hadn't been able to keep his lower extremities continually covered.

Fargo piqued her curiosity as no other man had done. After what had happened to her family, it had taken several years before she'd begun to trust men again. And that trust was limited to only a special few.

Sara smiled faintly. She'd learned other things about herself over those years. Though her heart had ached for her family, she was a survivor. Unlike Megan, she could accept what had happened and get on with her life. And it would appear she was now ready to take her life a step further.

Sara began drumming her fingers on the arms of the rocker. She knew she should be ashamed of her thoughts. After all, the man had almost died. Looking under the sheet would never even enter a proper lady's mind. Rose Halverson had never even seen her *husband* unclothed. Without exactly coming out and saying it, Rose had told her that all their coupling took place in the dark.

Sara closed her eyes, determined to rid her mind of anything and everything. She'd take a nap. How come men's private parts weren't all the same size? Sara's eyelids flew open. Feeling guilty at having such thoughts, she glanced around the room to be sure no one had entered. "Such silliness!" she told herself. She squeezed her eyes shut. But Mr. Tucker had such a beautiful body.... What harm would it be to take another peek?

She opened one eye and stared at the sleeping man. How could she possibly take a nap if she continued to let such thoughts eat at her rational thinking? On the other hand, though it had gotten her in trouble more than once, she'd never been one to deny herself anything. Maybe she'd just take one look and get it over with. But what if Mr. Tucker should awaken? She slid her slippers off and began rocking the chair. Each time she rocked forward, she worked her toes and her raised foot against the soft fabric. Inch by inch, the bed sheet moved to the side, until she had his body exposed. The rocking stopped, and she stared in open awe. She had never had the opportunity to take such a long look at a man's components. No doubt about it, Fargo Tucker was magnificent in every respect.

Fargo moved, and Sara's gaze shifted to his face. Her heart jumped into her throat when she saw his devilish grin. No doubt about it, he knew exactly what she'd been up to. She wanted nothing more than to go to the cellar and never come back out.

"Do you like what you see?" he asked in a low, honey-soaked voice.

Sara's mouth dropped open, and for once in her life no words spewed forth.

His grin broadened, and he motioned to her with his hand. "There's no need for you to be upset over those other women. I'm only human. And don't I always come back to you, Carrie Sue?"

Carrie Sue?

He raised up on an elbow and patted the bed. "Come on and lie here beside me. You know I'll make you forget everything. I want to feel you throbbing against me as I plunge deep within your glorious fountain of delight."

Sara knew her eyes were about to pop out, even though she now realized he was hallucinating again. His manly member had stiffened and grown in size, and she'd never heard such...such...*descriptive* words. There wasn't any doubt as to what he had on his mind.

"Damned if you don't have the prettiest set of breasts I've ever laid eyes on. They're big and full, just the way I like them. It delights me to suck on them and see your nipples become hard with longing." Chuckling, he lay back down and rolled over. Moments later he was sound asleep.

For the next five minutes, Sara didn't move a muscle. As she sat staring at Tucker, a slow anger developed. Big, full breasts? Sure he wouldn't awaken again, she raised her hands to her breasts. They weren't big and full, as he seemed to prefer, but they weren't flat, and it didn't make her any less a woman! Her bosom certainly didn't seem to bother the other men who tried to court and even bed her.

Suddenly she didn't care if Mr. Tucker did come to. She went to the bed, lifted the sheet, then flung it over his prostrate form. He groaned, but didn't move. And another thing, Sara thought angrily as she returned to the chair—Mr. Tucker couldn't be nearly as shy as she'd originally presumed. Penelope had been right when she stated, "Believe me, Sara, that man isn't shy. Not with those eyes." Sara gave up all thoughts of taking a nap. She was too angry.

She didn't realize she'd dozed off until a shuffling sound awoke her. To her surprise, her sister, Megan, had entered the room. She went to the far side of the bed, and after staring down at the stranger for a moment she placed her hand on his forehead.

"He's going to be all right," Megan commented before walking back out of the room.

Sara stared at the empty doorway. She'd never seen Megan touch any man except Will. Yet she'd touched Fargo—a total stranger.

After that, Megan reappeared about every hour. She never explained her thoughts, and Sara never asked. There were many things about her sister that Sara would never understand.

Once Fargo's fever broke, Sara and Carla ceased their constant vigil. Their guest spent all his time sleeping, and it became Carla's job to keep an eye on him. Sara returned to her daily duties. She hadn't told Will about the fight with Ocha. When he had asked why Tucker had been on Bar C land the day before he'd been invited to come, it became a question Sara also wanted answered. And what about that other little matter? How would she inform Fargo that she'd saved his life by committing him to a fight to the death—and with an Apache?

Sara kept the hem of her work skirt hiked up so that it wouldn't get caught in the spiny weeds that had grown thick around the wrought-iron fence she'd brought from Mexico several years back. The gate creaked a complaint as she opened it and stepped inside the small graveyard. Partially wilted flowers rested on top of each grave, which meant Megan had been there earlier that morning. She'd even started pulling the weeds.

Sara silently chastised herself for not visiting the plots as often as she once had. After all, it was on a small hill only a couple hundred yards or so from the back of the house. Today, for some unexplainable reason, she'd had a strong urge to be among her family and remember the anger, hate, hurt and uselessness she'd felt six years ago.

Sara studied each mound. Her two brothers, shot and killed; her sister, only eighteen, shot, killed and then raped; her father, Charles Carter, forty-one, shot and killed; and lastly, her beloved mother, thirty-nine, raped and killed by a knife to her throat. The memories flooded back, and for a brief moment Sara could hear the skinny man's sing-song voice, the screams and a gravelly voice asking her mother, "Why you fightin' me, woman? I'm better than that Injun you bed." Dodd's words had haunted Sara all these years. Her mother had held her head high and spit in his face. Had Dodd known something Sara didn't? Had her mother been unfaithful?

For a long time after that hideous day, Sara had wondered why Megan had black hair instead of red, like her brother and sisters. The questions faded for periods of time, but they invariably returned. Azul used to come to the house often. Could Megan be his daughter? It would explain, to some extent, why they were never attacked by the Chiricahua. But what if none of it were true, and her suspicions were only in her head? So many times she'd wanted to ask Azul, but she knew an answer wouldn't be forthcoming.

Sara rubbed her temples. At least Megan had survived. Back then, though, Meg had been like the living dead. But the good Lord had smiled on her. She'd blanked out everything that had happened on that fateful day. She remembered nothing about being raped, or about the deaths, and Sara had made a point of never mentioning those atrocities. Even Will knew to keep his mouth shut. However, Megan had her dark shadows. For a long time, there had been the nightmares. But, as of two years ago, even those had disappeared. Unfortunately, Megan's deep fear of strangers had never passed.

Sara shook her head. To this day, she didn't know how they had managed to survive. Back then, there had been no ranch hands, and no housekeeper. The family had handled everything themselves. She knew now that she wouldn't have made it if not for Will. Upon hearing what had happened, he'd left his father's small ranch and had come to work for her. His biggest asset had been his knowledge of cattle. He'd taken over the running of the ranch, with Sara right by his side, working and learning everything he knew. Yes, they owed him a lot. To her and

Megan, he had become family—like one of the brothers they'd lost.

Sara leaned down and settled a rock on her father's grave. There had been some positive changes from all this. She had made sure they would never be unprepared again. There were always several men working in the outbuildings. If any shots were fired, they would come running. She'd also insisted Megan learn how to take care of herself. Now Megan knew how to handle both guns and horses. If she ever had to point a gun at someone again, she wouldn't miss.

Hearing Phew's loud bark, Sara raised up and left the cemetery, closing the gate behind her. The dog came to a skidding halt, his tongue hanging out the side of his mouth. He looked up in adoration, wagging his tail so hard it made a slapping noise against the wrought-iron fence.

Sara laughed. "And just what have you been up to for the last hour?" She rubbed his ears lovingly. "You probably found a coyote bitch in heat. You're going to start a breed of coyotes that the Apache will mistake for horses!" With Phew following alongside, she returned to the house.

Sara entered the cool room and headed straight for Mr. Tucker's room. Though Carla had been doing the nursing, Sara still liked to see how he was faring. But so far they hadn't exchanged a word. Fargo was always asleep. Carla insisted that sleep helped him regain his strength. She also said Fargo had started eating some solid food. Another good sign. Even the bruises and cuts on his face had finally started to fade. But the deep cut above his eyebrow would probably leave a scar. Placing her hand on Phew's head to keep him from entering the darkened room, Sara peeked in, then released a quiet sigh. As usual, Mr. Tucker was asleep.

Disappointed, Sara continued out into the courtyard. She found Megan seated in a corner, enjoying the shade of a big tree their mother had planted over twenty years ago. Meg's back was turned, but Sara could hear her humming. Sara's heart ached for her sister. It was doubtful Megan would ever lead a normal life or marry. Especially if anyone ever discovered she might have Indian blood. But then, Sara's life didn't look much brighter. Having already reached the age of twenty, she could foresee a lonely future for herself, as well. Until she had met their guest, there had never been a man who had taken her fancy.

"Are you just going to stand there?" Megan called without turning. "You never told me if you enjoyed the dance at Schieffelin Hall."

Phew trotted over and lay beside Megan's chair. Her occasional second sight had developed after the massacre, and Sara had had to learn to live with it. "Yes, I did enjoy myself," she replied as she joined her sister. "You should have gone with me."

Megan set her needle work on her lap. "You know I couldn't do that."

Sara glanced around the large stone courtyard. There were plants everywhere. Large ones, small ones, some hanging, others in enormous Mexican pots. Many were blooming. There were now so many that the courtyard seemed to be disappearing. These plants were Megan's children. "Keeping to yourself isn't going to solve loneliness, Megan. One of these days you need to get out and meet people." Sara grabbed for the handkerchief tucked in her waistband, but a sneeze escaped before she could get it to her nose. Two more followed.

Megan returned to her needlework. "Did you notice the plants I've started putting in the house?"

Just picturing it in her mind's eye made Sara groan.

"Now don't get upset, sister. I'm determined to find out which plant makes you sneeze. The only way it can be done is by process of elimination." She tossed her long, thick braid back over her shoulder. "Is the man staying here until he's better?"

"His name is Fargo Tucker, and you know he isn't in any condition to travel to Tombstone. We have no choice but to keep him here until he can get his strength back."

"He's dangerous."

"Nonsense. You have no reason to fear him."

Megan closed her eyes and leaned back against the trunk of the tree. "Oh, Sara, I don't even know what I'm talking about. How could I know whether or not he's dangerous?"

Sara gathered Megan into her arms. "It's all right, Meg. I understand." She stroked her sister's glossy hair. "I should have moved us to town a long time ago. You need to learn to be around people. Staying out here in the middle of nowhere isn't good for you."

Megan jerked away, terror gleaming in her dark green eyes.

"It's not something that would happen right away. Believe me, being around people isn't so terrible. I know you'd need time to get used to it, but you *must* try. Have I ever let anything happen to you?"

Megan bowed her head. "No," she whispered.

"And I never will. You've been in the house too long. How about us going for a long ride? Like you, I also need to get out for a while."

Megan's expression brightened. "Its been nearly two weeks since we went riding. Let's go change clothes. While we're gone, you can tell me all about the dance."

Sara managed a smile before she sneezed.

Chapter Three

Fargo awoke, aching all over. The bright light entering through the open, recessed windows made him squint. Nevertheless, his head seemed clear and his appetite strong. Just the thought of a thick, juicy steak made his mouth water. He rubbed his chin, the growth of beard making him curious as to how long he'd been laid up. He certainly hadn't been able to get any answers out of the roly-poly Indian woman who fed him and dressed his shoulder. He had finally concluded that she didn't speak English. But, more confusing, since it was the Apache who had put him in this fix, it didn't make sense that one would nurse him back to health. And how was it that he lay in a comfortable bed in a clean bedroom? There were a lot of questions he'd like answered, including where the dark-haired angel he remembered had come from. Though he hadn't seen her since regaining consciousness, he clearly remembered her staring down at him. It could just have been his imagination, of course. That made a hell of a lot more sense than anything else.

He tried sitting up, but as before, he fell back in the bed. He lay still for several minutes, congratulating himself. He'd almost made it. Even the pain in his shoulder had lessened, and this time his head didn't reel, and there were no black spots dancing in front of his eyes. He was well on his way to recovery.

Hearing the rustling of skirts, Fargo looked toward the doorway. A moment later, the Indian woman waddled in carrying a tray of food. To his shock, none other than the prim Miss Sara Carter came in on Carla's heels. But what really caught his interest was the huge dog at Sara's side. The sheriff in Las Cruces had been right. The beast could easily be mistaken for a colt!

"Good morning, Mr. Tucker," Sara said cheerfully.

"Mornin', ma'am. This must be your house."

"Yes, it is. You're looking much better than when I brought you here. I believe you're going to live. Carla, why don't we prop some pillows behind Mr. Tucker's back, and perhaps he can feed himself?"

Fargo's eyes narrowed. The Indian woman, Carla, had fooled him. She clearly understood English. She placed the tray on the bedside table, then walked to the armoire and pulled out two pillows. He let her tomfoolery pass, because there were other, more important things on his mind. Like that bowl full of large chunks of meat and vegetables floating in a rich broth. Just the wonderful aroma alone already had his stomach growling with anticipation. Then he noticed the dog slowly making his way toward the bowl, his nose raised, sniffing the air. Fargo was ready to go to war. No way in hell would he let the beast have his meal! He looked for something to throw. He'd picked up a pillow and was ready to send it sailing in the dog's direction when Sara said, "Shame on you, Phew. You know you've already eaten. Go find Meg."

The dog obediently left the room.

Somehow the dog's ridiculous name sounded familiar to Fargo. He managed to lift himself up enough that the women could arrange the pillows for support. At last he could sit fairly comfortably without his ribs and shoulder giving him a fit. His mind flashed back to the dirt he'd eaten while being dragged on the ground behind a galloping Indian pony—brush slapping and cutting his face—and the sickening taste in his mouth when he'd felt his ribs crack against an ungiving rock. Carla handed him the bowl of stew.

"How did I get here?" he asked after he'd devoured several spoonfuls of the tasty food.

"I'd been on my way home from Tombstone when I happened upon a band of Chiricahua," Sara explained. "You were with them."

"And they let us live? They were stealing your cattle, Miss Carter." He finished off his last spoonful of stew.

"Not exactly, Mr. Tucker."

"I saw them."

"But with one difference. They had my permission."

Sara was still incensed at the hard look she'd seen Fargo give Carla several minutes ago. It had verged on contempt. She turned and looked out the window. "Carla, why don't you take Mr. Tucker's bowl and fill it again?" As soon as the housekeeper had left, Sara faced the big man and asked curtly, "Do you have a problem with my housekeeper, Mr. Tucker? Or is it just Indians that bother you?"

"After what happened to me, I'd be an out-and-out liar if I said I was fond of them."

"Even I fear the mighty Apache, Mr. Tucker...."

"I said nothing about fear."

"Please, don't try putting up a brave front on my account. And don't tell me that if you were an Apache you'd sit back and quietly accept your land being taken away while you were shoved on some reservation. Or maybe you would flee into Mexico as others have, and starve?"

"Why am I suddenly getting a lecture on Indians?"

Carla returned, and Sara made no comment.

Fargo found it amusing that when Miss Carter became riled, her cheeks became flushed, her voice became husky, and her large, wonderful green eyes flashed with indignation. Suddenly he found himself looking at her in an entirely different manner. As he accepted the bowl Carla handed him, he chuckled. Was this how the prim Miss Sara would look while partaking in a lusty—?

"Apparently you are improving quite nicely, so I'll leave you to your meal," Sara announced.

Even after she'd rushed from the room, Fargo could still smell the enticing odor of her perfume. It certainly didn't take much to get her worked up. Had she given him a chance, he might have informed her that he didn't dislike Indians—except for the one who had beaten the hell out of him.

Not until Sara approached her room did her anger begin to subside. She reminded herself that Tucker's attitude wasn't any different than that of most of the men and women of the frontier. She, too, had deep-seated concerns about the Apache. However, they were concerns of another nature.

Sara entered her bedroom, shut the heavy door, then continued on to the courtyard. The sweet aroma of flowers, at least, offered serenity, and at this moment that was exactly what she needed. She stopped near one of the rock benches and glanced around thoughtfully.

For some strange reason, she'd thought a lot about her family in the past couple of weeks. Now she was reminded of how many happy hours they'd shared out here. The hacienda had actually been built by a Spanish gentleman, and it had remained vacant for several years before the Carters had moved in. The Spaniard had had it built in the manner of a fortress, because of the hatred between the Mexican and Apache. Unfortunately, when the place had finally been finished, his family had refused to live in it. He'd had no alternative but to return to Mexico.

A three-foot-high adobe wall surrounded the house, the yard, and the natural spring. A pipe carried water to a large trough in a small shed at the back of the house, providing good drinking water. Between that and the cistern, water never had been a problem. Even gun slits had been cut in the thick outer walls of the house. Inside, most of the rooms opened onto the large courtyard, well protected by the wall. This was where Charles Carter had brought his wife and son, along with aspirations to a good life. He had thought they would be safe. Although several good men that knew how to shoot could hold off an entire army and never leave the house, Sara knew her father hadn't prepared properly.

"Are you still angry?"

Sara spun around and saw Fargo Tucker standing no more than ten feet away. "What are you doing?" she exclaimed. His face had become as white as the bandage under his arm and over his shoulder. He wore only the hip-hugging denim pants Carla had washed, and his boots.

"Once you had me sitting up, getting on my feet didn't prove to be that difficult. Excuse my lack of dress, but I couldn't find my shirt."

Sara didn't buy his shy look for a minute. Seeing him sway, she hurried forward. "Here, let me help you back to bed. Are you determined to undo all of Carla's work?"

"If you don't mind, I'd prefer to sit on the bench for a few minutes. After that I should be able to make it back on my own."

Sara placed her arm around his waist, then helped him to the bench. To her astonishment, touching his bare skin brought forth memories of his naked body and his words to "Carrie Sue." Knowing they were alone didn't improve matters.

Fargo eased himself down onto the bench. "This will do fine."

"I'm going to get some of the boys to take you back to your room. How could you do such a foolhardy thing?"

"Ah, I've made you angry again." He grinned broadly. "Or are you always of such a disposition?"

His grin, and the orneriness dancing in his blue eyes, made Sara relax. She sat on the bench across from him and returned his smile. "No, I'm not normally of such a disposition, but I do have my moments."

Fargo's gaze caressed her face. "I'm glad you were out here. I didn't thank you for saving my life."

"Carla saved your life, Mr. Tucker. Like it or not, you are indebted to an Indian. I simply brought you here."

"How about calling me Fargo?" He shifted his weight and grimaced.

"You shouldn't be out of bed yet," Sara scolded. "I knew I should have—"

"I'm fine. We both know the pain isn't going to leave overnight. Well?"

"Well what?"

"How about calling me Fargo?"

"All things considered, I don't think it would be prop—"

"I'll make you a bargain. As long as I'm here, we'll use Fargo and Sara. But if it makes you more comfortable, when we're in town we'll address each other as Miss Carter and Mr. Tanner." Fargo realized his mistake the moment the word slipped out.

"Did you say Tanner?"

"No," he replied smoothly. "The name is Tucker."

"Your voice dropped. I must have misunderstood you," she replied thoughtfully.

The big dog trotted up and rested his head on Sara's lap, capturing her attention. Fargo appreciated the distraction. "Tell me, Sara," he began as he gave her a mischievous wink for having used her name, "how did such a fine looking dog come to be named Phew?"

"Well, Fargo," Sara said, delightedly mimicking his use of her first name, "it's a rather embarrassing tale, but humorous. First of all, please remember that this is a big cattle ranch." She rubbed Phew's ears. "When I brought him home, he was the cutest, gangliest three-month-old puppy I'd ever seen. But to everyone's mortification, it didn't take him long to discover the joy of rolling in dung. He'd hurry home, so proud of how wonderful he smelled. To this day, I can still see him proudly wagging his tail so hard it made his rump move from side to side. Needless to say, no one else appreciated having him around. The first thing they'd all say would be 'Phew!'"

Fargo laughed. "And that's how he came by his name," he finished for her.

Sara nodded.

Though Fargo felt the need to go lie down again, he couldn't ignore an opportunity to gain information. "I swear, I've never seen such a dog."

"They're called Danes. A foreign gentleman who had stopped at the fort had a dam, a sire, and Phew. I was so taken with the pup that I bought him on the spot."

"Yep, a mighty fine looking dog. There can't be many like him around."

"Actually, he's been bred several times, and has some fine get to show for it." Sara stood. "You've been up far too long. Are you sure you can make it back to the bedroom alone?"

"I could probably use a shoulder to help me stand."

"I knew it. I should have made you go straight back to bed." She walked over and placed his arm around her shoulders. "Use me for support."

Fargo expelled a burst of laughter. She was so small that her offer verged on the ridiculous. He looked up and saw Carla waddling toward them, her face like stone.

"Too soon to be up," Carla snapped.

Fargo's lips remained curved in a smile. He could still find humor in the situation. Normally, he wouldn't be the least bit averse to having two women look after him. However, the women he'd have chosen certainly didn't fit the description of these two.

That night, Fargo awoke from a deep sleep, but his eyes remained closed. He could feel someone's breath on his face. Then soft lips touched his forehead. His eyes flew open, and he gazed at the face, which was hidden by darkness. He knew it was a woman, a woman with long, dark hair. He hadn't imagined it! She quickly straightened up and hurried out of the room. His angel hadn't been a dream. Angel? Not likely.

He yawned as he made himself comfortable again. He could never recall having been around a stranger assortment of characters: a dark-headed woman who drifted mysteriously from room to room without saying a word, a half-breed squaw who answered everything with a grunt, a brute of a dog with a gawd-awful name, and a lady who appeared to be friendly with the Apache. And somewhere, somehow, in the middle of all this, lurked a bounty hunter called Hawk.

Possibly a lover?

While he waited for his body to heal, he'd have to waste time on social games to procure information. He thought about the dance, and how he'd planned to abduct the redhead. Strange how things could change so quickly. He couldn't physically threaten her now that she'd saved his life. A life for a life. He owed her one.

For the next week, Fargo continued to strengthen, even though his little talk in the courtyard with Sara cost him three days flat on his back, unable to move. And with the healing came restlessness. Since his arrival in Tombstone, the higher elevation and the thinner, drier air had taken a little getting used to. Sara's ranch, which he presumed to be higher still, presented a similar problem—or at least that was what he wanted to believe. He grinned. What purpose did it serve to try to fool himself? It wasn't the altitude. His condition just wouldn't allow him to improve as rapidly as he'd like. He found it hard to believe he couldn't make himself get up and walk away this time, as he had on so many other occasions. But he'd never had the hell beaten out of him like this before. He might have accepted it a little better had he been allowed to defend himself!

His thoughts drifted to Sara. After their conversation in the courtyard, he'd seen her briefly a few times. The only other visitors he'd had were the will-o'-the-wisp, who continued to drift in and out of his room at night, Carla and Phew, who always welcomed a friendly pat. The dog certainly didn't fit the sheriff's description of being mean.

To add to his problems, his clothes had mysteriously disappeared. He knew Carla had to be the culprit. She'd made sure he couldn't take another visit to the courtyard.

Convinced it would be at least another hour before Carla came in to check on him, Fargo wrapped the sheet around his waist and slowly sat up. He didn't think staying in bed would help him regain his strength. So, for the past couple of days, he'd made a ritual of walking around the room and looking out the window. At night, after everyone had gone to bed, he toured the house.

He stood. It still took a moment for him to become steady on his feet, but he was in a hell of a lot better shape than when he'd first started walking. He walked around the room several times, working his shoulder as he moved. The pain had lessened somewhat over the past couple of days. As he passed the doorway to the courtyard, two female voices brought him to a halt. He moved closer to the open door and listened.

"I'm telling you, Meg, this can't continue!"

"Haven't you noticed your sneezing has stopped? I got rid of the plant that caused it."

The soft reply was in a voice Fargo had never heard before.

"Well, I'll be. You're right.... Meg, I need to talk to you about our guest."

"Why?"

"We know nothing about Mr. Tucker. I don't think you should go near him. He may start..."

Their voices faded, and even though Fargo inched closer to the opening, he couldn't make out what they were saying. He may start what? He returned to his bed, not wanting to take the chance of someone catching him eavesdropping.

The woman Sara had been talking to didn't have an accent like Carla's. Could she be his will-o'-the-wisp? Would she tell Sara about her many visits? He didn't know why he hadn't mentioned it. Perhaps because she always seemed so frightened, which had left him with the impression that her visits were a secret. For some ridiculous reason, he'd felt honor-bound to keep that secret.

He fluffed the pillows, lay down and spread the bed sheet over him. If he could meet "Meg," he might be able to get on her good side. Maybe she'd even prove to be another source of information. And getting to know her might not be an impossible task. Lately, she hadn't been hurrying away, even though she knew he was watching her. Then, yesterday, she'd stood just inside the doorway, smiling. Tonight, when everyone had gone to bed, he'd sit out in the courtyard. She had always entered his room from that direction. There had to be a way for him to communicate with her. After all, he'd never had a problem getting to know women before.

The full moon was on the rise, leaving deep pockets of night shadows, when Fargo walked out into the courtyard. He could have sworn he got a whiff of jasmine.

Unsure Meg would even make an appearance, he had almost changed his mind. Being wrapped in a bed sheet didn't help matters. But he had no choice. So far he'd wasted a lot of time, and he wasn't any closer to finding Jude's killer than the day he'd arrived in Tombstone. He sat on a bench, thinking that having only a sheet between him and the rock bench made it awfully hard on a man's fanny.

After only five minutes, Fargo impatiently began tapping a finger on his leg. In an effort to make the time pass more quickly, he centered his thoughts on Jude—the spoiled member of the family.

Because Mary Tanner had died giving birth to Jude, Tom had wanted nothing to do with the baby. He'd turned his back on everyone back then, including his seven-year-old son, Fargo. Losing his mother, and then having his father turn his back on him, had lit the first fires of anger. He had hated his father for what he'd done.

On the other hand, Fargo had considered Jude's birth to be the most wonderful thing that had ever happened. Though still a child himself, he became Jude's surrogate father, and proud of it. But when Jude turned three, Tom's guilt kicked in. All of a sudden he decided he should spend time with his youngest boy. This grew in importance when it became evident that Jude looked astoundingly like their mother. His skin never turned as dark as Tom or Fargo's, he had curly brown hair instead of straight black, and his features were small and refined. For a while, Fargo actually worried that Jude would grow up looking like a woman, and defended his brother in more than one fight because of it.

Even though Jude had obviously become Thomas Tanner's favorite, Fargo loved his brother dearly. Unbeknownst to the old man, Fargo had saved Jude's hide many a time. Because his arguments with the older man got worse, Fargo became harder, and concentrated on running the vast ranch. He and Jude drifted apart. Jude much preferred all the favors his father could give him to the work he'd have to do if he stuck around his older brother.

Everyone liked Jude when he was young. The boy had an appealing, outgoing manner about him. But by the time he was fourteen, he'd turned wild. He felt that there wasn't anything he couldn't get away with. After all, his father was the great Thomas L. Tanner.

Fargo shook his head. Now Jude was dead. No matter who said what, Fargo would never believe the boy could have done anything so bad as to warrant a high price on his head. For once, he agreed with his father. Nothing took precedence over seeing that the bounty hunter get his just reward.

Something caught Fargo's eye. The woman's high-necked white cotton nightgown and rigid features made her look like a statue, the only movement that of her loose, dark hair blowing in the breeze. She was watching him closely, but didn't back away. Fargo didn't move, either. He couldn't take the chance of scaring her away. "I couldn't sleep. Since I've only been able to smell the flowers, I finally decided to come out and take a look."

"You like flowers?"

The tone of her voice told him to say "Yes."

"If you can move around, you must be feeling a lot better."

Fargo gave her an ingratiating smile. "I'd look kindly on it if you didn't give away my secret." He kept his voice low so that he wouldn't be overheard. "I don't think I could take any more of Carla's scolding." Megan laughed. A full, throaty laugh that reminded him of Sara.

"I won't tell." She turned to leave.

"Maybe sometime you'd come visit me," he called quietly after her. "I get awfully lonely." But she had disappeared. Fargo wasn't the least bit disappointed, however. The initial contact had been made. The will-o'-the-wisp had talked to him.

The following week, Sara strolled down the hall, headed for Fargo's room. He would probably be pleased to know Carla had given the okay for him to have supper in the dining room. Sara was feeling guilty. Since it had become evident Fargo would live, she had seen him only on a few occasions, and those visits had been brief, because the man had a profound effect on her.

She stopped near his partially closed door, wondering if she should let Carla deliver the news. The more time she spent with Fargo, the more physically desirable he became. It wasn't just his body that attracted her—though that certainly had a great deal to do with it. It also had to do with his teasing, his almost daring orneriness, which made her want to meet his unspoken challenge. No man had ever had such an effect on her, and she wasn't sure how to react. All this combined made it difficult for her to act normally around him. But why worry? He'd certainly never indicated similar feelings. Quite the contrary. She might as well be one of the brass bedposts for all the attention he'd shown. Carrie Sue had had far more luck. Could he be married? She certainly hoped not. Why, Carrie Sue might even be his wife!

Sara smoothed out the skirt of her dress. It was white, with orange stripes. Not that it mattered, but more than one person in town had complimented her on how becoming she looked in the dress. She raised her chin and placed her hand on the doorknob.

She heard laughter coming from inside.

It wasn't a man's laughter!

How could Fargo have found a way to get a woman in his bedroom? she wondered angrily. She shoved the door open. Megan stood just outside the courtyard doorway with Fargo's arm around her shoulders! At least he had on all his clothes!

"What, may I ask, is going on here?" Sara demanded.

Megan spun around. Her face had suddenly turned pale. Without a word, she ran past Sara and disappeared.

"The way you act, one would think *you* were the older sister." Fargo leaned against the doorjamb and watched his intruder quickly close the gap between them. The bottom of her skirts, brushing softly across the hardwood floor, made a swishing sound.

"There are things about this family you know nothing about, nor is it any of your business. But there is one thing I want to make very clear. Keep your hands off my sister."

"You have a suspicious mind," Fargo told her mockingly. He shoved strands of thick black hair from his forehead. "Why would you think your sister isn't safe around me?"

Though Sara considered it a sin that a man should have such a come-hither look, she refused to turn away. If he had such an effect on her, heaven only knew what poor Megan must be feeling. The man was downright dangerous. She could only pray she'd not been too late in discovering the two together. "How long has Megan been coming into your room?"

Fargo's lips spread into a cocked grin. "As far as I know, ever since I arrived."

"Why didn't you tell me?" Sara demanded.

"Being sisters, I naturally assumed you knew."

"Assumed?" Sara crossed her arms over her breasts to keep from striking his smug face. "Has anything happened?"

"Like what?"

"You know what I'm talking about."

"No, can't say as I do, so you'll have to be more specific."

"Very well. Have you kissed her?"

"Uh-huh."

Sara's arms dropped to her sides, her hands balled into fists. "And have you . . . have you . . ."

Fargo arched a dark eyebrow and waited.

Sara stiffened her back. "Have you touched her . . . body?"

"Of course. When you came in, I'm sure you saw my arm around her shoulders."

"That's not what I meant, and you know it!" Sara had to fight to keep her temper under control. "Did you take her to your bed?"

Fargo chuckled. "Now where would you come up with such an opinion of me? I'm your guest, and beholden to you for saving my life."

"Dammit, just answer my question."

"Why don't you ask Megan?"

Sara spun around to leave, but before she could take two steps she felt him grab her arm and spin her back around. This time he wasn't grinning.

"Let me help you with your question. You want to know if I took Meg in my arms, held her breathlessly against me while devouring her with kisses and drawing sweet pleasure from the feel of her firm, ripe body against mine. And then, did I lead her to the bed and take her clothes off, piece by piece, eagerly anticipating the sight and feel—"

"That's enough!" Sara cried. She tried to free her arm, but he held her fast.

"Pray tell, could I accomplish such feats in my condition?" His condition wouldn't have had a thing to do with it, but no need bringing up that point. "The answer to your question is no, I did nothing. Contrary to what you obviously think, I *am* a man of honor. Nor would I enjoy taking a woman to my bed who obviously has problems. As for the kiss, I kissed the top of her head as a thank-you when she brought me some cut flowers. Now, is there anything else you'd like to know?"

Sara felt like a complete fool. "No," she whispered.

Fargo brushed past her and went to the washstand. He would have much preferred a strong shot of whiskey, but instead he poured himself a glass of water. "Tell me, Sara, since you're obviously a maiden who is cognizant of social graces and amenities, how did you come up with such base thoughts?"

Sara pulled the lace handkerchief from her waistband and raised it to her nose in an effort to hide her embarrassment. "I may be unmarried, but I do live on a—"

"You should have taken Meg to the dance in Tombstone. She would probably have enjoyed being around others."

"That is a family matter." Sara had wanted to leave the room as quickly as possible, but she suddenly remembered why she'd come in the first place. "Would you care to join us in the dining room for supper tonight?"

"I'd like that." Fargo smiled. "I should be able to leave for Tombstone in a few days—that is, if you'll lend me a horse."

Sara laughed nervously. "I apologize for asking such demeaning questions. I was so shocked to hear Megan laughing." Without thinking, she sat on the edge of the bed. "She hasn't done that in years. And she's never been friendly to anyone outside the ranch, so when I saw the two of you standing side by side, and your arm—well, I...jumped to conclusions."

Fargo studied Sara over the rim of the glass as he took a drink of water. He wondered what she would look like with that lovely auburn hair hanging loose and wild about her face. Though Sara certainly wasn't the type of woman he was usually attracted to, something about her definitely ignited lusty thoughts. He didn't much care for her almost huffy, ladylike qualities. He preferred someone more earthy, like Megan. Besides being unfashionably slender, Sara always kept a straight back, dressed stylishly, seldom had a hair out of place, and she always made sure she kept her temper under proper control—none of which were qualities he liked in his women. He couldn't help but wonder what she'd be like if she gave free rein to her emotions? If any other woman had propped herself on his bed, he would have considered it an invitation. Not Sara. Still, he had to admit that seeing her on his bed put ideas in his mind. He placed the glass back on the washstand. "There's no need to apologize. If I had a sister, I'd probably be even more protective than you are."

Sara's face brightened. "It's a beautiful day. How would you like to go for a buggy ride? I'm sure it would be all right." She rose to her feet. "You said you wanted to see the ranch."

"I can't think of anything I'd enjoy more. Perhaps Meg would like to go along."

Sara paused halfway to the door. *Why, all of a sudden, had he become so thoughtful of Megan?* Sara wondered suspiciously. "We'll ask her, if we can find her. She tends to hide at times." She turned and looked at the tall, striking man. "There is one thing I'm curious about."

"What's that?"

"Why were you wandering across my land when the Indians found you?"

"As I recall, you invited me. This is a bit embarrassing, and I'm certainly not implying you would be guilty of such a trick, but I've met ranchers who only show people what they want them to see. I wanted to check out your cattle on my own."

"You must have misunderstood. I invited you on Wednesday, not Tuesday."

Fargo looked shocked. "I thought it *was* Wednesday."

A plausible answer. Or maybe she just wanted to believe him. "Well, we all make mistakes. Are you ready?"

"More than you know." Fargo gave her his arm.

As they walked through the house, Fargo made a point of looking around. He had no desire for Sara even to suspect how well he knew every room by now. He'd kept himself busy over the past few nights. Unfortunately, it hadn't gained him any insight into Hawk.

They didn't find Megan, and a half hour later Sara and Fargo were traveling across the ranch by buggy. Sara kept the horse at a slow pace so as not to jar the big man.

"I told you at the dance I could picture you in a buggy," Fargo commented after they'd traveled several miles.

Sara laughed. "That you did."

"You certainly have some fat beef."

"My ranch foreman is working on a breeding program. He has the cattle divided up into three sections. You'll meet him tonight at supper. I'm sure you'll have a lot to talk about."

Thanks to Megan, Fargo already knew about Will.

The afternoon passed pleasantly, with the conversation centering on cattle, land, markets, and breeding programs. It quickly became apparent that Sara was quite knowledgeable in all fields. For the first time, Fargo began to think of her as a rancher, not just a lady of substance.

At supper that night, Fargo met Will Langdon. Though he was a good six inches shorter than Fargo, his barrel chest reminded Fargo of a mountain. Fargo found the sandy-haired man to be quite affable. Megan dined with them, too, but kept her head down and said nothing. Fargo felt sorry for her. Apparently she had no clothes other than the clean, crisp paisley print dress she always wore. "We looked for you this afternoon."

"Oh?" The light that momentarily leapt into Megan's green eyes quickly faded.

Fargo couldn't understand what had happened to her. When they were alone, she was far more talkative. With her seemingly having only the one dress, and being afraid to speak around the others, he had already started giving some serious consideration to the possibility that she was being mistreated. "I had hoped you'd like to go for a buggy ride with Sara and me."

"You did?"

Fargo nodded.

Megan looked suspiciously around the table. "You put him up to it," she accused Sara.

Sara shook her head. "No, Meg. I—" But Megan had already thrown her napkin on the table and left the room.

Watching everyone's expressions changed Fargo's mind. Megan's words had been belligerent, not cowed. Sara seemed concerned when she took off after her sister. Apparently, flying words were not uncommon in this household. But Will's reaction interested Fargo the most. Instead of looking at Meg, Will had looked at Sara, and in one brief moment his face had shown his love.

"Don't let this stop you from eatin'," Will said congenially. "Megan often gets upset. Most of the time, no one even knows what she's upset about."

"Does she only have one dress?"

"No, but to see her you'd certainly think so." He motioned to the large tureen in the center of the table. "Help yourself. Onion-and-watercress soup. It's real good."

It was apparent that Will felt quite at home. Was Will Hawk? "I'm surprised you don't have trouble with Indians here," Fargo said as he filled his bowl.

"Sara has been one of the lucky ones. At least so far. There's a chief called Azul, and he and Sara's pa had some kind of a bond between them. Accordin' to Sara, for some unknown reason, her pa never spoke of the relationship other than to say he'd once saved the chief's life. When Charles Carter—that's Sara's pa—was murdered, Sara had been scared to death that the Chiricahua would sweep down and kill her and Megan. But it didn't happen." Will took several sips of soup.

"Who killed her father?"

"Marauders. Anyway, her pa had often said that the Indians would never take more than they needed, and if he allowed them to slaughter an occasional steer or pig, the Apache would leave the family alone." Will smiled, appreciating the wryness of Charles's words. "Charles would say in that deep-chested voice of his, 'On the other hand, if I should choose to fight, the Apache would take what they wanted anyway, but everyone would be left dead.' So Sara has continued to follow his advice, and, so far, the rule of thumb has worked. But, in all honesty, she also has an advantage. She speaks Apache."

"So I gathered. I've heard her talking to Carla." Fargo changed the subject. "I saw the cemetery. What exactly happened to the family?"

"It's nothin' of interest."

Fargo found it interesting that Will avoided any discussion of the deaths. Yet with everything else, he seemed to be a continual source of information. "How did Sara learn to speak Apache?" Fargo nonchalantly finished his bowl of the surprisingly tasty soup.

"While ridin' across the range, her pa used to pass the time by telling of the Apache ways and teachin' the Apache language. Though her brothers considered it a waste of their time, Sara learned everythin' Charles had to teach. Azul didn't particularly like dealing with a woman, but he admired her for not runnin' scared, for the respect she showed his people, and for her willingness and ability to communicate with them in their own language. But to me it's like sitting next to a hot brandin' iron. One wrong move could quickly change a person's thinking. Sara's quite a woman."

Fargo found it hard to believe someone so small and dainty could hold her own among a bunch of wild Indians. "Is that why she has an Indian cook?"

"Carla just showed up one day and has been here ever since."

The following morning, Sara stood at one of the gun slots, watching Fargo and Megan stroll down the road. She hadn't been invited. It had become apparent that Fargo preferred her sister's company. Sara thought about the conversation she'd had with Megan after she'd left the supper table two nights ago. It had taken a lot of talking to convince the dark-haired woman that Fargo had befriended her without being prodded. Since then, the pair had seemed inseparable. And Sara couldn't say a thing. For the first time in six years, Megan actually appeared to be happy.

Sara turned and stared at the large room. It always seemed like Megan should be sitting in here, tending to her mending. But that might not last much longer. Slowly but surely, she was starting to live again. And it hurt. It hurt to know that a stranger had entered this house and accomplished something Sara had tried for six years to do. Now she could only wait, watch and worry. Would the dreams return? Worse yet, would Megan start remembering the past? The ramifications were frightening. What if Megan couldn't face the truth? Something else that bothered Sara was the possibility of Meg's falling in love with Fargo. He attracted even experienced women like Penelope. Sara knew instinctively that Fargo would never return Meg's love, and Meg would be faced with yet another hurt. But at what point should she stop trying to protect her sister? Sooner or later, Megan had to learn to deal with the knocks life handed out.

Feeling Phew lean against her leg, Sara reached down and scratched the top of his head.

Chapter Four

As they guided their mounts across the rolling land, Sara's gelding continually tugged at the reins, eager for a hard run. But Sara wasn't about to give the horse his head for fear that Fargo would follow suit. They had traveled at a leisurely pace, and she had every intention of keeping it that way. In truth, though, his wounds and injuries appeared to be coming along just fine. No one who saw him moving about would ever suspect what he'd been through.

Sara pulled her hat lower on her forehead to better shade her eyes. For a change, she and Fargo were actually alone. Maybe it had something to do with his leaving tomorrow to return to Tombstone. At least that was what she'd like to think. She loved her sister, but Megan always seemed to be by Fargo's side.... Though she wasn't with them today, she would still end up a topic of discussion. Once again Sara needed to broach the delicate subject of her sister. And with Fargo leaving, she could no longer put off telling him about the fight with Ocha.

Seeing that they were approaching the tall green trees that bordered the river, Sara just decided to spit it out about Megan. She brought her horse alongside Fargo's, and cleared her throat. "I would like to know what your intentions are toward my sister."

Fargo shifted in the saddle so that he could see her better. "What are you talking about?"

"You have spent a considerable amount of time with her, and though you have assured me nothing has happened or would happen, a good deal of that time *was* spent in your bedroom."

Eyebrows raised, Fargo stared in disbelief at the prim Sara Carter. "Is that why you seldom came to my room? Because it wasn't proper?"

"We're not discussing me, we're talking about Megan."

"Oh? Well, then, by all means, please continue."

Unable to watch the humor that had begun to dance in his eyes, Sara concentrated on the trees ahead. "Since you've been up and around, you've continued to spend time with her. As I see it, you've been sort of... courting her. As her guardian, I want to know if marriage is being contemplated."

Fargo broke into a coughing fit. "Marriage?" he finally managed to repeat. "Miss Carter, you're not proposing a shotgun wedding are you?"

"Heavens, no.... I mean—"

"At no time have I wooed your sister. Nor do I intend to. I have simply befriended her, and she's well aware of it. I've also spent time alone with you, and I certainly don't see anyone riding with us right now. So does this mean I also have to marry you?"

"You needn't get so testy! I was just asking."

"Does your mind often take you off in such directions?" Having reached the water's edge, Fargo dismounted and ground-tied his horse.

"I don't know what you're talking about. Megan is very naive, and—"

"I thought we'd already had this discussion. And if you feel she's naive, does that mean you see yourself as worldly?" He drew the revolver Sara had given him, turned it over in his palm, then held it up to check the sight. "I'll make sure you get this back as soon as I can buy another one in town." He slid the Colt back into its holster, which she'd also provided.

Come on, Sara, why don't you just flat ask instead of hemming and hawing around? Sara chided herself as she climbed off her horse. She stopped to straighten out her split riding skirt. When she looked up, Fargo was walking away. "Where are you going?"

"To see if the Colt shoots true."

Sara hurried after him. "But what about Megan?"

"What about Megan?"

As she drew nearer, Sara resisted the urge to plant her foot right in the middle of his behind. "Are you going to marry her or not?"

"I hadn't planned on it," he said over his shoulder as he strode on. "Would it make you feel better to know Megan wouldn't marry me if I asked her?"

She was still trailing after him, and a smug smile suddenly tugged at the corners of her full lips. "Oh! Then you're saying she turned you down?"

Fargo spun around, nearly causing Sara to run into him. "No! That's not what I'm saying. We're friends, nothing more. And from what I've seen, Megan can certainly use a friend."

Refusing to follow a step farther, Sara plopped down on the riverbank, her breath coming out in a swoosh as she hit the hard ground. For a brief moment, she allowed herself to wallow in self-satisfaction. It pleased her to know Fargo wasn't interested in Megan, and vice versa. A selfish reaction, she had to admit, but a true one.

The place Fargo had chosen to check the Colt's accuracy was thick with lush, green foliage, while the tall trees offered a canopy of shade. A shot reverberated through the peacefulness, followed by the frantic fluttering of wings, and birds calling out their irritation at the loud noise. The horses snorted, but continued nipping at the grass.

Sara plucked a blade of her own, and stuck it between her teeth. At least one of her problems had been solved. Now if only the other one could be resolved as satisfactorily.

Another shot resounded through the trees, drawing Sara's attention to the man standing downriver with his back turned to her. She suddenly found herself contemplating what it would feel like to run her fingers through the thick crow-black hair that hung just past his shirt collar. He had wonderful broad shoulders, and his back tapered down to jeans pressed snugly against tight buttocks. Sara sighed. It had been hard to think about her sister's welfare while fighting her own desire. At least now that had been resolved.

She watched with interest as Fargo turned and strolled back along the riverbank in her direction. There was nothing about him that didn't appeal to her.

"This is a fine revolver," Fargo commented to himself, as he sat on the ground beside her. "Sara, you really don't have to worry about Megan. She's a joy to be around, and a mighty fine figure of a woman. She'll eventually come into her own."

Interesting that he can mention Megan's qualities, Sara thought indignantly, *but never mine.* "I hope you're right." She leaned against the thick tree trunk. Her pride smarting, she pressed her shoulders back, which in turn pushed her breasts forward. She'd heard enough of his innuendos about her being flat-chested. Well, maybe that wasn't exactly what he had said, but he might as well have.

"It's going to seem strange staying at a boardinghouse again."

"I imagine so," she replied offhandedly. Never once had he looked down to her bosom. Maybe it was because of her loose shirt and rolled-up sleeves. "Do you have a woman in Texas?"

He chuckled. "Several."

"That's a conceited comment."

"You asked. I simply gave you the answer. Would you rather I had said no?"

"Of course not. Why would you think that?"

"Why did you ask?"

A lump formed in Sara's throat when his gaze traveled to her breasts. But it didn't linger. He gave her one of those devastating smiles, then picked up a rock and tossed it into the water.

Sara wasn't sure what should take priority—humility or anger. "There is another matter I need to discuss with you."

"Surely not Megan again."

"No.... It has to do with me saving you from the Chiricahua." *Well, she had his full attention now.*

"You mean there's something you haven't told me?"

Sara shifted uncomfortably. "The day of the next full moon, you have to fight a Chiricahua brave to the death."

"The hell I do!"

Lifting her eyes to meet his furious gaze, Sara stated calmly, "Yes, you do. I had to make the bargain to save your life!"

Fargo rose to his feet and started to walk away, then stopped and turned. "I guess that's supposed to make me feel better? Dammit! What else have you failed to tell me?'' He waved a hand dismissively. ''No, I don't want to know. I am *not* going into battle with an Indian.''

Sara scrambled to her feet. ''You *owe* it to me!''

''I didn't make any deals with anyone, Sara. You're the one who did the bargaining. Now you can live with it.''

Sara propped her hands on her hips and took a step toward him. ''You sniveling, no-account, ungrateful, uncaring...bastard! I wish I had let them have you! If I had my way....'' The words died in her throat. How dare he have the temerity to be laughing? ''You listen to me, Fargo Tucker!'' she said in a low, hushed voice. ''If you don't meet with Ocha, Will will have to take your place. Now, maybe you think that's funny, but I don't. I'll not risk his life for your miserable hide.''

''You should have thought of that when you were bargaining with *my* life!''

Sara gasped. ''Why has it taken so long for me to realize you're nothing but a coward?'' She spun on her heel and headed for the horses. Suddenly she felt herself being jerked back around to face a furious Fargo.

''No one, man or woman, gets away with calling me a coward,'' he growled.

Sara gave him a smirky look. ''More hot air, Mr. Tucker?''

To save himself from giving in to the urge to place his hands around Sara's neck, Fargo released her and stepped away. ''Where is this fight supposed to take place?'' he snarled.

''I'll have to take you there. But, please, I wouldn't want you to put yourself out for me. After all, we only nursed you and offered you the full hospitality of my home!''

''That does it,'' he snapped. ''You certainly don't make any bones about tangling with a rattlesnake, do you? I could crush you with one hand.''

For the first time, Sara realized she just might be in deep trouble. The civilized mask Fargo had worn since she'd first met him had been peeled away by his anger, leaving deadly eyes and a hard, cold mouth. "Then you'll fight him?" she asked, refusing to appear cowed.

"I'll fight him." Fargo strode to his horse and picked up the reins. After tightening the girth with quick, economical motions, he turned to Sara. "If you're ever inclined to bargain with my life again, check with me first."

"There won't be a next time," Sara retorted. "However, if there is, I'll ask. That is, if you still have a life to bargain with."

Fargo hooked his arm over the saddle horn. "You know, Miss Carter, I sincerely hope that the other ladies in Tombstone are of a less sassy disposition."

"I'm sure they are," Sara replied sweetly. "But they're not nearly as interesting."

Dumbfounded, Fargo watched Sara mount her horse. What Sara Carter needed was a man in her life. A strong one. Very strong. And patient. "I didn't see Phew this morning," Fargo commented, changing the subject. "Where does he disappear to?"

"Sometimes he goes with Will out on the range, other times he's with Megan. I've been told that when I'm gone he stays by her side constantly."

Interesting piece of information, Fargo thought as he swung up onto his horse.

Though Fargo kept his eyes open for any signs of trouble during his ride to Tombstone, he was also contemplating everything that had happened over the past five weeks. He had looked forward to his visit to the Carter ranch, but he certainly hadn't planned on being there so long, or on being turned into buzzard bait by a bunch of Apache. And it had all happened because of his impatience. He had thought to scan the area and hopefully find a paint horse prior to paying Sara Carter a visit the following day. Even when he'd spied the Apache slaughtering a steer he hadn't drawn his .45, because he'd had no intention of making his presence known. He had gotten careless, and it had almost cost him his life. He should have been aware that someone was coming up behind him.

Fargo nudged his horse into an easy lope. The dates of death on the markers in the graveyard had all been the same.... Why did everyone refuse to talk about it? Sara had once said something about Megan's problems having started six years ago. Whatever had taken place back then was certainly a well-guarded secret. Did any of that have to do with Hawk? He had long since given up on the possibility of one of the ranch hands being the bounty hunter. A rancher couldn't afford to have one of his men taking off for long periods of time. And if it was one of the hands, Sara would know about it. At this very moment, Hawk could be out hunting another bounty. That would explain why he hadn't shown up at the house. Right in the middle of all this was Sara Carter, a woman who had more backbone than a lot of men he'd known.

Picturing Sara's large green eyes becoming flashing emeralds when she grew angry made him smile. She was so small, but she was a real spitfire. He quite enjoyed getting her riled and watching her work to keep that temper of hers under control. She also wasn't averse to asking pointed questions, and, like him, she expected an eye for an eye. But not this time. He had no intention of fighting some crazy Apache. She wasn't going to like it one damn bit, but he could hardly tell her that finding Jude's killer took precedence over everything. He'd already wasted too much time, and he couldn't afford to risk the possibility of being laid up again. He'd come here to find the killer and put an end to his miserable life. Only then could he take Jude home to rest in peace.

Will stood at the window long after Fargo had ridden away. "Did you believe his story about accidentally comin' a day early?"

Sara sat on the shiny black horsehair sofa. Though she was definitely attracted to the handsome Mr. Tucker, she wasn't sure she trusted him. However, at this point in time, that needn't be discussed. "I have no reason not to. Everything he said was plausible. And what purpose would it serve for him to lie?"

"You know you can't afford to have anyone hangin' 'round here for periods of time. And what if he starts showing up unexpectedly. Hawk has a lot of enemies. How do we know Fargo's not part of the Clanton or McLaury gang? Maybe he's a rustler. With Tombstone being such an infamous boomtown, it's attracted every thief, cattle rustler, gambler and gunman known to man, and he could be any one of the above." Will paused. "How did he explain not comin' by way of the road?"

"I didn't ask."

"Do you think he'll buy Ed Harris's ranch?"

"I don't know that, either. Why do you keep asking me questions about him, Will?"

"Maybe I'm jealous."

"Now who's making up lies? You worry too much, Will. No one has watched over Hawk as well as I have. You know I'm not about to let anything happen. I doubt that it matters, anyhow. After the fight, chances are we'll have seen the last of Mr. Tucker."

"Do you honestly think he'll keep his word and fight Ocha? If I were in his shoes, I damn sure wouldn't."

Sara leaned her head against the back of the sofa and closed her eyes. "I guarantee he'll be there. Even if I have to get the boys to hog-tie and deliver him. Something I'm sure Mr. Tucker hasn't taken into consideration."

The following week, Fargo slept a lot, or rode to the hills, where he tossed large rocks to strengthen his shoulder. He read the local newspaper, the *Tombstone Epitaph* faithfully, from front to back. But Hawk was never mentioned. Nor had the locals offered any information about the bounty hunter. Fargo decided to tackle the saloons.

The legends surrounding the infamous dens of pleasure in Tombstone stretched all the way to the East Coast. They were many and varied. Fargo didn't know how much was fact and how much was fiction, but he suspected that if the name Hawk was to be mentioned, it would be in one of the saloons. The one name that rang in his mind was the Bird Cage Theater, reputed to be the wickedest spot known to man. A place no lady would even walk past, let alone dare to enter.

All this and more went through Fargo's mind that evening as he tied his horse to the hitching post outside the Bird Cage Theater. Even from outside he could hear the sounds of revelry inside. As he entered through one of the tall, open doorways, loud music and an occasional shrill laugh hit him like a blast. He paused to look around. Immediately to his left stood a polished cherrywood bar that sported a large French mirror.

Fargo strode over and leaned against the smooth wooden surface. "Give me a bottle of your best whiskey," he said.

"We only serve the best," the red-coated bartender replied. "Will you be wanting a chip?"

Fargo shook his head. "Maybe later. I'm not sure I'll be gambling."

The graying man laughed. "This must be your first visit. A chip is for the ladies."

"I'm not expecting company, either," Fargo stated. "I'm alone, as you can see."

The bartender set down a bottle of whiskey, and a shot glass, leaned his arms on the bar, and looked up at Fargo with a smile that could almost be called a smirk. "The 'ladies' I'm referring to, son, are part of the entertainment here. See them steps over there?" He pointed across the room. At Fargo's nod, he went on. "Those lead to the bird cages. Within a week after this place was built, those steps were worn down to less than the thickness of a dime. That's 'cause we have such beautiful women. Had to put a whole new set of stairs in. Now, do you want the chip or not?"

Fargo released a low, good-natured laugh. "If you had told me what kind of ladies you were referring to, you could have saved yourself a lot of talk. I just spent several weeks with the other kind of lady, so I guess that's what I had on my mind. I don't think I'll be buying a chip. However, maybe I'll take you up on it another night."

Fargo slapped some money on the bar, picked up the shot glass and the bottle and entered the spacious main room, where all the noise was coming from. He looked around in awe. On the large stage straight ahead, three lovely women were singing and dancing. They were accompanied by a man playing the grand piano in the pit. To the side, a juggler showed off his skills with pegs. But it was the swing suspended from the high ceiling that drew Fargo's attention. A scantily clad woman was balanced precariously on it, swooping back and forth over the gambling tables, executing contortions that would have put ideas in any man's head.

An image reared up in Fargo's mind that had him laughing out loud, drawing a few interested stares from the patrons. Fargo had suddenly pictured Sara on that swing, and the portrait that it drew in his mind was so ludicrous he couldn't control his laughter.

The Bird Cage Theater played host to men from all walks of life. They crowded around the gambling tables or stood in groups talking, drinking and enjoying the entertainment. The shuffling of cards could occasionally be heard over the steady drumming of voices. Along both of the remaining walls were recessed booths, and above those the famous bird cages that held the women of pleasure. The grandeur of the place was something to behold. Fargo knew no one in Texas would believe him if he even came near to describing the place.

The sheer size of the crowd made Fargo realize that his chances of getting information here were practically nil. He decided to call on Nellie Cashman the next day. He hadn't seen her since returning to town. She might have additional information that she wasn't even aware of. Spending time with a mighty pretty woman could only be looked upon as pleasure. At least she wouldn't always be jumping to conclusions or making accusations, like a certain other lady he knew.

Fargo wandered about the room, sometimes having to shoulder his way through the crush of people. He stopped at one of the poker tables and watched with interest for quite some time. When one of the men suddenly scooted back from the table and stood, Fargo quickly moved to take his place. Maybe he would gather some information, and maybe he wouldn't, but at least he'd have a full night's entertainment. He set his bottle and glass down. "How about a drink on me, fellows?" he said with a smile.

Unable to sleep, Sara paced the bedroom floor, her bare feet making a patting sound on the hardwood. She had expected Fargo to pay them a visit, if only to find out the details regarding the fight. But so far he hadn't shown his face. It wasn't like her to be taken in by honeyed words that meant nothing. Yet, even now, she could see in her mind's eye those cool blue eyes watching her, almost as if he were in the room. Always taunting her...luring her....

She had been a fool to think Fargo might find her attractive. He hadn't even tried to kiss her. She considered whether or not she should forgive him for that. Why she even concerned herself with him was beyond her understanding. But there was no denying that just being near him created desires she had thought herself incapable of.

Even so, she had not allowed her attraction to cloud her perspective. Was he a man of honor? A man who possessed the necessary grit to meet Ocha? Time would tell. Unfortunately, she couldn't afford to wait around to find out. Will's questions a couple of weeks ago had weighed heavily on her mind, so she'd done something about it. When Fargo had left the ranch, she'd had him followed. Tex had orders to get a room at the San Jose House, where Fargo was staying. If Fargo left town, Tex would send a message, then stay with him.

Tapping her chin with a tapered fingernail, she pondered the feasibility of traveling to Tombstone herself. Too much time had elapsed, and the day of the fight was drawing near. She had to make sure Fargo would keep his appointment. Tomorrow she'd take several men with her to help Fargo keep his word.

Sara went to the chiffonier and pulled out her valise. As long as she couldn't sleep, she might as well pack.

By noon the next day, Sara had her buggy headed for Tombstone—five men following in her wake. A sixth man had been sent ahead to inform Rose and Cyrus Halverson that Sara would be spending a little more than a week with them. She had fretted enough over her problems. Now all she wanted to think about was spending a few enjoyable evenings with friends. If for just a short time, she needed to hear something besides Will's constant grumbling about one thing or another, and Megan's questions about the past, which she wasn't ready to answer.

As Tombstone came into view, Sara grinned. Even after all this time, it still excited her to know that, seemingly overnight, a rip-snorting town had sprung up in the middle of nowhere. The town had even built up again almost immediately after the fire earlier that year that had nearly leveled it.

Sara stopped her horse in front of the Halversons' two-story white house and stepped down from the buggy. She immediately set to dusting off her blue traveling suit. A moment later, Rose, smiling from ear to ear, hurried out the front door, with her lanky husband, Cyrus, right behind her.

"Are you planning on hanging someone?" Rose teased as she stared at the five hard-looking, well-armed men still mounted.

Sara laughed. "Not unless it's necessary. Oh, Rose, it's so good to see you."

"Cyrus, put Sara's things in her usual room."

While Cyrus unloaded the luggage, Sara watched her men ride off toward town. They already had their instructions.

"Let me take a good look at you." Rose pursed her thin lips and shook her head. "I don't know how you do it. You've traveled all this way and you're still beautiful!"

Sara laughed. Though Rose would never be considered a raving beauty, Sara thought her friend's flawless olive complexion and rich brown hair unequaled. But because of Rose's lack of self-esteem, and the drab clothes she chose to wear, people tended not to notice her prettiness. "I'm not feeling particularly beautiful."

"Oh, Sara, I'm so pleased that you'll be staying longer this time," Rose said excitedly as they walked up the flower-bordered path. "My life has become too boring."

"Shame on Cyrus. Here you've only been married a year and you're already complaining. Perhaps I should have a private talk with your husband."

"Don't you dare!"

Sara laughed.

"How is Megan?" Rose asked as they entered the house. "Any improvement, or is she still as quiet and withdrawn as ever?"

"Not exactly," Sara replied with a hint of dryness in her voice. "We had a visitor."

Rose's face lit up with interest. "Oh?"

"I'll tell you about it after supper."

They moved aside to let Cyrus carry the cases upstairs.

"Mems will be right up to help you unpack. Then you get some rest. We'll have supper in about an hour. I've sent a note to Penelope inviting her to dine with us. After, we'll have an old-fashioned get-together, like we used to."

Sara nodded and started up the steps.

Fifteen minutes later, Rose joined Cyrus in the parlor. He had poured himself a glass of port and made himself comfortable in his favorite chair.

"Sara is up to something."

Cyrus lifted the *Tombstone Epitaph* from the end table. "Why do you say that? This isn't the first time she's ridden into town with her men. I'd rather she did that than make the trip alone, like she did the last time. It's just not safe these days."

Rose stared at the newspaper, which was now hiding her husband's face. "I've known Sara too long. There's something she hasn't told me." Receiving no reply, she stared into space. "Cyrus," she said softly, "do you ever wish Sara had accepted your proposal, and you hadn't ended up married to me?"

Cyrus laid the paper on his lap and looked at his wife. "That's a foolish question. Are you looking for a way out of this marriage? If so, my dear, it won't work." He gave her an impatient smile. "You should know by now that I am quite satisfied with our arrangement. I wouldn't have wanted it any other way."

"But she's so pretty, and sometimes I think—"

"You're letting your imagination run away with itself. Now go see to supper, and stop worrying about ghosts that aren't there. You said Penelope will be joining us?"

"Yes. She should be arriving any time. I so enjoy the rare times when the three of us women can be together."

"Hmm...."

Rose knew she had been dismissed. Cyrus had raised the newspaper and was already absorbed in some article. She sighed and headed for the kitchen. Though it was sinful to have such thoughts about one's husband, she never felt as close to Cyrus as she would like. He seemed to keep her at a distance. It was something she intended to discuss with Sara during her friend's visit.

After supper, the three women gathered in the parlor with their sewing, dying to tell each other what had happened since they'd last met. Rose started it off, talking about the growing successful of Cyrus's mercantile store, then elaborating on the huge amounts of silver being taken from the earth.

"Haven't you anything more interesting to talk about?" Penelope complained.

Sara smiled. The three of them were so very different, yet they had been friends almost from the moment they'd met at a women's luncheon several years ago. They were absolutely tenacious about keeping each other's secrets.

"Nothing that would be of interest to you ever happens to me, Penelope. Obviously you have something you're itching to say," Rose retorted with a grin.

"I do indeed." Penelope set her embroidery in her lap. "Remember that handsome man at the Schieffelin Hall party? The one I *thought* was so smitten with Sara?"

"Yes," Rose replied.

"I've seen him escorting Nellie Cashman around town!" Her eyes took on a feline gleam. "I would love to get my hooks into that one, I can tell you. Did he ever come to your ranch, Sara?"

"Indeed he did. In fact, he was there for nearly a month."

Penelope licked her lips, and Rose leaned forward in her chair.

"Don't leave out a thing," Penelope said.

Chapter Five

Fargo stepped out the front door of the San Jose House, determined to spend the day searching out Phew's get. He had to be sure he covered all other possible angles before centering his attention on the Carters. When he'd returned to Tombstone a couple of weeks ago, he'd considered paying Marshall Virgil Earp a call. But when he remembered how friendly he and Sara had been at the dance weeks ago, the idea left his mind as quickly as it had entered.

Fargo stopped, pulled a cigar from his vest pocket and lit it as he looked up and down Fremont Street. Even so early in the morning, the town had already become a beehive of activity.

Last night he'd escorted the lovely Nellie Cashman to the Can Can Restaurant in Hop Town, the large Chinese section of Tombstone. The food had been excellent, and the service without flaw, but Fargo had been disappointed to hear that Nellie's inquiries about Hawk had produced nothing. He took a long draw on his cigar and watched the milk wagon pass by. Too much time has already passed, he thought as he slowly blew the smoke back out. He'd already had his fill of running into brick walls. Someone had to know Hawk's identity—or where he could be located.

If it wasn't for the dog, he would be convinced that the sheriff in New Mexico had deliberately set him up. Fargo had to give Hawk credit. The man certainly knew how to keep his identity a secret.

All things considered, Fargo thought as he headed for Jack Crabtree's livery stable to fetch his horse, last night certainly hadn't been a waste. He smiled. Spending the evening with a lovely Irish miss, and having Nellie tell him about a woman named Hazel Broom, could hardly be termed as uneventful. Miss Broom had two of Phew's pups.

By the time Fargo had mounted his horse and was riding down Fourth Street, he'd begun questioning the wisdom of seeing Nellie again. She could be deliberately keeping information about Hawk from him. But why would Nellie have anything to do with Hawk? He had reached the point of suspecting everyone. He tipped his hat and returned the smile of a lady standing on the corner.

Fargo found Hazel Broom's place on the outskirts of town. He had just dismounted when a pair of large, barking dogs suddenly charged from around the corner of the small, wooden house. Fargo was ready to swing back onto his horse if the shaky-looking fence didn't hold them. He'd be damned if he'd let those white fangs sink into his flesh.

"Buck! Hog! Down!"

People hereabout sure had a strange way of naming dogs, Fargo thought. He relaxed when the dogs turned and trotted to their master, who had stepped onto the small porch. The tall, rail-thin woman wore men's denim overalls and boots, and, had it not been for obvious breasts under the purple shirt, Fargo would have mistaken her for a man. Even her gray-streaked hair had been cut short. But what drew Fargo's attention was the double-barreled shotgun tucked beneath her arm. He grasped the front edges of his vest so that she could see his hands.

"Morning, ma'am. Would you be Hazel Broom?" Fargo called.

"That's right, but you can just climb back on your horse."

"Came to talk to you about those dogs." Fargo tipped his hat back. "The Carter dog sired them, didn't he?"

"That's right."

"I was quite taken with Phew when I stayed at the ranch, and I've been trying to find another dog like him. Sara said he'd sired some pups."

"How do I know you're tellin' the truth?"

"You don't, but it's not important," Fargo said. "I can see your dogs don't even have the same coloring."

"Sara could of told you that."

"Well, ma'am, I'm afraid I didn't make my mind up until a couple of days ago. I just figured I'd kinda like to take a dog like that back to my ranch in Texas. It was a whim, and not really that important." Fargo tipped his hat. "Thanks for your time. I'll be on my way." He shoved the toe of his boot into the stirrup.

"Hold on there. I reckon if you was lookin' for trouble, you wouldn't be so all-fired anxious to leave. Come in and have a cup of coffee. You can tell me how Sara's doin'."

Fargo cautiously lowered his foot. Never taking his eyes off the dogs, he tethered his horse and slowly opened the gate. The dappled dog growled, and Fargo stepped back out.

"Cut that out, Hog. I invited him in." Hog sprawled at her feet. "A woman can't be too careful these days," Hazel stated as she motioned to Fargo to come in.

"I absolutely agree." Fargo had to duck his head to keep from hitting it on the doorframe as they went into the house.

When they entered the kitchen, Hazel motioned to a table covered with a clean, red-checked oilcloth. "Have a seat, and I'll have coffee fixed in no time."

"Don't go to any trouble on my account."

"Ain't no trouble. Havin' a visitor is always a treat. I don't get many." Hazel tossed coffee into a kettle, then filled it with water. "I'm sorry to tell you this, but you ain't gonna find another dog like Phew around these parts." She lit the stove.

"Why do you say that?"

"'Cause I had the bitch that birthed 'em. She's dead now. Anyways, there were only ten pups in all. The one with Phew's coloring was born dead, I got two, a drifter took one, a lady in town another, and the rest are on ranches."

Fargo leaned back in the wooden chair and smiled. He'd come to the right house. Hazel Broom had finalized any doubts he might have had about the possibility of there being two Phews.

"So you was out to the ranch? How's Sara and Megan doin'?"

"Fine."

"Sara seldom comes to town, but when she does, she always spends a day with me."

Fargo remembered the man at the dance who'd told him Sara was everyone's friend.

"After what happened to them girls, they deserve all the good fortune they can get."

"Was there a town here back then?"

Hazel placed a steaming mug of coffee in front of him. "Cream?"

"No thanks. I take mine black."

"Same as my Gordon did, God rest his soul." The thin, neatly kept woman joined Fargo at the table. "No, there weren't no town back then, but there was people tryin' to raise cattle and fightin' off marauders an' Apache, and later all them men searchin' for the great mother lode."

Fargo sipped the surprisingly good coffee. "So you were here when Charles Carter was killed?"

"Not me. Gordon. He told me all about it"

The graves at the Bar C ranch flashed into Fargo's mind. Maybe he'd lucked out again. Here was the very person who could tell him exactly what had happened on that fatal day. "Poor Megan," he said thoughtfully, hoping to draw Hazel into talking about it.

Hazel nodded. "That's a terrible thing to have to live with. Thank God nothin' happened to Sara. To this day I don't know how that young girl managed to bury her family and get Megan taken care of. Did you know a whole week had gone by 'fore anyone found out what happened?"

Fargo shook his head before taking another drink of coffee.

"Seems Will was a real good friend of them Carter boys. Will, his pa, and some other men rode over to pay a visit and tend to some business. When they arrived, Gordon said Sara had tended to everything. The stock had been fed and taken care of, there was food in the kitchen, and the house was spotlessly clean. Accordin' to Gordon, Sara thanked them for comin' but said she didn't need any help except for the cattle. She couldn't get 'em branded and to market by herself. Will wanted to stay and help Sara, so his pa let him. Come brandin' time, Will's pa and brothers returned to get the job done."

* * *

During his ride back to town, Fargo contemplated how he'd still failed to find out exactly what happened to the Carters. There seemed to be only a few people who knew the details, and they weren't talking. But apart from that, the afternoon had been quite fruitful. He'd found out that when Will's father had taken his family back East, Will had taken over the family ranch, which was adjacent to the Bar C. He'd also agreed to pay his father for the land, as well as the cattle. Being a bounty hunter would help supply that money. So there was a strong possibility that Will was Hawk. He thought about the fact that Will and Sara ran their cattle together, then dismissed it as unimportant. He had known other ranchers who had done the same thing.

Fargo brought his horse to a halt on the crest of a hill and looked down at the valley below. There was another possibility. What if all the brothers hadn't died? All the bounty hunters Fargo had ever known made their profession a full-time job. The brother might not want anyone to know he'd survived. Then the men responsible for the Carter killings wouldn't suspect they were being chased. Far-fetched, but damn sure possible, Fargo decided, and at this point he'd grab at any straw he could get his hands on.

When he'd heard what all Sara had accomplished at the young age of fourteen, Fargo had gained some insight into the reason behind her straightforwardness, self-control and determination. His opinion of her had continued to escalate—this time by a good ten notches.

Fargo released a long, tired sigh. He'd come here to face his brother's killer. He'd sure as hell never thought that first he'd have to find out the man's identity. One thing was certain. All the answers were at the Bar C ranch—which meant he'd have to fight that damn Apache after all. He had to stay on good terms with Sara.

Sara sat in the Halversons' parlor, only half-listening to Rose expound on what it took to keep good help. Though Sara had only been in town a week, she had already become restless. Coming to Tombstone had been a mistake. Her men didn't need her. If Fargo chose not to leave for the ranch early Tuesday morning, they had their instructions to take him, even if it meant using force.

A call of "Hello" startled Sara. A moment later, Penelope waltzed into the room, looking the height of fashion in a brown linen town suit and gloves, with a small chapeau perched atop a mass of blond curls, and a matching parasol.

Rose greeted her. "You are out and about early this morning."

"I had planned on doing some shopping, but when I saw Fargo Tucker riding down the street, I rushed right over here. Sara, you know Rose and I are absolutely fluttering with excitement that you're actually showing interest in a man. Isn't that right, Rose?"

Rose smiled and nodded.

"So when I saw that fine-looking Mr. Tucker, I decided we needed to do something to make him aware of what a splendid catch you would be."

"Penelope! I'm not some fish in a pond! And you make it sound like I'm considering marriage." Sara stood and walked over to the long mirror. It aggravated her to know that Penelope had seen Fargo, especially since she'd made at least a half dozen trips to town and had never once laid eyes on the man. "I believe you've deliberately forgotten why I'm in town. Right now, I have only one thing on my mind. To get Fargo Tucker to that fight Tuesday. I still haven't told Will that he will have to meet Ocha if Fargo doesn't. I do believe he would be even more upset than Fargo at hearing the news. Will doesn't care for fights."

Penelope settled herself on the small brocade settee. "You openly admitted you're interested in the tall, handsome devil."

"Yes, but—"

"And you said you doubted that he'd even noticed you were a woman."

"Well, I—"

"So, we have to make him notice."

"How are we going to do that?" Rose interjected.

"Even I would like to hear this." Sara studied her reflection in the mirror. "Was he with anyone?"

Penelope pulled off a glove. "If you mean a woman, the answer is no."

"Do you like this dress?" Sara asked.

Rose didn't even bother to glance at Sara. "It's fine. Penelope, we—"

"I think this shade of green is rather becoming, don't you?" Sara turned sideways and ran her hands along her tiny waist.

"Sara, I like the white lace collar, and the trim at the bottom of your skirt." Penelope removed the other glove. "And I adore the clever way your skirt drapes to the side and brushes the top of your shoes. I also like the printed bows in the material.... I even like the matching bow in your hair. Can we now discuss my plan?"

"What about my bust? Do you think it's too small?"

"Sara, what are you talking about?" Penelope suddenly clapped her hands together. "Aha! It's that devil, Tucker! Oh, Rose, what a wonderful couple Mr. Tucker and Sara are going to make!"

"Penelope, you know Sara won't marry. Are you suggesting what I think you're suggesting?" Rose asked, wide-eyed.

"You needn't look so shocked," Penelope replied. "I would rather Sara have a liaison than become a shriveled-up old maid without wonderful memories."

Sara rolled her eyes.

"But that's terrible!" Rose gasped. "What if she were to get pregnant? She would be looked down upon as a tainted woman."

"Really, Rose, you should know there are all sorts of ways to keep from getting in a family way. We've discussed condoms enough times."

Rose nervously dabbed her nose with her lace handkerchief. "I don't think that is something we should speak of so openly," she said behind her handkerchief. "My maid may hear, and they're so terrible about carrying tales." She leaned forward and whispered, "Did I ever tell you I heard that pregnancy could be prevented by squatting over a pail of boiling onions?"

Penelope and Sara glared at Rose in disbelief.

"Does it work?" Sara finally asked.

Rose fell back in her chair. "Mother said it did, but she could never explain how she still had five children."

Sara suppressed a giggle. "You'll save yourself a lot of unnecessary trouble if you stop your scheming right now, Penelope. I have no intention of pursuing Mr. Tucker. I've far more important priorities at this time."

"You haven't even heard what I have to say. As your best friends, Rose and I are absolutely dedicated to helping you with this little problem."

"We are?"

Penelope ignored Rose's question. "I see no harm in inviting the gentleman to a small dinner party."

"No," Sara said flatly.

"Come, come," Penelope continued, "it will have him again looking at you as a lady. I still can't believe you actually straddled a horse and went riding with him."

"I wore a split riding skirt and it was perfectly proper. I do run a ranch, Penelope!"

"Which Will and all your other ranch hands take care of competently. Really, Sara, you know it is a lady's proper mannerisms that attracts men." Penelope's lips spread into a kittenish grin. "We are quite capable of enticing gentlemen, without them even being aware of it."

"Speak for yourself," Rose chided.

Sara walked to the window and, for a brief moment, watched two children playing across the street. "I'm not sure I would refer to him as a gentleman."

"I assume 'him' is Mr. Tucker?" Penelope cooed.

"I think having him for supper is a wonderful idea," Rose commented.

"The answer is still no. Besides, I've decided to return to the ranch tomorrow. Now, if you ladies will excuse me, I'm going upstairs. After I change clothes, I shall ride to town. I have a new dress to pick up. As soon as I've taken care of that, I'll return and start my packing."

"I don't know why you have to be so stubborn," Penelope complained. "I'm only doing it for you."

"You're doing it because you love to meddle, and you know it," Sara replied as she headed for the stairs.

"But must you hurry back to the ranch?" Rose asked. "Has Penelope upset you?"

Sara paused and turned. "Of course not. And it's not that I haven't enjoyed your hospitality, for indeed I have. But I worry about Megan, and there are things that need attending to at the ranch."

Rose and Penelope sat staring at Sara's back as she ascended the stairs. The moment she disappeared from view, Penelope turned to Rose. "I think there is something Sara isn't telling us. I'm dying to know what it is. Rose, aren't you going to offer me tea?"

Two hours later, Sara stood in the dressmaker's shop, her new dress draped over one arm. After complimenting Mrs. Trumpington on her marvelous creation, Sara quickly left.

The moment Sara stepped outside, she saw Fargo Tucker leaning against the hitching post. Somehow it made perfect sense that he'd be there. When she'd looked for him, he hadn't been available. Now that she had given up, there he stood.

Sara acknowledged with a "Good morning" before placing her garment in the buggy. Fargo looked wonderful. All the bruises and scrapes that had been on his face were gone. Even the cut that Carla had had to stitch closed gave him a devilish—or perhaps more of a rakish—look. The horse she had lent him had been tied to the back of her buggy, and the borrowed gun and belt lay on the seat.

Realizing he'd actually missed the minx caused Fargo to smile. "I've been waiting for you."

"Whatever for? And how did you know I was at the dressmaker's?"

"I saw you enter. Actually, you've saved me a trip. I had planned to ride to the ranch tomorrow. I believe we have an appointment, my dear. If I remember correctly, I'm supposed to meet some Indian at a designated place and time."

His smile warmed Sara, and his eyes sent tingles of delight running up her spine. She was inordinately excited to know she had misjudged him. "Can I count on your being there?"

"Oh, I'm sure you've known all along that I'd be there, whether I liked it or not."

"What do you mean?"

"I think you know exactly what I mean. I've been followed for over a week, and I can only think of one reason why. You're making sure I stand by my agreement."

"That's ridiculous."

"You put up a good bluff, Miss Carter. But since staying with you, I've come to learn that you don't gamble. No, that cowpoke is one of your men. You have no idea how saddened I am to know you didn't trust me to keep my word."

"All right," Sara confessed, "I do have a man watching you. And you're right, I don't take chances. Too much depends on you." She gave him a full smile, and then, with the help of his hand, perched herself on the buggy seat. "When you think of how I can repay you for the insult, don't hesitate to let me know."

"I've already thought of a way."

"Oh? And what would that be?"

"Let me take you out to supper tonight."

Sara was sure he could see her heart pounding against her ribs. Still, she didn't want him to get the impression that his invitation excited her. After all, a lady didn't reveal such things. "I have a better idea. I'm staying at a friend's house. Why don't you come over tomorrow night and have supper with us?"

"Are you afraid to be alone with me?"

"That's a ridiculous question. If you remember, we've been alone on more than one occasion."

Fargo frowned. "There's something about you that seems different."

"Tombstone has a way of making me feel more alive. Maybe that's what you're noticing. Others have made the same comment. Can I expect you tomorrow night?" She clamped her hands around the reins so that he wouldn't see them trembling. If he refused, she had half a mind to have her men drag him to the Halversons' house.

"It would be my pleasure."

Even after Sara had given Fargo directions to the house and had the buggy headed toward the Halversons' house, she still couldn't be sure she wouldn't swoon. Something about Fargo Tucker always had this effect on her. Penelope was right. She'd been in the shadows far too long. The time had come to start living again. Desire had been stirred, and she intended to do something about it. She smiled, then laughed out loud. Just thinking about what Fargo's kiss would feel like had her imagination running away with itself. She couldn't wait to see the shocked look on Penelope's and Rose's face when they found out she wouldn't be returning home right away. And they'd be speechless when she told them Fargo would be coming for supper.

As Sara left her bedroom and headed for the stairs, she felt like a queen. She had chosen to wear her new dress, a shimmering green taffeta affair only a shade darker than her eyes. The low-cut neckline and formfitting bodice left no doubt that she did, indeed, have breasts. With the help of Rose's personal maid, her thick auburn hair had been piled atop her head, with short, soft tendrils framing her face and sausage curls dangling down her back.

A loud knock on the front door caused Sara to pause halfway down the stairs. The maid opened the door, and Fargo stepped into the foyer. Sara clutched the banister when she saw the dark man handsomely dressed in a gray suit. As if he knew she would be standing there, he looked up. His eyes momentarily held hers before lazily taking in her every feature, from head to toe. His slight smile and pleased look were far more than Sara had hoped for. She opened her green fan and began waving it in front of her as she continued down the stairs, hoping she wouldn't make a complete fool of herself by tripping. When she reached the bottom, Fargo offered her the crook of his elbow. Sara placed her arm beneath it, welcoming a means of stability. Without uttering a word, he led her into the parlor, where Penelope, Rose and Cyrus were waiting patiently with their glasses of brandy.

It quickly became apparent that Cyrus had given Fargo his approval. They spent a good part of the evening discussing business—primarily mercantile stores and cattle. But at the supper table Fargo made sure the ladies were included in the conversation. He discussed Tombstone with Rose, inquired as to how long Penelope had been a widow, and asked Sara about Megan. He was the perfect gentleman. Only Sara saw the subtle, ravishing glances he bestowed on her. Enticing glances . . . or were they? Surely she couldn't be making something out of nothing simply because that was the way she wanted him to look at her.

When it came time for Fargo to leave, Sara already had decided that Penelope had been right. Fargo would, indeed, make an excellent lover. Without saying or actually doing anything, Fargo had somehow drawn her into his web, and she no longer cared to deny the feelings he stirred. The problem being, she had no idea how she could relay this message to Fargo without ending up embarrassed should he not feel the same.

After Fargo thanked the Halversons for an enjoyable evening and a delicious meal, Sara escorted him outside. It was a warm, lazy evening. The kind of evening that—

"When do you plan on returning to the ranch?" Fargo asked when they'd reached his horse.

"Monday. The day before your meeting with Ocha."

"Why don't I accompany you? At least you would no longer be concerned about whether or not I'd show up."

Sara thought of the six men she had in town. Six men who would make damn sure he arrived. Six men Fargo knew nothing about. "I'd welcome the company." Sara stopped breathing when Fargo raised the back of her hand to his lips and kissed her knuckles.

"You are truly a vision of loveliness tonight, my dear." He stepped away. "I'll be looking forward to our trip, Monday."

Fargo untied his horse, and, as he swung his lithe body onto the saddle, Sara grabbed the hitching post for support. Her breathing still hadn't returned to normal after that kiss on her hand.

Fargo tipped his hat and rode off.

Aggravated by her jellylike condition, Sara pushed away from the post and squared her shoulders. Her reactions to Fargo were like nothing she'd ever experienced before. If she didn't hurry and do something, she would surely end up with apoplexy.

Sara returned to the parlor and found Rose and Penelope waiting. "Where is Cyrus?" she asked before sitting beside Penelope.

"He's gone to bed," Rose answered. She leaned forward in her chair and asked excitedly, "Did he kiss you?"

"She means Fargo, not Cyrus," Penelope clarified.

Sara had already anticipated the questions. "He kissed my knuckles."

"How romantic," Rose fell back in her chair. "No man has ever kissed my knuckles."

"Don't you think it's strange that Fargo is suddenly showing me so much attention?" Sara rationalized. She could still feel the sensation when, during the meal, he'd practically seduced her with his eyes. She'd become light-headed just from the joy of it. "He certainly never acted like that at the ranch."

"There you go, trying to analyze everything," Penelope scolded.

"Monday he'll ride to the ranch with me."

"Thank goodness your men will be along." Rose began picking at some imaginary piece of lint on her skirt. "Although I find Fargo's company most enjoyable, there is still a strange, brooding quality about him that bothers me."

"It bothers you because you've never known a real man." Penelope rose to her feet.

"How can you say that, Penelope Stewart? I have Cyrus."

"My statement stands. I really must be going. It's getting late and my driver might fall asleep on the way home." Penelope looked down at Sara and smiled. "You know, my dear, you should send your men home early. Ta-ta. I'll see you ladies tomorrow."

A few minutes later, Sara and Rose heard the front door open and close.

"Sara, don't you listen to a word Penelope says." Rose fidgeted in her chair. "Just because she has an occasional male friend doesn't mean you should do the same thing. Penelope may be a widow, but she's far too promiscuous for my standards. That she is deliberately trying to lead an innocent young lady astray is unforgivable. Why, every decent woman knows to save herself for the man she'll someday marry."

It amazed Sara that Rose and Penelope could have remained such good friends, what with Rose being so pious and Penelope so free. Maybe there was a quality in each of them that the other secretly admired—or desired.

"And if I never marry?"

Rose looked Sara straight in the eye. "Believe me, Sara, you won't have missed a thing," she said, without so much as a hint of embarrassment. "Someone has to tell you the truth. Being with a man is not nearly as gratifying as Penelope would have you think. Furthermore, the first time is extremely painful."

"Thank you for your well-meant words, Rose, but after seeing what happened to my family, plus growing older, I've become a firm believer that one should take what few pleasures life offers. I'll be equally honest. I want Fargo Tucker to make love to me. No man has ever walked into my life and ignited passionate feelings the way he has, which makes me think it may never happen again. It's time I start tasting the fruit in the basket, Rose. I deserve it. Can you understand that?"

"Yes, and no...." Rose said sadly. "I have never experienced such ardent feelings." She stood and hugged Sara. "I just couldn't bear to see you get hurt again."

Sara slowly pulled away and smiled. "I once heard someone say that with pain comes healing. I'd like to believe that's true. I have to admit, though, it bothers me that, come Tuesday, I may be taking the one man I ever desired to his grave."

Sunday night, Sara and Rose sat staring at Penelope in total shock. Somehow the blond widow had managed to purchase a colorful Mexican peasant blouse and black skirt for Sara.

"I went to a lot of trouble to get this. It's really quite comfortable," Penelope assured her friends. "It allows a woman much more freedom."

"No." Sara stated emphatically. "I am not going to wear that outfit on the trip tomorrow."

Penelope tossed the skirt and blouse onto the settee and headed for the doorway. "Suit yourself." As she passed Sara, she stopped and leaned close to her ear. "Coward."

Sara gave her a whimsical smile. She hadn't had a good challenge in some time. "If these clothes are so comfortable, I'll make you a bargain."

"Oh? What kind of a bargain?"

"You know that for me to get to the road leading to my land I have to go through town. Which means I'll be seen by a good many *upstanding* citizens. So, a turn for a turn. I'll wear the clothes tomorrow, but when I return, you will take your turn parading through town on foot."

To Sara's shock, Penelope agreed. As a matter of fact, Penelope seemed to be delighted with the idea.

Chapter Six

Fargo arrived at the Halverson house Monday morning wearing a Stetson, a red shirt and jeans. A new gun belt rested low on his slender hips. To Sara, he looked handsome, dangerous and altogether too tempting for any woman's peace of mind. Why was she putting herself through all this? It wasn't as if she loved Fargo, or even planned on their marrying. She already knew the answer to her question. Wittingly or unwittingly, he had fanned a desire in her that had turned into a ferocious storm. It only made sense that if he could start it, he certainly ought to be capable of calming it down.

Sara covered up her embarrassment over the clothes she wore—plus the absence of a girdle—by hurrying about, making sure everything had been properly packed in the back of the buggy. The morning air proved to be unusually crisp, and Sara's abnormal lack of covering caused her to shiver. Somehow she managed to hide her embarrassment. But she couldn't make the chill go away.

In her heart, Sara was glad Penelope had bought the Mexican skirt and blouse. Yesterday, she had decided to seduce Fargo during their trip—a decision she hadn't shared with Penelope or Rose. Nor had she told her friends she had sent her men back to the ranch a day early.

Once the picnic basket had been placed into the buggy, it was time to leave. Fargo helped Sara onto the seat, then circled around and climbed up beside her. He'd already tied his horse to the back. Sara waved goodbye to Cyrus and Rose, and Fargo gathered the reins between his fingers. He flicked the leather across the horse's shiny rump, and they took off down the road.

"I like your outfit," Fargo commented. "It reminds me of home. The Mexican women in my part of the country wear those blouses and skirts."

Sara gave him a half smile. Maybe the women in Texas wore them, but not the ladies in Tombstone. But she'd sworn she wouldn't give a single man or woman an inkling of her embarrassment. As they traveled down the streets in town, Sara held her head high, and at times even waved at gawkers. She refused to hide the low-cut peasant blouse embroidered with bright flowers, or the black skirt. She had even left her auburn tresses hanging loose down her back. Nevertheless, as they left town, she was convinced she would never again be welcome in any self-respecting woman's house.

As the sun rose higher, the day grew hot. Sara found that her clothing was much cooler than the travel dress she would have worn had it not been for Penelope. Later, however, Sara could definitely feel a burning sensation on her virgin skin, where the tops of her shoulders and chest were exposed. Sara tried to ignore the discomfort.

She and Fargo had remained silent. Sara had no idea what he was thinking, and her thoughts were in a turmoil. Now that she'd made her mind up to seduce him, how should she go about it? They were well away from town, and from all humanity, so she'd best get busy and do something. Anything! Why should so natural an act be so complicated?

Sara considered her blouse. It scooped low in the front and back, allowing a peek of the swell of her breasts. And she did have breasts! Maybe not cantaloupes like some people she knew, but definitely tomatoes. Perhaps Fargo needed a better look. She placed her hand next to Fargo on the black leather seat and leaned over, allowing the neckline to fall over her shoulder. It gave him a clear view of her creamy flesh. "What a wonderful day," she commented cheerfully.

"Hmm . . ."

"Actually, I always feel my best of a morning. I guess that's why I'm an early riser."

Fargo kept the horse at a steady trot, and Sara enjoyed the soft breeze blowing across her face and body. She reached up and raised her heavy mane, letting the breeze cool the back of her neck, as well. With a hidden smile, she watched Fargo flex his shoulders. It was a nervous reaction she'd seen more than one man make. At least her latest effort had gotten a reaction. What could he be thinking? She had always had the distinct feeling that Fargo was a man who took what he wanted without offering an explanation or an apology—one of the many things that had attracted her from the very beginning. So why didn't he say something, dammit?

"Stop the buggy!" Sara suddenly shouted.

Fargo brought the horse to a halt. Sara climbed down. "Look there," she said excitedly, pointing to a tall, graceful plant with beautiful orange blossoms at the end of each long finger, "the ocotillos are starting to bloom. Soon most of the plants will be in full color."

"What kind of plant is that?"

"A cactus." Realizing Fargo was standing right behind her, Sara turned and, hoping it would appear to be an accident, came against his hard, solid chest. As she looked up into his fiery blue eyes, his arms were already encircling her waist. "Oh, I'm sorry," she said breathily. Time seemed to stand still as he looked down at her. Would he do it? Would he kiss her? She watched him slowly bend his head. Her blood was pumping so fast she thought she would surely die of heart failure. She couldn't take her eyes off his lips. They looked soft and compelling. Then, slowly—too slowly—he lowered his head even more.

"If there are redheaded gypsies, you must be one of them." He ran his fingers through her hair. "You should wear your hair down more often," he whispered before his lips claimed hers.

If there had been any doubt in Sara's mind about Fargo being able to satisfy her longing, it had disappeared. Her eyes closed as she became lost in the pleasure of his tentative, yet compelling, kiss. He drew her closer, sucking on her lower lip, then tracing the inside of her mouth with his tongue. She felt herself being pulled deeper into a vortex of pleasure. Then, even though she knew she was being a fool, she drew upon every bit of willpower she possessed and gently pushed Fargo away. She didn't want him to get the impression that she fell easily into a man's arms. The real truth being that she couldn't handle the sudden raw burst of emotion she had experienced. It frightened her.

Fargo didn't try to prevent her from leaving his arms. When she finally looked at him again, he had that half smile that had become all too familiar.

"You taste good." Fargo reached up and brushed his thumb across her swollen lips. "Have you ever had a man make love to you?"

Sara backed away. How had everything gotten twisted around? She was supposed to be the aggressor. "Why do you ask?"

Fargo placed his hands on his narrow hips and shifted his weight to one foot. "Because I want to know how gentle I have to be when I make love to you."

"I..." Not only was Sara dumbfounded, but she was uncomfortable, as well. "You seem awfully sure of yourself," she said in a huff. She watched his eyes travel across her face, down her neck and over the swell of her breasts. The lazy journey made her knees weak.

"Are you going to tell me you don't want me?"

Sara was getting angry. She didn't like his arrogant self-confidence. "I don't know what type of woman you're used to being around, but I don't fall into bed—"

"Just answer the question. Have you ever had a man make love to you?"

His eyes held hers, and that deep, honey-coated voice was almost Sara's undoing. She felt confused. She wanted him, God knew how much she wanted him. But she kept pushing him away. Why? A sudden, sickening momentary picture of a man's face flashed in her mind. No... No! It had been six long years, and she'd be damned if she'd let the past keep her from what she desired! Why now? Never before had Dodd's face come to mind—his voice, yes, but never his face. The vision had stolen her romantic thoughts. "I'm a lady, not—"

"Oh, there's no doubt about that. However, things are a lot easier if two people just come out and admit that they want each other."

Sara wasn't sure what to say. Fargo's straightforwardness had a way of lighting a flame in her, and it was working again.

"We desired each other from the first time our eyes met," Fargo continued, "and now the question is, how long is it going to be before it happens?" He reached forward and trailed a finger from her shoulder, down across the rise of her breasts.

Sara slapped his hand away. None of this was going the way she'd envisioned it. Since the first time their eyes had met? Her ridiculous efforts hadn't even been necessary! He had been toying with her all along! "Of all the no-account—" He swallowed her words with a kiss. Then, as she started to lean into him, he moved away.

Seeing her eyes flash and her hair blowing in a sudden gust of wind, Fargo suddenly broke out laughing. He turned and walked back to the buggy. "What a hell of a pair we're going to make, Sara. Just tell me when...." He climbed up, lifted the reins, then sat waiting for her to join him.

Sara was still shaken by his kiss, and her steps weren't as steady as she would have liked. What a mess everything had turned out to be. Avoiding his eyes, she made herself comfortable on the seat. Would he think her a tease because of the way she encouraged him, then turned around and said no. She had no idea why she had acted in such a manner. It had all seemed so simple when she'd thought it out. Her mind had been absolutely set on having him make love to her. Yet now she almost hated him for his blatant assumption that they would eventually couple. At the same time, it was unbelievably titillating to know that such an appealing man had every intention of taking her to his bed. This couldn't continue. She'd go insane. It would be better to just get it over with.

Sara looked at Fargo, ready to inform him that he could have her body. Fortunately, at that moment he flicked the reins and started the horse moving, and her resolution weakened again. It was all too confusing. In order to save Fargo's life, she'd accused Ocha of running with his tail between his legs. In order to get Fargo to fight, she'd accused him of being a coward. But today, she had been the biggest coward of all. She'd deliberately set out to seduce Fargo, and yet, when her passion had become so strong that she could taste it, she'd backed off. At this rate, she'd never experience the pleasures that were supposedly shared by a man and a woman.

Sara tried to concentrate on the road ahead. She had underestimated Fargo. His statement made it apparent that he was a man who noticed a lot of things, even if he made no comments. In what other ways had she underestimated him? Even the silence they now shared was uncomfortable. He'd brought everything out into the open, and his words just hung there in front of her, more tempting than the biblical apple, she thought, yet too truthful to be deceptive.

He was like a mountain lion, she decided. He had made his move, and now he was waiting for the prey to come to him. Over the years she had met a lot of men, but none quite like Fargo Tucker.

By high noon, the temperature had risen considerably. As Sara continued to battle with herself over what to do about Fargo, she could clearly feel the burn on her shoulders and neck worsening.

When they reached the San Pedro River, Fargo brought the buggy to a halt beneath a large tree. Sara immediately climbed down, and as soon as her feet touched the ground she hurried to the water's edge. She knelt and drank from her cupped hands. Satiated, she soaked her handkerchief in the invigorating water, and then with slow, long strokes, bathed her face and her shoulders. She shivered as the cool water trickled down the heated valley between her breasts.

Fargo removed the straw basket containing their food from the back of the buggy, and turned. Seeing Sara made him pause. Since the night he'd been to the Halversons' for supper, he'd known Sara felt an attraction to him. Thinking about her obvious confusion as to whether or not she should give way to her desire brought forth a smile. A difficult decision for a woman who worked very hard at keeping her life well under control. Oddly enough, none of her efforts even began to compare to the innocent view of her he was looking at right now. Seeing her eyes closed and the look of pleasure on her face as her hand glided down her body to cool her flesh proved to be far more sensuous than anything she had deliberately tried so far. The water had soaked the front of her blouse, leaving her breasts molded against the material and showing nipples that were firm and inviting. He longed to feel them pressed against his hand while he licked the river water from her body. Oh, yes, he wanted her, there was no doubt about that. But he couldn't force it. He couldn't afford to alienate the one person who could lead him to Jude's killer. He would have to wait and let Sara come to him, or be damn sure that when he made his move it was exactly what she wanted. He had to gain her confidence before he'd be able to get her to tell him about Hawk.

He grabbed the throw from the back of the buggy and headed toward Sara. "What do you say we take a rest and have something to eat?" he asked as he spread the small blanket on the ground. He placed the basket next to Sara.

"That's a wonderful idea," Sara replied cheerfully. She felt considerably more in control, now that the water had cooled her off.

She spread out several napkins, then unpacked from the basket crisp fried chicken, a loaf of crusty bread, cheese, and a variety of fresh, plump fruit.

Fargo sat directly across from Sara, and they proceeded to enjoy their meal in silence. Fargo didn't fail to notice that Sara kept averting her eyes. Knowing she was still discomfitted by their earlier conversation, he deliberately waited until they'd finished their meal before trying to break the tension. "It was good of you to put me up tonight," he said as he picked up the last piece of cheese.

The statement eased the anxiety Sara had been feeling. Apparently Fargo had dismissed what had happened at their last stop. The satisfying meal also helped her to relax. "It's the least I could do. Especially since I'm the one who got you into this mess."

"Well, now, you did save my life. This man I'm supposed to fight . . ."

"Ocha."

"If I remember correctly, didn't you say he's the one who had thought to end my life?" Fargo asked.

"I believe so. Did you get a good look at him?"

"No." Fargo stared at the river. "I don't remember too much." As he thought back on the hell he'd suffered, a deep, hitherto-suppressed anger began to build. "I remember the sharp pain when the arrow lodged in my back. I had just raised up from lying on my stomach when it hit. I scrambled to a sitting position, and the next thing I knew someone hit me in the face with a rifle butt. Everything went black. I didn't see the man who struck the blow. I remember the kicks, my wrists being tied, and a horse dragging me along the ground for what seemed like miles before I was finally forced to stand." He remembered a hell of a lot more, but chose not to talk about it. He realized that his anger had made Sara temporarily fade from his mind. "Maybe this fight was inevitable, after all." He laughed. "I've been told that these Indians are rather small, so it shouldn't last long. You just keep the rest of them off my back. Are there any rules I'm supposed to abide by?"

"Only one or two."

"Like what?"

"There's a long rope," Sara began. "One end will be tied to Ocha's wrist, the other end to yours. You'll both be given knives. Then anything goes."

"Knives, huh?" He picked up a peach and broke it in half. "How long is this rope?"

Sara shrugged her shoulders. "I have no idea. I've never seen the fight. I've only heard about it."

"And what determines the winner?" He sank his teeth into the sweet, juicy peach.

"The one who is still alive."

Fargo rose to his feet, and a moment later he sent the peach pit skipping across the top of the water.

He could hear Sara cleaning up the remnants of their lunch, but he didn't turn and look at her. He didn't want her to get so much as a hint of how furious he felt. Being in a fight didn't bother him. Dying didn't bother him. But the possibility of dying and Jude's murderer getting away free bothered the hell out of him. Here he was, in a situation he had no business being in, and with no way out. He needed Sara. She held the key to everything. If he could spend enough time at the ranch, possibly even Megan could answer his questions. But none of this would happen unless he met Ocha tomorrow. He was damned no matter which way he turned.

As soon as Sara had everything ready, Fargo folded the throw and put it in the back of the buggy, then placed the basket on top. He sat beside Sara and made some off the shoulder comment about the weather. Neither his expression nor anything else revealed his anger about tomorrow's date with destiny.

To Sara's surprise, when they arrived at the house, Megan stood waiting out front. She exuded excitement and happiness. Her eyes were on Fargo, not Sara. Apparently, when the men had returned home yesterday, they had spread the word of Fargo's arrival.

One of the ranch hands came forward and took the horse's reins. As soon as Sara and Fargo had climbed down, Megan ran forward. Laughing, she jumped up and threw her arms around Fargo's neck.

"I'd begun to wonder if you'd ever come back to visit me," Meg said playfully.

Both of them laughing, Fargo swung her around in a wide circle before putting her back on her feet. "I told you I'd be back." He placed a big arm around her shoulders, then walked with her into the house.

Sara remained standing by the buggy.

"Where do you want me to put the luggage, ma'am?" one of the hands asked.

"I don't care where you put it!" She marched into the house, ashamed of herself for being angry. Wasn't Megan expressing the very attitude that Sara had prayed she'd see one day? Still, Megan didn't have to be quite so capricious. It seemed she had decided to come out of her shell. Sara had thought it would be a much slower process. When she heard Megan and Fargo out on the patio, laughing, she felt alienated. Apparently, Fargo made a habit of plying his charm on whatever woman was available.

Refusing to stand around and listen to the two of them, Sara went straight to her room. Maybe she shouldn't have saved Fargo's life.... What would happen to Megan if Fargo lost tomorrow? Could her older sister handle the death of yet another person who was dear to her? It might set her back so far that there would be no hope of her returning to normal.

* * *

That evening, Fargo, Megan and Will dominated the conversation. Sara wondered if Megan had been saving up all her words over the past six years and had now chosen to spew them all out. She talked about how much she enjoyed going hunting and taking long rides, pushing her horse to its fastest speed and allowing her hair to blow wild in the wind. Sara could only stare in disbelief. Where in the world had Megan come up with all of this? It had to be from those books she read.

Fargo asked Will questions about the ranch, and if Will left something out, Megan filled it in. Apparently Megan had acquired a lot of information over the years. Through it all, Sara sat properly at the table and smiled when necessary. Even Will seemed bewildered and kept looking at Megan as if he didn't know her.

Later that night, Sara tossed and turned in her bed. Sleep was an impossibility. She kept telling herself that she should be happy at Megan's sudden transition. Fargo had accomplished a miracle. But the fight for Megan's sanity wasn't over. How would Megan react to others? Could she handle going to town and seeing all the traffic, all the people? She seemed fine around Fargo, but he was only one person.

Unable to sleep, Sara sat up, pounded her pillow and flopped back down. The sunburn on her shoulders didn't help matters. After tomorrow, there might not be any questions. Fargo could be dead. She didn't want Fargo to get hurt or killed. But she had no choice. She had a ranch to run and people to take care of, and that took priority over everything else.

Sara kept screaming, trying to warn her mother not to leave the house, but no sound came forth. Her beautiful, unsuspecting mother came out and there were shots. But when Sara looked at the ground, it wasn't her mother lying there dead, it was Fargo.

Her face covered with perspiration, Sara jerked upright in bed and glanced around the dark room. It seemed to take several long minutes before her mind began to clear. It was a dream. Just a dream. She rose from the bed and went to the washstand to rinse off her face. Was it an omen?

Tomorrow would tell.

Chapter Seven

Will, Sara and Fargo stood on the dirt flat, their horses' reins held in their hands. In a state of nervousness—exacerbated by the memory of her dream—Sara had suggested bringing a wagon in case Fargo should be badly injured. The suggestion had been quashed by Fargo's surly response. At a little past one in the afternoon, the sun looked like a bright orange ball in a field of clear blue sky.

Fargo pulled his hat down farther on his forehead and scanned the area. "Well, are they coming?"

"They'll be here," Will muttered.

After another five minutes, Fargo squatted on his heels, anxious to get the confrontation over with. Hearing a horse whinny, he stood and turned. The corner of his mouth twitched. There had to be at least thirty mounted Chiricahua coming down the road, from both directions.

Fargo's instincts told him the three of them should jump onto their horses and get the hell out of there. Even the cavalry wouldn't want to be caught in the middle of this many Apache, none of whom would give a second thought to taking a scalp. He glanced at Will. The blond man kept nervously wrapping and unwrapping his horse's reins around his hand. His face had turned so pale, he looked as though he'd pass out at any moment. Sara, on the other hand, stood calmly watching the Indians approach. Fargo found himself questioning the validity of her confidence.

Fargo took several deep, stabilizing breaths. There was nothing he could do at this point to prevent whatever was about to happen, other than to be ready to draw if one of the Apache made a wrong move.

Having recovered from his initial shock, Fargo scanned the group, wondering which one was Ocha. None of them appeared to be nearly as small as he had heard. When the Indians parted and one lone rider came forward, Fargo knew this was the man he was to fight. As Ocha slid from his pony's back, Fargo sized up his opponent. The brave was every bit as tall as Fargo, but where Fargo tended to be lank, Ocha looked to have the strength of a bull. Fargo knew he was facing the fight of his life.

As the Chiricahua made a wide circle with their ponies, Ocha and Fargo faced each other. Ocha's face expressed loathing and contempt. The more Fargo looked at his enemy, the angrier he became. The cocksure bastard had put him through a living hell, and he had every intention of doing it again. But Fargo had other ideas. He didn't plan on dying by this man's hand, and he did plan to make sure Ocha got back what he'd doled out. But Fargo knew he'd have to do it quickly. He wasn't sure he had the endurance of his adversary.

Sara twisted her hat in her hand as she watched the two men strip to their waists. Upon seeing the anger build on Fargo's face, she tried to console herself with the belief that the fight probably would have happened anyway.

Another brave, carrying a rope, entered the circle. As the two men continued to take each other's measure, the end of the rope was tied to Ocha's wrist.

"You will die," Ocha uttered in broken English.

"Don't count on it."

The other end was tied to Fargo's wrist.

Satisfied the knots were secure, the brave handed each man a long, deadly knife. As he backed away, the two enemies began to circle each other. Sara flinched. She wanted to call off the fight, but she knew it wasn't possible.

Ocha swung his knife first, but Fargo managed to dodge the sharp blade just in the nick of time. He retaliated, but missed. Ocha leaned down. Too late, Fargo realized what he was up to. Grabbing a handful of dirt, Ocha flung it in Fargo's eyes.

Sara thought the fight was over. But, somehow, Fargo managed to stay on his feet and dodge the brave's continuous slashes. Finally his eyes cleared, but Ocha grabbed the rope and jerked it forward, flinging Fargo toward him. Fargo made a dive to the ground, but not in time to prevent a searing cut on his arm. Ocha tried wrapping the rope around Fargo's neck. Fargo managed to kick the big man's feet out from under him. They rolled on the ground, each holding the arm that gripped the other's weapon of death. A cloud of dust had risen in the air by the time the men scrambled to their feet. Again, they moved to the ends of the rope, cautiously circling. Fargo had discovered he could move faster than his adversary, and that gave him an advantage.

For another ten minutes, they slashed at each other, circled, fell to the ground and knocked each other down. Blood flowed from cuts, but neither man gave an inch. Yet, the way their chests heaved as they gasped for breath indicated that neither man could remain standing much longer.

Ocha's ploys were no longer working on Fargo as well as they had at the beginning, and Sara could see that the big man had become more cautious. For the first time, her hopes slowly started to build.

Another fifteen minutes passed, and Sara couldn't believe either man was still standing. Muscles bulged, sweat and blood soaked their dust-covered bodies, and wheezing sounded from their lungs. Then Fargo yanked the rope, and Ocha moved forward, ready to attack. Fargo suddenly moved backward and to the side, his knife held low. Ocha realized his mistake too late, and couldn't stop his forward movement. As he passed Fargo, a knife was buried deep in his gut. His face showed his shock. He tried charging Fargo, but again Fargo yanked the rope, knocking the warrior off his feet. Ocha's body twitched, and a moment later, lay still.

Fargo had won the fight. But he wasn't satisfied. Ocha's chest was still moving, which meant he wasn't dead. Fargo knelt. In two quick slashes, he cut both Ocha's wrist and his own. Raising Ocha's hand, he held the two cuts together.

"Now, you son of a bitch," Fargo spit out, "if you live, you'll be cursed with the reality that we're blood brothers. And don't you forget it." He released Ocha's arm and stood.

Once he'd returned to the center of the circle, Fargo looked directly into the eyes of one brave, then another. It was a silent dare for any one of them to challenge him. He'd take them on if necessary, even though he wasn't sure how much more he could stand.

A man of indeterminable age raised his staff. Gasping for breath, Fargo tried to wipe away the sweat burning his eyes. He was still waiting for the others to attack. But it didn't happen. Except for the braves who collected Ocha's body, the Chiricahua turned their horses as one and rode away. Fargo staggered, then fell to the ground. He rolled onto his back and stared at the sky, not caring what happened next. A moment later, Sara and Will were leaning over him.

"Get the water canteen," Sara told Will.

As soon as Fargo had drunk his fill, Sara bathed and bandaged his arm. Satisfied, she washed and assessed his other cuts. "Congratulations on your victory."

"Where did you get the rags?" Fargo finally managed to ask, his breathing coming considerably easier now.

"I hid them inside my blouse. I knew you'd get upset if you saw them."

Fargo replied with a grunt.

Sara's relief was overwhelming. He wasn't in nearly as bad a condition as he'd looked. "You'll be glad to know that you're going to be all right. I knew we should have brought that wagon. Will, return to the house and fetch the wagon and some men."

Fargo looked at Will and shook his head. "If I can survive that fight, I can damn sure get on my horse."

Will reached down and helped Fargo up. Though still exhausted, Fargo made it to his horse. He raised his foot, slipped the toe of his dusty boot into the stirrup, and then, with the strength of his arms alone, pulled himself up into the saddle. There wasn't a muscle that didn't ache. But he felt good. Though he had always enjoyed a good fight, he had no intention of going through another one like this. At least not if he could help it.

Sara handed Fargo his shirt, which he tossed across the saddle in front of him. His hat followed. He shoved it on his head.

"Is there anything I can do for you?" Sara asked worriedly.

Fargo smiled, and Sara blushed. "I mean, would you like another drink of water or—"

He butted in, a grin still spread across his dirty face. "I could use a hot bath."

Sara shook her head and mounted her horse. "You know, Will, I think he's going to be all right."

The three laughed and moved their horses toward home.

When the hacienda came into view, Megan was once again waiting out front. The worry etched on her face quickly melted away when she saw Fargo smile at her.

Half laughing and half crying, she watched Fargo slowly dismount. "I knew you'd win. I'm so proud of you but you look terrible! Come along. We'll have Carla tend to your cuts."

As had happened before, the two took off into the house, leaving Sara standing alone.

Sara glanced at Will, but he was already headed for the bunkhouse. Probably can't wait to tell the men about the fight, Sara thought bitterly. Have Carla tend to the cuts, indeed. She had already done a pretty good job of taking care of him!

That night at supper, Megan continued her ongoing flow of words.

"I'll be heading back to Tombstone tomorrow," Fargo told Megan while he enjoyed a slice of chocolate cake, "but how would you like to go for a ride early in the morning?"

Sara curled her lip at having been excluded from the invitation.

Megan reached across the table and squeezed Fargo's hand. "I'd like that."

Sara was absolutely livid. She'd seen enough. Since when had her sister become so excitable? She'd be damned if she'd let the two of them go riding alone. "That sounds like a good idea. I think I'll join you."

"How about you, Will?" Fargo asked. "Would you care to join us also?"

What was Fargo trying to do? Sara wondered angrily. Pair everyone off?

Will looked at Sara, then shook his head. "No, I got to head out on the range. There's too much work that needs to be done." He placed his napkin on the table and stood. "It was a good meal, Sara. I have to get up early tomorrow morning. I probably won't see you before you leave, Fargo.... You sure you're in good enough condition to travel all that way?"

"Carla's tender nursing to my cuts and bruises and that hot bath were all I needed." He looked at Sara. "Well, just about all I needed." He winked, discreetly. "But thanks for asking."

Sara was sure her face must have turned every possible shade of red. Was he suggesting—? A strong quiver of excitement worked its way up her spine. In one brief second, Fargo had made it clear he'd been thinking about her. She tried to remain calm by reminding herself that all his attention had been centered on Meg. But that didn't keep her hands from becoming clammy, or an ache from forming in the pit of her stomach. She glanced at Will, and then Megan, to see if they had seen the wink. Apparently not.

Sara swung her legs over the side of the bed and placed her feet on the cold floor. She couldn't sleep. Like it or not, knowing Fargo was only three doors down the hall continued to play havoc with her overactive imagination. Fargo probably hadn't meant a thing by what he'd said or by the wink. She'd only thought he had, because, as usual, that was what she'd chosen to think.

She stood and walked out into the courtyard, which was lit by a brilliant full moon. She caught sight of a falling star, and made a wish that Fargo find her irresistible.

As she enjoyed the cool air perfumed with Megan's flowers, she strolled to the far side of the yard, deliberately walking in the opposite direction of Fargo's room. At least tomorrow he'd be gone, and she'd no longer have to put up with this insanity. Unthinkingly, she ran her hand over one breast, surprised at how taut the nipple was. Shocked, she dropped her hand back down to her side.

She'd only gone a few feet farther when she realized Fargo was out in the courtyard, too. She didn't see him, but she could sense his presence. She stopped and turned. He stood no more than five feet away, dressed only in a pair of worn jeans that hung low on his hips.

"I see you couldn't sleep, either."

Sara smiled nervously. "No, I—"

"You're beautiful."

"I think I should—"

"I want to make love to you, Sara. I haven't thought about anything else since the night you invited me to supper at the Halversons'." He ran his fingers through his tousled hair. "You make it awfully hard on a man, standing there in the moonlight. Did you know that the outline of your hair glows, and your nightdress is almost transparent?"

Sara sucked in her breath. Her feet seemed planted to the ground as he slowly came to her. "This isn't right. Megan—"

Fargo placed his hands on her slender shoulders and slowly drew her to him. "Megan has nothing to do with you and me." He leaned down, allowing her every opportunity to pull away. Instead, she looked up at him, waiting. "Let me make love to you, Sara," he whispered before claiming her lips.

Sara was already lost in an abyss of unfulfilled passion. She couldn't have turned away, not even if the sky had broken open. His lips seared hers. His hands slid down her back and over her hips, molding her to him, while his tongue burned a trail of fire down her neck. The sensation of his bare chest pressed against her lightly clad body made her feel deliciously wicked. She didn't resist the temptation to kiss his chest and then reclaim his lips. When Fargo swung her up in his powerful arms and headed for his room, her heart sang. This was what she'd dreamed of. For tonight, Fargo Tucker would be hers.

Fargo gently laid her on the bed, and then Sara could hear him removing his clothes. Though the courtyard had been lit by the moon, the room was too dark for her to see. She felt the bed sink, and then he was beside her, nibbling on her ear, creating wonderful sensations.

He asked, as he had before, "Have you ever had a man make love to you, Sara?"

His hand had moved to Sara's breast, and she wasn't sure she could speak. A whispered "no" was the best she could manage. She wasn't even sure he heard the word.

He drew her to him, causing her to shudder with anticipation. As he pushed the hem of her nightdress up, his hand trailed along the bare flesh of her leg, higher and higher.

"Then I'll teach you," he murmured, and again claimed her lips.

Sara grew taut. Every nerve, every thought, was concentrated on his hand moving up her inner thigh, then coming to rest between her legs. Gently parting the folds, he stroked the sensitive area.

"Let your body relax and feel, Sara," Fargo said, his lips brushing against hers. "Take pleasure in what I can give you."

When Fargo again claimed Sara's lips, she returned his kiss with a fervor that surprised and delighted him. He had expected her to suddenly jump up and put a halt to any more touching. But Lady Sara was coming alive. Little moans of pleasure were now escaping her lips, and she was rocking her hips ever so slightly, encouraging him to continue moving his finger, loving the feel of what he was doing to her.

Fargo's own desire had started to build. He nibbled gently on the firm bud of her breast, which was still hidden beneath her nightgown. "I want to undress you, Sara. I want to glory in the feel of your body next to mine."

Caught fast in the clutches of passion, Sara wasn't even sure what he'd said. But when Fargo went to pull her gown over her head, she stopped him.

"Is something wrong?" Fargo asked, his deep voice husky with desire.

"I..." Sara pushed her hair from her face. "My..." She wasn't sure how to say it. His fingers were toying with her sensitive nipple, making it difficult to think. "Are they too small?"

Fargo's hand stilled. "What?"

"My breasts. Are they too small? I mean, if they are, there isn't much I can do about it." She felt like a fool. Why hadn't she just kept her mouth shut?

"You have wonderful breasts. I can't think of a single thing wrong with your body. You're beautiful."

"Oh?"

He removed her gown, all the while spreading delicious kisses all over her body. Then bare flesh clung to bare flesh, and Sara thought there could be no greater rapture.

Yet she felt a need that she didn't understand, and it continued to build. She became obsessed, wanting more, while at the same time convinced he was driving her out of her mind.

When Fargo entered her, Sara was prepared for the painful tearing sensation. But it wasn't nearly as bad as she had anticipated, and only moments later, Fargo had her again moaning with desire. He showed her the pleasures of moving her hips, and he encouraged her boldness. Her hands roamed his magnificent body, and her body became damp with perspiration. She didn't feel she was giving nearly as much as she was taking. She became a woman possessed, demanding and receiving. Her breathing became shallow as the sensations continued to build. Then, right at the moment when she thought she would surely die, everything exploded. Fargo's mouth covered hers as one magnificent wave cascaded upon another. She had discovered the indescribable secret shared between a man and a woman. Then, she passed out.

When Sara came to, she was surprised to see Fargo leaning over her. It was too dark to see the expression on his face.

"Are you all right?"

"Oh, yes," Sara purred. "I'm just fine."

Fargo rolled onto his back and chuckled. "I thought I had hurt you." A moment later, when his breathing had returned to normal, he asked, "Why did you want to know if your breasts were too small?"

Sara smiled. "I guess I just didn't want you to be disappointed."

Laughing, Fargo rolled her over on top of him. "Believe me, my kitten, nothing about you was disappointing.

* * *

Astride her horse, her dress hiked nearly to her knees, Megan urged her mount to a faster speed. The dilapidated shack that someone had once used while searching for gold drew closer and closer. Just a little bit more and she would have won the race. Not until the last minute did she jerk back on the reins, bringing her horse to a sliding stop. Laughing, and paying no heed to her unladylike position, she leapt off her horse.

"I won!" she said as soon as Fargo joined her.

"That you did, my dear." Fargo pulled off his hat and slapped it across his knee, knocking off the dust. "I had no idea you could ride so well."

Reins dangling from her hand, Megan started walking to cool down the horses. Fargo fell in alongside her.

"I also happen to be a very good shot."

"Is that right?"

"You don't believe me, do you?" Megan asked.

"I didn't say that."

"I'll prove it."

Seeing her hand held out to him, Fargo raised a questioning eyebrow.

"Hand me your gun."

Fargo wasn't sure what he should do. If she was lying, she could end up shooting herself—or him. However, she'd certainly told the truth when she said she knew how to ride a horse. His curiosity getting the better of him, he pulled the gun from his holster and handed it to her.

Megan stopped and gazed across the land, looking for a target. "See that limb coming off to the side of that salt cedar?"

Fargo looked toward where she pointed. "If you can hit that, I would say that you're a lot better shot than most *men* I know."

Megan raised the gun and pulled the trigger twice, each time nipping the limb back a little closer to the tree trunk. Smiling, she handed the revolver back to Fargo.

"That, my dear, was some mighty fine shooting," Fargo commented as he returned the gun to his holster. "Who taught you to shoot like that? Perhaps a boyfriend I haven't met?" Fargo smiled. "Why, I would be surprised if he didn't ride a paint horse."

"Don't be silly. No Indian is going to spend time teaching me how to shoot." She leaned down and picked a wildflower by her foot. "Isn't this beautiful?"

"Indeed it is." Fargo hadn't even paid any attention to the flower. "Are you going to tell me that you just picked up a revolver one day and started shooting?"

"Something like that." Megan suddenly grew serious. "In this land, you never know when you're going to have to protect yourself."

Fargo's patience was wearing thin. He would have liked to reach over and give Megan a good shaking for continually holding back information, but he didn't. Like Sara, Megan appeared quite able to avoid giving any direct answers. Didn't they realize the type of man they were protecting? Hawk had to be a brother or some relative. It was the only answer that made sense. "Well, you certainly know what you're doing. I wish whoever taught you could teach me. I'm not half as good as you are."

Megan looked at him with bright eyes. "Maybe I could teach you."

Fargo decided to take a gamble. After all, he sure as hell wasn't getting anywhere at the rate he was going. "Have you ever heard the name Hawk?"

"Of course. I see them quite often flying overhead, searching for a mouse or something else they can feast on."

Fargo decided not to pursue it any further. If he made an issue of the name Hawk, she might mention it to Sara, and in turn, Hawk might hear about it. The way things were going, the bounty hunter would eventually find out someone was asking questions about him. "I think the horses are rested enough by now. We need to be getting back to the house."

He turned and took her arm, ready to help her back onto her horse when she jerked around and said, "Don't you touch me! Don't you ever touch me!"

Fargo started to move forward.

"Keep away from me!" Megan screamed. Fury, hate and stark terror twisted her lovely features.

Fargo backed away. Tears streamed down Megan's cheeks. She sat on the ground and wrapped her arms around her chest, then began rocking, crying and whimpering at the same time. Fargo wanted to go to her, but instinct told him that was the worst thing he could do.

"Don't...don't do this. Please, Mama, don't let them do this."

"Megan," Fargo said gently. "It's all right. No one's going to hurt you."

But Megan was beyond hearing anything he said. "Oh, God," she moaned, "please make them stop."

Any fool would have known that something had happened to Megan in the past, and Fargo was no fool. He might very well have discovered what had happened six years ago. Will had said marauders had killed the family. Now Megan called to her mother, who had died on the same day as the rest of the family. Something must have happened to her for Megan to act this way. She had either witnessed it or had been part of it. Fargo could only imagine her nightmare.

Suddenly Megan looked up and smiled, and with her hands still wrapped around her she said in a low, quiet voice, "They're not going to get away with this."

"Who isn't going to get away with this?" Fargo asked, not daring to ask what "this" was.

Megan shook her head as if to clear it. She stared off into the distance for a long moment, then shook her head again and looked up at Fargo, her eyes clear. "You're right. I think we'd better go back."

Though the spell seemed to be over, this time Fargo didn't try to help her onto her horse.

Once they were mounted and on their way, Megan chattered on and on about the various plants in the area. Fargo found it difficult to discuss things on a normal level after what he'd just witnessed. Something else had now started gnawing at the back of his mind. What if the person he had been looking for turned out to be a woman? Perhaps a woman with long brown hair so dark it appeared to be black. A woman who'd had something terrible happen to her in her past, and desired nothing but revenge.

Sara opened her eyes and stretched languidly. Her room was partially immersed in sunlight, which told her that she must have slept much later than normal. Fargo had to have carried her to her bedroom after she'd fallen asleep. Fargo. Just the name made her warm all over. Laughing, and feeling better than she had in years, she jumped out of bed and hurriedly dressed.

Sara was in such a happy mood that she practically danced down the hallway as she searched for Carla. She longed to shout to the world how glorious it was to have a man make love to her and how it made her feel like an entirely different woman. Of course, she didn't dare. Instead, she burst out in another exuberant fit of laughter.

When Sara entered the kitchen, she found Carla busily hanging herbs to dry, and Megan sitting at the table, peeling potatoes and singing.

"Where's Fargo?" Sara asked as she snitched a freshly baked cookie from the counter.

"He's headed back to Tombstone," Meg informed her. "He told you that last night at supper."

"You mean he didn't wait until I got up?"

"Apparently not."

Sara gave her sister a keen look. "You seem to be in an awfully happy mood."

"I am. I had a long ride this morning. Fargo has to be the most wonderful man I've ever met."

Sara's good humor faded, giving way to suspicion. "I'm so glad to hear everything is so wonderful. But how can you judge? You haven't met that many men." She pulled out a chair and sat across from Megan. "Did you ride for long?"

"About two hours." Megan's eyes brightened. "Oh, Sara, it was wonderful. He even let me win a race."

Megan had a look in her eyes that Sara had never seen before. Had Fargo made love to *her,* too? "Megan, I think you should know a few things about men. Compare them with hogs. Some are friendly. Some are good. Some wallow in their own pleasures. And some are just plain mean. But for the most part, it's the others you have to watch out for."

"What others?"

"The ones that you don't dare turn your back on." Sara shoved her chair back and stood. Placing her hands on the table, she leaned forward and looked at her sister. "Megan, is there something you want to talk to me about?"

"Like what?"

"What I'm trying to say is...did Fargo try anything with you?" Sara shook her head. "No, that's not what I mean. I mean, did Fargo...did he kiss you?"

"Why would he kiss me?" Meg asked.

Sara straightened and began pacing back and forth. "You're a very attractive woman and men are going to find you appealing."

Megan picked up another potato.

"Aren't you going to say anything?"

"I'm sure you're trying to tell me something, Sara, but I haven't a clue as to what that something is. So why don't you just come out with it?"

Sara stopped dead in her tracks. How could she say anything when it might mean throwing Megan back in time? She couldn't. "I guess I'm just trying to tell you that Fargo is a stranger, and you should be careful when you're around him."

Megan laid the potato down in the bowl. "Well, I wish you'd make up your mind, Sara. You say you want me to be friendly around people. Then, when I am, you start criticizing me for it."

"I'm not criticizing you. I'm just warning you to be careful. Fargo is very...experienced, and knows just what to do to make himself appealing to women."

Megan stared at Sara, her face showing her confusion.

"I want you to be around people, and I want you to have friends. But you also have to realize that not everyone is as good as you are." In exasperation, Sara looked up at the ceiling. She'd never thought of having to explain this aspect of life to her sister. Perhaps Megan's sudden change wasn't a blessing after all. "I'm just telling you to be careful. When you go into the hog pen, don't you keep an eye on the boar? When you go into a corral of fresh horses, don't you watch to see what they're up to? It's the same way with people. You have to feel them out, to get to know what they're like before you start trusting them."

"All right." Megan shrugged.

"Is that all you have to say? All right?"

"What else am I supposed to say? But you're wrong about Fargo. I don't have to worry about being around him. He'll take care of me."

"Please, Megan, just be careful."

"Fargo said he'd be back in a couple of days."

"We'll see."

Megan laughed. "He told me to tell you good-morning."

Sara's whole world suddenly became bright again.

That night Sara lay in her bed, staring at the empty space beside her. All day she had moved around in a cloud. What would it be like to wake up and find Fargo still next to her? Would he take her into his arms and whisper sweet nothings, as he had last night? Her woman's instincts had been right. Fargo was a magnificent lover. Not that she was that knowledgeable, but from the things Penelope had told her, and Rose's complaints about Cyrus, it hadn't been difficult to conclude that all men weren't the same in bed. Or that all men were as good as Fargo in bed. Just thinking about him stirred desire. She rolled onto her back and peered into the darkness.

Three men sat around the crackling campfire, staring at the orange glow and watching the flames lick at the dry wood.

"Well, are you going to ride with me or not?" Dodd asked Lou Duncan.

"Did you hear Clayborne shot James Hickey in the head 'cause he kept insistin' Clayborne have a drink with him?" Lou took a drink of the strong coffee. "He was buried up on Boot Hill."

The big, barrel-chested Dodd snorted. "Old man Cantrell was murdered by a man named Brown."

"Hell, I'd rather get killed starin' down a Colt than by workin' in some mine," Bud, the third man, stated.

"Bobier's dead. He and his partner disagreed over a cockfight. Three-Fingered Jack got killed robbin' an express car," Lou added.

Dodd looked at the skinny man. "You thinkin' about goin' straight, Lou? Is that why you're talkin' about all these men dying?"

Lou tossed a twig into the fire. "I'm pointing out that a lot of men I've ridden with have ended up on Boot Hill. I ain't aimin' to join them. Heard some news I thought you might like to know about, Dodd."

"What news is that?"

"One of my men was telling me about a stranger in town. Seems you ain't the only one lookin' for that critter Hawk. Gus overheard this feller asking one of the Bird Cage girls about him. Gus said he'd never laid eyes on the feller before. Said he was definitely a gunman 'cause of where his holster hung. Right at his fingertips. Gus was sure he'd be a fast draw. Said the man was tall, dark, and looked like he could be a mean one. Anyone you recognize?"

Dodd shook his head. "Did Gus find out why he's lookin' for Hawk?"

"Nope. No one seems to know."

"The damn fool's swimmin' in mud." Dodd spit tobacco juice into the fire and listened to it sizzle. "Hell, if I couldn't find out anything in six years, I don't know what the hell he expects to do."

"I heard you almost got Hawk the last time." Bud's pockmarked face looked even more pitted in the light from the campfire.

"Also heard you ended up killing one of your own men," Lou added.

Dodd curled his lip and shrugged. "You think I killed him on purpose? Hell, that kid, Jude Tanner, was one of the best men I ever had. He was a mean son of a bitch." Dodd dug his spurs into the soft dirt, remembering the scene.

"Just exactly what happened?" Lou asked.

"Seems like that damn Hawk has always been on my ass. He's almost caught me more than once. So I decided to lay a trap for him. I got word he was in the area. Me and my men set a ranch house on fire, knowing the smoke could be seen from miles away. We enjoyed ourselves with the women—of course, we tied and gagged them so they couldn't holler out any warning. Then me and the boys hid and waited. Hawk came riding in on that painted horse, and his dog following right behind him. There was some other feller, too. Hadn't never laid eyes on him before, but he sure could shoot." Dodd spit again into the fire. "Found out later it was Wyatt Earp. The two of 'em pulled up in front of the house, then slowly dismounted. I dropped my hand to signal the boys to start firing, but before a shot could land, that damn dog started barking and Hawk and Earp hit the ground. A couple of my men came running toward them from behind, and one of them was Jude. When Hawk dropped, my bullet got the kid right between the eyes."

"There's been a lot of hard feelings over that little incident," Lou stated. "I heard tell that some of the boys ain't wantin' to ride with you anymore. Guess you haven't been doin' too good on your raids. Men are gettin' killed around you, more than they are if they just ride out on their own."

"Ain't my fault," Dodd growled.

Lou rose to his feet, and Bud followed suit. "Tell ya what, Dodd. Me and my men will help you hit that payroll, but until you get Hawk off your ass once and for all, I ain't ridin' with you again. As I see it, right now you're as hot as a lizard's ass resting on a rock in the middle of summer."

Dodd started to draw, but Lou was too fast. "You're plumb lucky I don't just blow your head off." Still keeping his gun pointed at Dodd, Lou tossed his tin cup onto the ground. "Now, I know you got some men watching us, Dodd, so unless you want to be a dead man, you'd best call 'em off."

"You got me all wrong." Dodd grinned, showing three missing front teeth. "You just rubbed me the wrong way. You know I ain't gonna do nothin'. I need you and your men to get that payroll.

Lou lowered his revolver. "Next time you go to draw on me, Dodd, you're a dead man. Come on, Bud, let's get out of here."

The two men mounted their horses and rode off in a spray of dust.

A tall man with a floppy-brimmed hat stepped into the circle of firelight. "Want us to go after them, Boss?"

"Naw, let 'em go." Dodd stuck another wad of chewing tobacco in his cheek. Hawk had caused him more trouble than he cared to admit. He wanted the man dead. He thought about the stranger Lou had mentioned. The one also searching for Hawk. Dodd shook his head. The bastard wasn't going to learn a thing.

Chapter Eight

Sara had been waiting anxiously and passionately for Fargo's return. She had just entered the dining room to clean when Phew's friendly barks announced that someone was approaching the house. Hoping that someone would be him, she quickly licked the palms of her hands and ran them across the sides of her hair to make sure there were no flyaway strands. Then she yanked her apron off, rolled it into a ball and looked around for a place to throw it. At that moment, Carla walked in, and Sara handed it to her. She smoothed the material along her tiny waist, making sure that the dark green dress with the flowered print fit smoothly. Then she pinched her cheeks for color.

"I think that rooster Miguel brought is a fighting cock."

"Not now, Carla. We'll talk about it later." Sara hurried toward the door. She had just started to walk outside when, to her disappointment, Will bounded in. Agitated, she complained, "You almost knocked me over."

Will strode past Sara into the parlor, and she followed.

"Is something wrong?" she asked when Will went to the wall case. He opened the door and took out the whiskey decanter. After he'd poured himself a stiff drink, he gave Sara his attention. "We lost three good breedin' cows today. They were shot."

"Rustlers again?"

"Yep. The boys came on them by accident, so they didn't get away with anything. They did shoot the three cows though, apparently as a means of gettin' even." Will downed his drink. "Haven't you talked to Virgil about this kind of thing before?"

"Yes," Sara replied, "but we both know he can't be everywhere. We need to catch them."

"Oh, I intend to catch them, but when I deliver 'em, they're goin' to be dead." Will poured himself another drink. "I thought you might like to know that we're fixin' to have a visitor."

"Who?"

"That new friend of yours, Fargo Tucker. Are you takin' a likin' to him, Sara?"

"Don't be silly." Sara turned a complete circle. "Do I look all right?"

"Perfect, as always. I don't like havin' him around, and I don't believe his story about buyin' old man Harris's place. I think he's using that as an excuse to bide his time."

"Why would he want to bide his time?"

"I don't know. That's what bothers me."

"I thought the two of you got along."

"You know we can't afford to have him stayin' anywhere near here. It was dangerous enough with him laid up in bed. We can't afford it, Sara," he stressed again. "And you know it. Furthermore, I don't think he's a cattleman, like he says he is."

"Why do you say that?"

"He doesn't carry himself like a rancher. I'm telling you, Sara, you need to get rid of him."

"How is a rancher supposed to carry himself? For the life of me, Will, I have no idea where you come up with these things. But, assuming you're right, how would you describe the way Fargo carries himself?''

"Like a gunfighter."

Sara returned to the doorway. "Maybe in Texas they're one and the same. You're being oversensitive, Will. He has no reason to suspect anything."

"You're not being cautious enough. What's gotten into you, Sara? This isn't like you."

Sara turned and looked at the man who was like a brother to her. "Will, I—" Upon hearing a horse approach, she hurried out the door.

Just watching Fargo swing from the saddle warmed Sara's heart. Her life had seemed dormant over the past two days. Now there wasn't a single part of her being that didn't feel alive. She fought the temptation to run to him, wrap her arms around his neck and kiss him. She clasped her hands behind her. "Welcome back to the Bar C."

Fargo smiled broadly, then took his time tethering his horse to the hitching post. He turned and gazed at her slowly, from the top of her head to the toes of her shoes, not skipping a single detail. He was about to tell Sara that he had missed her when Will walked out of the house.

"Hello, there," Will said. "I'm curious. Have you made your mind up yet about buying Ed Harris's place?"

"I bought it this morning."

Will felt like a mouse that had just been devoured by a snake. And he had to admit that Sara had apparently been right about Fargo all along. Will wasn't unhappy, though. He not only liked Fargo, he had a growing respect for the Texan. Especially after the fight with Ocha. And Fargo had long since proven his knowledge about cattle as well as ranching. But for some reason, Will just couldn't shake the nagging suspicions he felt toward the tall man. Maybe it was just jealousy.

"How wonderful," Sara exclaimed. "It looks as if we're going to be neighbors."

Fargo smiled. That was exactly the reason he had purchased the run-down place. Now he'd be close enough to the hacienda to keep an eye on any strange happenings.

Will didn't like the way Sara's cheeks flushed in the near-stranger's presence, or how her green eyes sparkled like precious jewels. She'd never blessed him with that look. "I'm goin' over to the bunkhouse. I want to check and see how Charlie's doing."

"Charlie?" Fargo asked.

"A rattlesnake got him," Sara replied.

"I've thought about you," Fargo said softly, when Will was out of hearing range.

"And I've thought about you." Just remembering the way his lips had glided across her flesh, the way his hands and body had unveiled previously unknown mysteries of bliss, made Sara light-headed. She looked into his wondrous eyes. "I want you to make love to me," she said truthfully.

"Here and now?" Seeing Sara blush broadened his grin. "You've changed, Miss Sara Carter. I can no longer look at you and think of the prim and proper lady who has yet to be awakened."

Standing apart from him, not touching, was very titillating, and his words had a caressing quality to them that she could feel in every fiber of her being. "I don't think even you would be willing to make love to me here and now," she returned with a saucy grin.

"Don't count on it. Miss Carter, I'd take you in a trough, or in front of man or beast, if that was what you wanted."

Sara broke out laughing. "Even on top of a cactus?"

"Yep, even there. But with one difference. I don't think either of us would last very long. Come here and kiss me, Sara."

"But I'm—"

"Afraid someone might see?" he challenged.

Sara could see that devilish gleam dancing in his blue eyes. He brought out a daring in her that she hadn't known she possessed. She walked slowly forward, stood on tiptoe and placed her arms around his neck. She didn't have to kiss him. He'd already lowered his lips to meet hers. When their lips met, time stood still for Sara. He caught her tongue between his lips and sucked gently on it, bringing forth memories of what had happened several nights before. Desire ran rampant through her. For just a moment, she would have allowed him to make love to her, then and there. But the moment passed, and she stepped away.

"I imagine you're thirsty after such a long ride."

"Coward," he teased, releasing her and following her into the cool house. A moment later, they were joined by Megan. And though Fargo asked Megan how she was doing and if she had been riding lately, his eyes lingered on Sara's, holding them in a silent promise.

Because of the distance from the ranch to Tombstone, and because Ed Harris hadn't moved his family out yet, Fargo was welcomed at the hacienda until he could move to his new home. Each night, after everyone had gone to bed, Sara unashamedly went into Fargo's room. He showed her wonders that she had never dreamed of, and took her to heights she had never suspected possible. Each night was a new experience. . . . Making love to Fargo became an addiction; during the day, she waited only for the night.

Suddenly everything seemed to be in a turmoil. Will remained upset about Fargo staying at the house, Carla was giving Sara strange looks, and Megan hung around Fargo as if he were the only man on the ranch. Sara suffered pangs of jealousy. The only one who didn't seem affected by all this was Fargo.

Sara's biggest problem turned out to be trying to appear normal—to be exactly as she'd been prior to Fargo's arrival. She certainly didn't want the others to know of the wild, uncontrolled passion she experienced each night. But hiding her feelings took every bit of acting skill she could draw upon, especially since Fargo kept finding places to steal hungry kisses...or caress her breast while nibbling on her neck...or perform other acts that made her desire soar.

A week after his arrival, Fargo left the ranch. Sara had known all along that her bliss eventually had to come to an end. She had even mentally prepared herself for the occasion. But when Fargo actually left, she didn't know how she'd manage without him. He had started a fire burning deep within her, and every night he had tended to that fire. But, with him gone now, would it consume her?

"I'm glad he's gone," Will stated bluntly when Sara returned to the house after seeing Fargo off. "You're playin' with fire, Sara."

More than you know. "I don't know what you're talking about," she said instead.

Will slammed the whiskey decanter down on the end table. "The hell you don't. From the way you're acting, I'm wonderin' if wedding bells will be next."

"That's ridiculous. You know I can't marry." Sara went over and sat on the black horsehair sofa. "I don't want to argue with you, Will."

"Have you enjoyed having him make love to you?"

Sara sucked in her breath. "I don't know what you are talking about."

Will spoke through gritted teeth. "Did you honestly think you could do something like that and no one would notice? Hell, it's written all over you."

"What I do is my business."

"It's also my business, and you know it. Did you tell him about Hawk?"

"Of course not." Sara placed her fingers on her throbbing temples. "Why are you doing this, Will? Why are you even bringing up these things? You know I will never, ever desert Hawk. I've told you before, and I'll say it again. There is nothing that would take precedence over that situation."

"I just need to know where you stand."

Sara looked sadly at Will. "I have a right to think about my life, too, Will."

"That's what I've been tryin' to tell you for years. Let Hawk go, Sara."

"I can't," she said sadly. "Hawk is the only real justice we have."

As Fargo rode toward the old Harris ranch, his anger ate away at him like acid. Buying Harris's run-down place had been just one more thing he'd had to do to discover Hawk's identity. Would this never end? He couldn't think of a damn thing that had gone right. A smile suddenly played at the corners of his mouth. Well, maybe he could think of a couple of things. Who would have believed that the righteous Sara Carter would end up having a sexual appetite every bit as strong as his, or that the same Miss Carter would become unabashed in her lovemaking? Many times, when he had her at the very brink of fulfillment, he'd asked if there were other men in her life. She always said no, and once again he was left knowing no more than he had known before.

Fargo kneed his horse into a lope. With the passing of time, he'd become more and more convinced that Will couldn't be Hawk. He just wasn't the type to tackle something that didn't disturb his everyday life. And while Fargo never thought of Will as a coward, he didn't think that the man had the guts or the hunter's instinct to track wanted men. Hawk had to be Megan. Now he had to prove it. Knowing he'd be chasing a woman failed to temper his cold determination to find Jude's killer. The days were ticking by, while Jude remained buried—waiting to go home.

Not having much to begin with, Fargo settled quite quickly into his new home. Actually, it was hard to call the dilapidated two-room house a home. But it suited his purposes. For the next week, he checked out the cattle, assured the ranch hands they still had their jobs, and took stock of what exactly he owned. It proved not to be a hell of a lot. His men were quick to inform him of the Mexican raiders who came across the border, the Apache and the ever-threatening rustlers. Just what Fargo needed to hear.

At times, Fargo would ride to the Bar C ranch, stay hidden in the hills and wait all day to see if a paint horse ever came or left. He watched every man who came to the house. He watched Will, often following him, and he watched Sara and Megan. He finally came to the conclusion that Hawk had gotten rid of the paint horse. But eventually the no-good would make his move. Fargo would catch him either leaving or going to the house, or if someone went to meet him. And when that happened, he'd be ready.

* * *

Filthy and worn-out after spending two days watching the branding, Sara turned her horse over to one of the hands, then headed for the house. Branding had to be the hottest, smelliest, dirtiest job that could be asked of a man. But Sara always made a point of being there. She made sure none of her calves accidentally ended up with a Crazy L brand on its flank. As long as she hung around and watched, no one would be tempted to make an error. Not that she had any reason to distrust Will. Caution had just been her basic nature for a long time.

She smiled as she entered the house. There wasn't any doubt in her mind that Will watched his stock just as closely. But for now she didn't want to think about cattle—or anything else. All she wanted was a hot bath, food and a bed to fall into. At least the branding had taken away her need for Fargo.

The next morning, Sara awoke refreshed and ready to tackle another day. She was about to leave her room when Megan rushed in. "You have a visitor."

Sara's eyes lit up. "Fargo?"

"No. Sara, why hasn't Fargo come to see us? It's been over a week since he left."

"I guess he's busy with his new ranch." Sara sounded more sarcastic than she meant to. "Whoever wants to see me probably wants to discuss cattle. Tell him to ride out to where the men are branding and talk to Will. I'm going down to eat breakfast."

"It's the one you call Azul. He wants to talk to you."

Sara grabbed her soft riding gloves from off the chest, then hurried down the stairs. As they reached the landing at the bottom, Phew scrambled from the floor and followed Sara outside.

The Apache had always remained outside the wall, with the exception of Azul. Even he had quit coming inside when Sara's parents were killed. But there he sat on his pony, looking every bit the proud warrior he'd once been. Though they had never expressed such feelings between them, Sara had a strange sort of affection for the ageless man, and she wanted to think it was reciprocated. She glanced around, but, to her surprise, there were no other braves in sight. "It has been such a short time since we last talked. Is something wrong? Does your visit concern Ocha?"

"There is someone I would have you meet."

"Who would that be? You've brought no one."

"You will bring your sister and follow."

Sara stepped next to the water trough to get out of the sun, then looked down at the murky water. "How can you ask this of me, Azul? You know I worry about my sister. She leaves my heart heavy."

"There is no need to worry about Broken Wing," he replied. "Come, we must go."

"Azul, I am becoming frightened," Sara admitted. "Does this have something to do with Ocha? Does he live?"

"He lives."

Azul's eyes shifted, and Sara jerked around to see what had drawn his attention. Megan had come out the door. Sara wanted to tell her to go back inside, where she'd be safe. Something was very wrong. Azul had never made such a request. Sara didn't know what to do. Azul hadn't brought anyone. Apparently, he expected her to put her faith in him. And she probably would have willingly done so had he not insisted Megan go with them.

"You will need horses," Azul declared.

"I'll get them," Megan replied. She turned and headed for the barn.

Megan's calmness came close to being Sara's undoing. Megan would have to learn not to be so trustful. Sara looked fleetingly at Azul. "She doesn't know. If I must, I'll tell her you're her father. Just give me time and let me do it my way." For the first time, Sara actually saw a surprised look on Azul's face.

"We will go." Azul moved his horse toward the barn. "You need not fear. You and Broken Wing will be safe."

Sara ran after him. "I'm asking you not to do this."

"I have no choice."

When Megan brought out two saddled horses, Sara had to fight to keep her composure. She had to do something. She looked at Phew. Having sensed trouble, he stood in readiness, waiting for a command. Sara was torn by indecision. Why weren't Will and the other men around now that she needed them? In a matter of seconds, Sara made up her mind. Although Azul looked frail, she instinctively knew she could never overpower him, and she could not believe that he didn't have his men waiting somewhere outside the compound. She raised her hand, and Phew obediently dropped to the ground. She couldn't even help him if he charged Azul. She had no weapon.

"You will let me tell Megan the truth?"

"You may tell her what you think is right."

It wasn't what she wanted to hear, but it would have to do. Now she'd have to trust Azul's word that she and Megan would be safe. Telling Megan about her father wasn't going to be easy. She would never be able to accept that she had Indian blood.

As the three prepared to ride away, Phew rose to his feet, ready to follow. Sara's strong "no" changed his mind.

* * *

Sara wondered where Azul was taking them, and how long they would have to travel. It had already been over two hours since they'd left the house. The rolling hills had given way to deep valleys and crevices. Several minutes away from the hacienda, a brave had fallen in behind them, then another, and another. Now there were at least fifteen following. It had become apparent that whatever Azul's mission was, her refusal had never been an option. And she now knew why he had appeared alone. He'd allowed her the opportunity to come peacefully. Sara blessed her decision not to have Phew attack.

As the towering, rocky cliffs drew closer, Sara could see Indians standing on huge rocks, their rifles held in readiness. Her concerns continued to escalate. Putting her trust in Azul might be the worst mistake she'd ever made. She had one comforting thought, however. All conversation would be spoken in Apache, a language Megan didn't understand.

They were following a rocky path that trailed along a trickling stream. As it curved around the base of a cliff, a small, lush canyon was revealed to them. Water poured off tall rocks, causing a fall that flowed into a small pond below. But Sara could hardly tear her eyes away from the fifty or so Indians standing about, and she could hear weeping coming from different areas. Women stood quietly, while young children clung to their skirts, their large brown eyes solemnly watching the two white women. Sara smiled at one, and he ducked behind his mother and giggled.

Sara looked at Megan. She appeared to be taking nothing more than a pleasant stroll! How could Megan not be frightened?

The braves who had been following stayed at the mouth of the canyon, as if to guard it. Azul dismounted and walked toward a large gathering. Sara and Megan leapt from their mounts and followed closely behind. As they neared the group, the people silently backed away until Sara saw a litter on the ground and an old man lying on top of furs. His eyes were closed, and he appeared to be dead. She stopped and stared down at him, wondering what any of this had to do with her and Megan.

The woman of regal bearing standing at the side of the man leaned down and whispered something to him. He opened his eyes and whispered something back to her. The woman straightened and, in perfect English, said, "The great Keno would have you come closer. He wants to see his granddaughters before he dies."

Sara looked at Azul. There had to be some mistake. His nod wasn't what she wanted to see. She looked at Megan. Her sister had gone chalk-white. "No!" Sara insisted. "My mother wasn't Indian. She—"

"Speak the language of the People," the woman commanded. "My husband and your grandfather, Keno, chief of our people, cannot understand the white tongue."

For the first time, Sara realized that the woman's eyes were blue. Sara choked back the desire to scream and get Megan and herself back on their horses and ride away from here! But she couldn't. Chanting had started.

"Grandmother? Grandfather?" Megan whispered, her voice sounding like a child's.

Seeing Megan's tear-filled eyes, Sara put her arm around her older sister's shoulders. They should never have come, but there wasn't anything she could do about it now except wait for the first opportunity to get the hell out of here.

"Help me to sit," Sara heard the weak, wrinkled man say. "I will welcome Princess Hair of Fire and Princess Broken Wing."

Two braves immediately rushed forward and propped him up with furs.

Keno reached out his hand to Sara. "I am pleased."

Sara stiffened. "There has to be some mistake."

"We have both suffered. You have been strong. Azul has kept me informed. You are a warrior, and worthy of a warrior's praise."

Though she didn't want to feel anything, Sara's heart went out to the gray-headed man, as it would have to anyone old and dying. And what harm would it do to let him think they were his granddaughters? It might even be to her advantage. Sara released Megan, then knelt beside the wrinkled old man and took his hand in hers.

"Bring my gift," the chief instructed a brave. "I would see her face before I die."

A moment later, he raised a badly gnarled finger. Sara looked in the direction he was pointing. The brave held a rope that circled the neck of what looked to be a yearling. He was the most magnificent horse she had ever seen. His withers were brown and faded into a white rump with brown spots. With his full mane and his ears pricked forward, he reminded Sara of a painting.

"I took the liberty of naming him Wings of Air. I have saved him for you. Ride him with pride."

Keno closed his eyes. Sara heard weeping, and realized that it came from the woman standing on the other side of him. Sara stood and backed away. When she reached Megan, she motioned toward their horses, but discovered right away there would be no escape. Three mean-looking Indians stood guard over the animals.

The day passed into night, and still the old man clung to life. A shaman danced around and worked with things that Sara couldn't identify; nor did she care to try. She didn't realize how hungry she was until she and Megan were handed food. Knowing that Apache supplies were sparse, she felt guilty. She also knew that refusing to eat would offend the Apache.

"That's our grandmother and grandfather?" Megan asked Sara, when they were momentarily left to themselves.

Sara looked at her, ready to make some sort of excuse, but when she saw her sister's open curiosity she decided to answer truthfully. "I don't know, Megan. I don't know what this is all about. I'm as confused as you are. Hopefully we'll get some answers. Now eat up—it may be a while before we eat again."

"Won't the men come looking for us?"

"They'll never find us."

As the hours passed, Megan seemed to blend in with those she now considered her relatives. The possible stigma that few men would accept a woman with mixed blood didn't seem to matter. She appeared to welcome the way the people treated her with friendship and acknowledged her as one of them. Sara didn't believe for a minute that she could have Chiricahua blood. She not only didn't believe it, she didn't want to believe it. Unlike Megan, she chose to remain distant.

As the great chief and warrior Keno lay dying, Sara found a quiet spot well away from the others. It was all too overwhelming.

"Would you walk with me?"

Sara looked up at the regal woman she'd been told was her grandmother. Sara liked her name, Smells of Flowers. "Shouldn't you stay by your husband?" Sara knew she was being snippy, but she couldn't help herself. She raised her knees and wrapped her arms around them, making it clear she had no intention of going anywhere.

"My husband has asked me to speak to you. Though I would rather spend my time with him in his last hours, I will abide by his wishes."

Sara looked up at the woman. Her hair was gray, her face deeply lined, and her figure tiny. "You are a white woman, and yet you choose to live with the Apache."

Smells of Flowers raised her head proudly. "I am Apache."

Tired, and feeling defeated, Sara stood. She'd wanted answers. Maybe now she'd get them. Without saying a word, the two women fell in step and walked away from the others.

"We did not know our son hadn't told his family of his heritage."

Sara almost tripped over her own feet. "Son? There must be some mistake."

"My name is Velma St. John." Smells of Flowers looked at Sara and smiled fondly. "Though I may not look it now, at sixteen I was considered very pretty."

Sara noticed that her features had softened.

"And very stubborn. I insisted on teaching school in a place called New Mexico. When I arrived in Santa Fe, it wasn't what I had expected. Being a young girl, I became restless. Then, one day, although I had been warned against it, I rode my horse out of town and into the desert. I never was much of a rider. Somehow the horse got its bit free, and he ran away with me. I finally fell off. When I raised up, this magnificent man stood over me, and I loved him from the moment our eyes met. Though it wasn't easy, I became a Chiricahua for him. I won't go into detail, but let it suffice to say that our love has lasted throughout the years. I think I love him even more now than I did when I first saw him."

They had walked up an incline and now stood looking at the valley below.

"It was different then." She looked across the vast land. "There were no boundaries. All belonged to the Apache. We lived well and happy. At first we were friends with the white man, until they started shooting and forcing us away. Then it became a matter of survival." She leaned against a large rock for support. "Are you aware that an Apache man can have more than one wife?"

"Yes."

"When I became Keno's second wife, he already had a son. That son is Azul."

Sara, who had also been looking across the land, jerked around and stared. "But that would mean—" Sara couldn't finish the sentence.

"None of the tribe could understand why, when Keno's first wife died, he kept only me. But that was his choice. He wanted only me.

"We had a son whom we named Chuta. Keno was very proud of him. But when Chuta became a young brave, he left. He longed to know of the white-eyes' ways. We were heartbroken. We did not see him for years. Then, one day, the gods spilled their love on us, and Chuta returned. Now he was known as Charles Carter."

"No!" Sara cried, "not my father! I thought my mother had— No, not my father!"

"Is it so hard to believe that you have Indian blood?"

Sara was furious. "But he would have said something. He would have told us."

"He had lived among the white men too long. He knew that if anyone suspected he had Indian blood, he could not own land, and he would be an outcast. He was ashamed. I do not know if your mother even knew."

Sara collapsed onto the rock beside Smells of Flowers. Dodd's words came back to her. "Yes, I think she knew."

Sara could no longer deny the things she'd heard. Now she understood the bond between her father and Azul. She understood why the Chiricahua always left them alone, and she understood how her father knew the Apache language and ways so well that he was able to teach them to his children. Had he planned on always keeping it a secret from his children, or had he planned on telling them of their heritage when they grew older?

"Your grandfather would send Azul to see how you were, and I believe he even mulled over never telling you about your ancestors. But he is proud of our people, who have been and are being forced from their land and will probably not survive. It is a heritage he wanted to share with you before the gods called him to them."

Sara felt as if her blood had been drained from her. She had suspected her mother of unfaithfulness, and all the time it had been her father's heritage. She should have known. Certainly all the signs were there, and she had chosen to ignore them. She turned to her grandmother and saw tears in the older woman's eyes. Sara was deeply touched. "When Keno dies, you must come live with Megan and me. I would consider it a privilege and an honor."

Smells of Flowers shook her head. "These are my people, and I shall die with them."

Her simple words pulled at Sara's heartstrings. "Will we see you again?"

"Perhaps."

"Please, if you are near, send Azul to get me. Promise me."

Smells of Flowers patted her granddaughter's knee and smiled. "I promise."

Sara wasn't sure she would ever be the same after this night. Her visit to the Chiricahua encampment had affected her deeply.

In the wee hours of the morning, Keno died.

Chapter Nine

Seven men gathered around the strongbox, their faces gleaming with anticipation. Stealing the Glory Mine payroll hadn't been as difficult as they'd thought. Their eyes settled on the balding man with the wide mustache and barrel chest.

Dodd drew his gun and shot the lock off. He opened the lid. The box was empty.

"What the hell is going on here?" Lou demanded. "Dammit, you said you searched it out. This box was supposed to be full."

The other men started grumbling.

"I was told—"

"Raise 'em high, boys."

Dodd looked up. "Hawk," he whispered.

The men went for their guns—all except Dodd, who made a dive to the side. As bullets were exchanged, he half ran, half crawled into the bushes. A moment later he leapt onto his horse, pushing the animal to top speed. That damn bastard Hawk had almost caught him again. The empty strongbox should have told him it was a trap. After this, no one would ride with him.

When the firing had ceased and the smoke had cleared, only three of the outlaws were left, and they lay on the ground wounded.

A bandanna hid the face of the stranger on the paint horse, so the three men couldn't see Hawk's anger. Because of the unexpected nature of Hawk's appearance, the gunfight had ended quickly. But Dodd had escaped.

The men glanced nervously at the big dog standing over them, its lips curled back, showing long, white canines.

"Hell, mister, you wasted your time!" the pale, red-headed man with the pockmarked face stated angrily. Keeping an eye on the dog, he cautiously pulled himself to a sitting position, his bullet-riddled arm hanging limp by his side. "There weren't nothin' in the strongbox, so you might as well holster your gun."

"Too bad everyone got away but you three. You boys are going to fit right in at Yuma Prison. However...if you don't fancy spending a few years with a ball and chain around your ankle, tell me where Dodd hides out."

"How're we supposed to know?" the redhead asked. "Hell, he's always movin' 'round."

"You must have met him somewhere in order to plan this holdup."

"We always met him at the Cactus Saloon on the outskirts of Elgin. But he ain't gonna be showing up there anymore. Now call your dog off. I told you all we know."

"Get on your horses," Hawk ordered. "We're going to go see Marshall Earp."

The one wounded in the leg jerked up, then froze when the dog snarled at him. "Burt's told you the truth. Why the hell are you gonna turn us in?" he whined.

"He ain't gonna turn us in," Burt said confidently. "He's bluffing. He's wanted, too, or he wouldn't be hidin' his face."

"I'll tell you one more time. Get on your horses."

Burt, who had done most of the talking, turned his head away and didn't move an inch—until two bullets hit the ground by his leg.

"Now get mounted, or I might lose patience and pull this trigger again. Next time it's going to hit flesh."

The men rose painfully to their feet, then headed for their horses. A few minutes later, they all rode away, leaving the opened box behind.

It was dark when four riders pulled up in front of the jail. The door swung open, and Virgil Earp stepped out of the lit office, followed by Wyatt.

"They tried robbing the Glory Mine payroll."

"This has gotta stop, Hawk," Wyatt said angrily as he had the outlaws dismount.

Hawk swung a leg around the saddle horn. "What do you mean? I'm just helping clean up the place."

"Dammit, you've already pushed your luck too far. Or maybe you're wanting to get yourself killed!"

Virgil watched Hawk lower his leg, and then, without saying a word, back his horse up.

"You can't let him go!" Burt shouted. "That son of a bitch helped us rob the payroll!" But Hawk had already disappeared into the night, taking his dog with him.

It was claimed that the Nellie Cashman Hotel had the best restaurant, with the best pies in all of Tombstone. It was also a well-known fact that Nellie would never turn away anyone who was down on his luck. The beautiful young Irishwoman with the proper brogue was well-thought-of in town. Sara considered all this as she sat across the street in her buggy, waiting for Nellie's return. Not more than five minutes ago she had entered the hotel and been told that Nellie should be back shortly.

Sara slowly pulled off her riding gloves and tried to make herself comfortable on the leather-cushioned seat. Earlier she'd had a talk with Virgil Earp. He had informed her that the bartender at the Crystal Palace had overheard a man asking Nellie Cashman about Hawk. To Sara's astonishment, the man's description fit Fargo Tucker. Now she intended to find out what kind of questions he'd been asking Nellie. But this time she'd hear it from the source.

Seeing Nellie approaching the hotel, Sara stepped down from the buggy. "Nellie!"

Nellie waited for Sara to cross the street. "It's been a long time since we last talked," she said when Sara had joined her.

"Oh, I'm sure you'll search me out when you start another of your charity campaigns," Sara replied good-naturedly.

"Why don't you come into the restaurant and let me get you a slice of pie and some coffee?"

"No, thank you, perhaps another time. To be truthful, I'm here to ask you some questions."

"Oh? What kind of questions?"

"I want to talk to you about Fargo Tucker."

Nellie's eyes scanned Sara's face. "He can be a charmer, can't he?" Nellie lowered her parasol, which matched her yellow dress. "If you're wondering about our relationship, we're just friends."

"No, no," Sara lied. "It has nothing to do with that." She slapped her gloves against her hand, not wanting to admit that Nellie's comments had made her feel quite smug. "What reason did Fargo give you for coming to Tombstone?"

"I believe he said something about a cattle ranch."

"That's all?"

"He asked about a dog that met Phew's description, so I told him about you. If I remember rightly, I also told him he would probably find you at the Schieffelin Hall dance."

The importance of what Nellie said struck Sara with the force of a cannonball. And Fargo had said he was mesmerized by her beauty! "Did he want to know about anything else?" Sara's throat had constricted, making it difficult for her to speak.

"No, other than that bounty hunter he's been looking for. I've asked all around, and no one I know has heard anything about someone called Hawk. Why are you asking all these questions?"

"It's very important to me. Nellie, please don't tell Fargo we discussed this."

"If he asks, I'm not going to lie, Sara. You're sounding as if he's an outlaw. I happen to be extremely fond of Fargo."

Sara nibbled at her lower lip. "No, I'm not saying he's wanted. Would you please not mention it unless he brings up the subject?"

"All right," Nellie said warily. "I guess that's the least I can do, after all the money you've donated to my charities."

"Thank you, Nellie." Sara climbed into her buggy and drove off.

"Megan, where have you been for the past week?" Sara demanded as her sister entered the house. She stood, paying no attention as the book she'd been reading dropped from her lap onto the floor. Sara also ignored the fact that she had also only returned today.

"While you were in town complaining to Marshall Earp about the rustlers, Azul came by. Grandmother was near. I went and joined my people."

Sara stared at her sister. "You might have left a message with Carla." Megan's face and clothes were smudged with dirt, and her hair was in wild disarray. "Even the Indians stay cleaner than you do. How can you do this, Megan? How can you just take off? And those aren't your people. You're only one-quarter Indian." Sara went to her sister and began tugging her toward the hall.

"That's not the way people will look at it," Megan retorted.

Sara came to an abrupt halt. "What are you talking about? What people?"

Megan walked past Sara and entered her bedroom. She began to undress. "White people don't like others with Indian blood."

"Where did you hear that?"

"Mama."

Stunned, Sara stared, openmouthed, at her sister. "She told you we have Indian blood?"

"She said that I must never reveal the truth to others. That we would not be accepted if anyone knew Papa was a half-breed."

Sara dropped onto the edge of the bed. "Then you've always known this?"

Megan let her dress fall around her feet. The petticoat followed.

"Dammit, was I the only one who didn't know?" Sara demanded angrily. "Papa didn't look Indian."

Megan unlaced her corset.

Sara fell back on the bed and stared up at the ceiling. She thought of her tall, handsome father. He'd had very chiseled, refined features, and his hair had been dark brown, not black. Now that she looked back, it occurred to her that two of her brothers had borne the features of the Apache.

"I also went by to see Fargo."

Sara sat up, jealousy grabbing her with the strength of a bear. Fargo wasn't worth an ounce of jealousy, but she couldn't help it. She watched Megan move to the washstand and pour water from the pitcher into the bowl. Reaching for a washcloth, she dunked it into the water. "And you went over there alone?" Sara asked.

"Of course." Megan lathered the cloth with the sweet-smelling lavender soap, and proceeded to give herself a spit bath.

"Megan, you know there's every crooked face and name known to man in these parts. As long as you're near, I can protect you. But when you take off without telling me where you're going, my hands are tied. Do you have any idea how much I worry when you take off like this?"

"You sound like mama. You know I can take care of myself, Sara."

By the time Megan had dressed, Sara had given up trying to explain anything.

Carla entered the room. "The big one has arrived."

"It's Fargo," Megan said excitedly as she ran out of the room.

Sara's green eyes became icy, and the normally soft contours of her face hardened. Now the roles were going to be reversed. Fargo had gone to a lot of trouble to get acquainted with the family, including bedding her. Yet never once had he mentioned anything about Phew or Hawk, and that made it apparent that everything he'd done so far had been a ruse to gather information about Hawk. Sara checked her hair to make sure it was still in place. Fargo wasn't the only one adept at playing games. She left the room and headed for the parlor. Now it was her turn. She'd find out what Mr. Fargo Tucker wanted.

The moment Sara stepped into the parlor, her face looked the very picture of delight. She gave him her best smile. It wasn't difficult. No matter what the sneaky dog was up to, Fargo still had the ability to turn her into a fluttering mess.

"I would have come by sooner, but I've been busy trying to figure out exactly what I own," Fargo began. He placed his arm around Megan's shoulders, but his eyes were on Sara. "When Megan came by to visit me, I'd hoped you'd come along."

Sara's heart fluttered, and she had to remind herself that the man was a deceiver. She ran her hands down her calico skirt, searching for the right words. She couldn't tell Fargo about Hawk until she found out why he felt the need to track him down. Only Hawk could bestow the family's vengeance. "It's been a long two weeks."

Fargo took his time studying each perfect feature, as if committing it to memory. When his eyes reached her bust, he smiled. The lady should have never had any concerns. Her breasts could never be considered large, but she was more of a woman than any he had ever known. But something—an intangible something—had changed. She acted friendly, and at the same time withdrawn. Could it be because he'd taken so long to return after they'd made love? "I agree. Two weeks can be an awfully long time. I saw your new stallion. He's quite a horse."

"Yes, I'm very proud of him."

"Where did you get him?"

"It's none of your business," she said, giving Megan a warning look.

"I've asked Fargo to go with me to the Indian encampment next time," Megan said matter-of-factly.

Sara was thunderstruck. How could Megan do this? "I see." She looked at Fargo. "And has Megan told you everything?"

"Why are you acting this way, Sara?" Megan asked. "Fargo doesn't care that we have Indian blood. He said it clarified a lot of things."

"Really." It was plain to see that Megan had no intention of keeping the information a secret. In fact, she apparently had intended to blatantly declare it. Any hope of no one knowing disappeared as quickly as a mosquito.

Sara's eyes shifted to Fargo. Indeed, the information didn't appear to bother him. But who could guess what thoughts ran through his head? At least she now had a better understanding of the snake. He kept things hidden. What were his *real* feelings? "Will you be staying for supper?" Sara was tempted to ask him if Indian bread and corn pudding suited his taste.

"If I'm welcome." Fargo removed his arm from Megan's shoulders.

"Of course you're welcome," Megan assured him.

"I'll tell Carla." Sara left the room, heading for the kitchen. As angry as she was at Fargo's deception, she couldn't deny the tremor of excitement she'd experienced when he said he would stay. He wasn't even in the same room, and she already longed once again to feel his hands on her body, his lips searing hers, and the explosion of raw passion when he took her to ultimate fulfillment.

Sara stopped and looked back toward the parlor. What if she played Fargo's game? What if she used him the same way he'd used her—with one little exception. After they'd made love, Fargo would receive a big shock.

Sara paid little attention to the conversation during supper. Fargo's smoldering looks took away any appetite she might have had. How could she feel such desire for a sneaky, untrustworthy man? It wasn't fair that every time his lips curved over his fork she was reminded of how his lips felt on hers. Even before Carla had placed the dessert on the table, she was awash with a driving hunger that had nothing to do with food.

Sara had thought to take Fargo for a walk after the meal, but, to her annoyance, Megan and Will insisted they have a game of dominoes. Will warned Fargo that the women were good, and that he would have to watch his p's and q's.

Sara's annoyance increased when one game followed another. She finally had to accept the inevitable. Her planned evening had been shattered. With that realization, she settled into the game with a vengeance. Several times she mentioned that Fargo had a long ride home, but because it didn't seem to bother him, they played late into the night.

By the time they'd completed the last game, Sara had a splitting headache. Irritated by the way things had turned out and Fargo's apparent lack of interest, she bade everyone goodnight, and retired. Megan and Will could see Fargo out, she decided.

In her bedroom, Sara quickly shed her clothes, donned her nightgown, blew out the candle and climbed into bed. The crisp, clean sheets helped her relax. She so badly had wanted Fargo to make love to her again... She had two choices: either wait until he made another visit or go see him at his place. She decided on the latter. Patience had never been one of her better qualities.

Hearing a strange noise, Sara lay still and listened. Suddenly a hand clamped over her mouth. Before she could put up a fight, she heard Fargo say her name. Fargo had come to claim what he apparently considered rightfully his. Her anger immediately vanished and was replaced with adrenaline, pumping through her veins. Even so, he needed to understand that this was a mutual decision. "I thought you were on your way home," she said as soon as he'd removed his hand.

"Will and Megan think the same thing."

"You seem awfully sure that I would welcome you to my bed." She moved her legs over the side and sat up. Touching him presented too great a temptation.

"From the looks you gave me tonight, I had the distinct impression you were extending an invitation. Did I misunderstand?"

"Well, I—I mean—"

He placed his hand on her shoulder and gently pushed her down on the bed. "I can't even begin to tell you what a hard time I had trying to concentrate on the game. All I could think about was making love to you."

"You hide your thoughts well." Sara's pride had been hurt by his seeming lack of interest. "I've wanted you all night, too," she said when he lay beside her. "I thought—"

Fargo kissed her—it was a hungry kiss that showed his need for her—and Sara fell into the pit of their mutual desire.

Satiated, Sara lay languidly in Fargo's arms, wondering who was using whom. Whichever it was, the other one certainly wasn't getting the short end of the straw. She closed her eyes as Fargo trailed his hand across the flat of her stomach, over her breasts and upward, then pulled her hair back and kissed the curve of her neck.

"You always smell so wonderful," he whispered. "For two weeks I've thought of nothing but possessing you again."

Sara wanted to believe him; however, she didn't particularly care for the way he used the word *possessing*. "When did you plan to get around to asking me about Hawk?" To her surprise, he did nothing to indicate that her question had taken him by surprise. She didn't feel his body tense; nor did his hand pause, even momentarily, on its way to resting on her breast. It did, however, seem to take an eternity before he spoke.

"When did you find out?"

"When isn't the issue." He'd asked the question in such a nonchalant manner that Sara was twice as offended. Angry now, she climbed off the bed, wrapping the sheet around her. After a moment's fumbling in the dark, she had lit a candle. She walked to the rocking chair and sat. With her eyes resting steadily on Fargo, she waited.

Fargo sat up, not bothering to hide his nakedness. He had known that with all the inquiries he'd made it was highly likely that word would get back to the Bar C ranch. "This seems very important you."

There's that honey-coated voice again, Sara thought. "That's putting it too mildly. Why didn't you ask *me* about Hawk, instead of wheedling your way into my family—or, worse yet, into my bed?"

"Whoa, now, just one damn minute," Fargo said, raising his hands, palms out, toward her. "I didn't force you to do a thing."

"Just answer me. Why do you want to know about Hawk?"

Though her question had taken him off guard, somehow he'd managed not to show it. He certainly hadn't thought it would come right after they'd coupled. "All right, I'll tell you why I'm looking for Hawk. I've heard he's a no-account bounty hunter who brings all of his prisoners in dead." He watched Sara's face closely. Her nostrils were already flared with indignation. "I've also heard he keeps his identity a secret, has a big dog that fits Phew's description and is known for getting his man." Fargo could see the corners of Sara's eyes twitching. Still, he had to give her credit—she managed to keep her countenance. "Now, this Hawk may be a bastard, but he's good, and I want to hire him to do a job for me."

"I don't know of anyone by that name, so your efforts have been a waste of time, Mr. Tucker."

"I think you do know who he is. There is no dog like Phew for miles around, possibly even hundreds of miles around. So someone on this ranch is Hawk, and you know who that person is. Why keep it a secret? He'll not only get the bounty for the man I want him to catch, he'll also get a wad of money from me."

"Why don't you go after the outlaw yourself?"

"He knows me. His men even know me. I wouldn't get within ten miles of him. But someone like Hawk could, and he could tell me what needs to be done to catch him. Then I'll take my men and we'll get rid of the whole gang.

"Like I said, you've wasted a lot of time for nothing." Fargo sat on the edge of the bed and picked his shirt up from the floor. A moment later, he had a cigarette rolled and lit. He inhaled deeply, then let the smoke slowly trail from his lips. "No, I didn't waste my time. Being with you has been worth every moment." He looked at her glorious auburn hair. It was shimmering in the candlelight, wild and disheveled, with ringlets falling onto her forehead. Her lips were still swollen from his kisses. He could feel his desire growing again. "You're very beautiful, you know."

"The compliment won't work."

Fargo took another long drag from the cigarette, then flicked the butt out the door into the courtyard. "Tell me,

Sara, if you think this was all just to get information about Hawk, why did you let me make love to you tonight?''

"If you expect me to say I don't desire you, you're in for a surprise. I always wondered what it would be like to have a man make love to me, and you were without a doubt the most fetching man I've met."

"Fetching?" His eyes darkened. "Are you saying you used me?"

Her hands were busy, pleating and unpleating the edge of the sheet she'd wrapped around her. "I'm saying exactly that."

To Sara's surprise, Fargo burst out laughing.

"What, may I ask, do you find so funny? Doesn't it bother you to know that you've been used?"

"Why should it? I consider it a compliment." Fargo gave her a devilish grin. "I hope I lived up to your expectations." He reached down and picked up his trousers, then proceeded to dress. "Apparently you don't look at it the way I do."

"Are you saying you used me?"

"Not at all. But I have a strong hunch that's what you think." He sat on the bed and pulled on a boot. "Are you going to tell me where I can find Hawk?"

"I know nothing about someone called Hawk. However, if I did, I can assure you he wouldn't be the type of person you've described."

Fargo pulled on his second boot and let his foot fall to the floor. He released a heavy sigh, then looked at Sara, who still had the sheet wrapped around her. "Is Megan Hawk?"

"What? I've never heard of anything so ridiculous!" Sara scrambled out of the rocking chair. "How dare you even think such a thing! I don't ever want to see you on this ranch again."

Within two strides, Fargo had reached her and pulled her to him.

"Keep your hands off me." Sara tried pulling away, but he held her firmly. She was furious.

Fargo wrapped his hand in her thick auburn hair and slowly forced her to look up at him. "Whatever our reasons are for wanting each other, Miss Carter, it's not something that can be dismissed lightly anymore. You're no longer the prim little miss sitting over in the corner, my dear. You're a woman, with strong appetites, and like it or not, you want me every bit as much as I want you." He leaned down, but didn't claim her lips. He kissed each eye, her nose, the corners of her mouth. He felt the sheet fall to the floor, then her naked body press against him. He ran his hands along her spine, drawing pleasure from the feel of her smooth flesh. When he finally claimed her lips, she was as eager for the kiss as he was.

"You are a—" she kissed his neck "—worthless—" she trailed her tongue down his chest "—snake." Her tongue circled his nipple.

Fargo groaned. "Damn, woman, you drive me wild." He was already unbuttoning his pants again.

Sara laughed, drawing strength from the effect she had on him. "It's good to know that it's not all one-sided." She went over and lay on the bed, waiting for him to undress. He knew nothing about Hawk. He could only make wild guesses. So what harm would it do to spend a little more time enjoying the fruits in the basket?

Not until the first rays of dawn lit the sky did Fargo finally dress, mount his horse and head for home.

For the next two weeks, Fargo and Sara shared a passion that had no bounds. Fargo teased Sara, telling her that it had to be her hot Indian blood. Because of his teasing, she began slowly to accept her heritage. She had to keep reminding herself that Fargo was only seeking one thing. To locate Hawk. Yet, all she had to do was look at that now-familiar fire in his eyes and she eagerly would go to him. They rode together, laughed together, talked a little and made love a lot. He inquired about Hawk, and she denied knowing such a person. They had an understanding that didn't need to be put into words. And Sara was content to leave it that way. In the meantime, she worked with her new horse, Wings of Air. She called him Wings for short. He had been gentled by the Apache, and Sara worked at keeping him gentle.

Sara sat in the courtyard, toying with the idea of riding over to Fargo's ranch. Phew lay sprawled out at her feet, and Megan sat across from her, darning socks.

Megan placed the sock she was working on in her lap. "Sara, I worry about you."

Sara looked surprised. "That's a strange thing to say. If I remember correctly, I'm the one who always watched after you, not the other way around." She smiled fondly at her sister.

"I don't know why, but lately, when I look at you, I feel saddened. Smells of Flowers says it is a gift, but if feeling sadness and worry is a gift, I don't want it."

"I'm not sure I would, either. But you needn't worry about me." As if she'd just opened her eyes for the first time in weeks, Sara suddenly realized that Megan had changed. Her sister possessed a maturity that Sara had never seen before. Megan was beautiful. Sara became overwhelmed with guilt. She hadn't even noticed that her sister dressed differently. In fact, Sara recognized the dress as her own. And Megan no longer wore her hair wild or in a braid. It had been pulled up into a smooth, becoming knot on the top of her head. Where had she been that she hadn't even seen what was sitting right beneath her nose? She hadn't paid attention to her sister! The thing she'd sworn would never happen *had* happened. Her obsession with Fargo had taken precedence over everything. Mere moments ago she'd been absorbed with thoughts of going to him. She had been living in a fool's paradise.

Sara watched Megan darn the sock for a moment, then looked toward the sky. It was a cloudy day. Rather appropriate, given the way she felt. It looked as if they were finally going to get some much-needed rain. Who was she kidding? Fargo didn't care for her, at least not in a romantic way. He wanted Hawk. As soon as he accomplished that, he'd be out of her life forever. Just that quickly. Yet she had foolishly fallen in love. An unforgivable mistake. Apparently Megan had been right again. Her future did indeed look bleak. But there was that one, omnipresent obsession that kept her going. It had always taken, and would always take, precedence over everything else. And nothing, not Fargo or anyone else, would interfere with it.

She looked back at Megan, and her heart reached out to her sister. Another priority. She would do anything on God's earth to protect her.

"Megan, we haven't had much of a chance to talk."

"That's because you haven't been around."

"I want to know—I need to know—how you feel about Fargo."

"What do you mean?"

Sara stood, unable to remain seated a moment longer. Phew rolled onto his back, and, with his legs in the air, watched her. "What I mean is . . . do you think you're in love with him?"

Megan's eyes widened, and her cheeks flushed. "That would be rather foolish, don't you think? Especially when he only has eyes for you."

Sara plucked a hedge rose, then held it to her nose, inhaling the faint, sweet odor. "You didn't answer me."

Megan hesitated. "I thought I was," she said at last, "but I'm not so sure now. More than once you've told me I haven't seen enough of life to compare it with anything. I believe you're right. Sara, when you have time, I think I'd like you to take me to Tombstone. And maybe we could stay with your friend Rose."

"You know I would do anything to make you happy, but are you sure you're ready to make such a trip?"

Megan laid her darning in her lap again and stared into space. "Sara, I remember the past."

Sara clutched at her throat. "When did this happen? When . . . How did it happen?"

"Seeing you and Fargo together started bringing back memories. It was the looks he gave you, the same looks that Papa used to give Mama." She bowed her head. "Remember the morning Fargo and I went riding?"

Sara clenched her fists. "Yes. Did he do anything?"

"No, I did. He started to help me onto my horse, but I began yelling at him. I didn't even remember what had happened on our ride until that night. Then everything—the past—started coming back to me in waves. I thought I was going insane. I left the house and saddled my horse. I rode for hours. At dawn, I came to my senses."

"Oh, my God, Megan, I'm so sorry. Why didn't you come to me? Why didn't you tell me?"

"And what could you have done? Do you remember that week I was gone?"

"You have taken off many times without my knowing where you were. Are you talking about the last time?"

"Yes. I was feeling so down, and I felt as if I had no family. Then Azul came and told me our grandmother was near. I realized then that I did have family. Not one, but many. As Grandmother said, they are our heritage. I thought about what the People had gone through, and then the pain didn't hurt so much."

Sara felt a growing uneasiness.

"I told Grandmother everything, and she understood. It was spending time with her, and her wise counsel, that has helped me learn to accept the past."

"Why couldn't you come to me? I'm your sister."

"Don't be angry with me, Sara." Megan reached out and placed her hand on Sara's. "I know you have watched over me and have taken care of me, but somehow I felt the need for advice from another direction. I thought about going to Fargo. I probably would have, if Azul hadn't shown up."

"Megan...you're not thinking about going to live with the Chiricahua, are you?" Sara hated to ask the question, but she knew she had to.

Megan picked up her darning and stood. "No, Sara, I'm not going to live with the Chiricahua. I'm going to have enough trouble learning to live with myself."

"Megan, it wasn't your fault."

"I know, and yet, when I watched the wonderful little Indian children playing, I thought about how I'd like to have children of my own someday, but who would marry a woman who is no longer a virgin—and a half-breed to boot?"

"I guess our father wondered the same thing. No one has to know, Meg."

"I'm not ashamed of it," Megan said fiercely, walking away.

Sara followed after her. "Megan, I don't expect you to be ashamed. Would you stop and listen to me?"

Megan turned and waited.

"Why did Papa not tell anyone? Because he couldn't own the land. Megan, it's the same for us. We could lose everything. Is that really what you want?"

Megan looked confused. "No. I love this ranch. This is *our* land."

"Have you said anything to Will?"

"Yes, but—"

"Don't worry. Will is one of the few people I know who can be trusted. He won't tell anyone. Have you said anything to anyone besides Will and Fargo?"

"No."

"So that only leaves Fargo to worry about." Sara began pacing. "Fortunately, I don't think he's aware of the weapon he's holding."

"Why do you say that?"

"It's not important. Just don't say anything to him about how we could lose the ranch. We'll just sit back and see what happens." Sara stopped and smiled. "In the meantime, you and I are going to Tombstone. If the people frighten you, we'll just turn around and come back."

"I have another confession."

Sara looked questioningly at her sister.

"I've seen Tombstone."

"How?"

"On more than one occasion I've ridden up near Boot Hill and sat staring down at the people moving about," Megan blurted out.

Sara was shocked. "That's a five-hour ride!" She started to tell Megan she could have been killed, but then she realized it would serve no purpose now. "Well, what's done is done. At least I'm starting to have some insight as to where you disappear to. We need supplies from the feed store. What do you say you and I take the ranch wagon and go to town and get them ourselves?''

Megan grinned. ''Tomorrow?''

''First thing in the morning.''

Lightning suddenly lit the sky, followed by a loud clap of thunder. Phew darted past them into the house. Before Megan and Sara could enter, heavy sheets of rain were already pouring down.

Neither woman tried ducking for cover. They stood, loving the feel of the much-needed water. ''If this keeps up, it's going to take a day or so for the ground to harden back up. Sorry, Megan, but we may have to wait a couple of days before we can go to Tombstone.''

Megan laughed as she enjoyed the flashes of lightning streaking across the sky. ''I've already waited a long time, and a couple of days isn't going to make a bit of difference.''

Chapter Ten

Three days later, one of the cowhands delivered a farm wagon to the front of the house, climbed off, then helped Sara and Megan onto the seat. Both women were holding shotguns, and gun belts were buckled just below the waists of their skirts. Phew jumped in the back.

"You sure you don't want me to drive that team for you, ma'am?"

"Tim, I'm quite capable of handling a two-horse team."

"Well . . . how about some of the men ridin' along with you."

Sara looked at Meg and smiled. "I don't think that will be necessary either, Tim."

Sara pulled her hat down to shade her eyes, took the reins in her gloved hands and slapped them across the horses' rumps. It was a glorious day for Megan Carter to get her first taste of life in town. They did have an advantage. Megan had met Rose, Cyrus and Penelope on more than one occasion when they'd visited the hacienda. But this time, Megan wouldn't be able to find privacy in her own room.

"Sara," Megan said when they were about two miles down the road, "do you think we'll ever marry?"

"Who would have us?" Sara teased.

"I'd like to think that someday I'll marry and have children. If we do marry, do you think we should tell our husbands about our Indian blood? Papa told Mama."

"I guess it depends on the man." Sara grinned mischievously. "We could always buy us some husbands."

"What?" Megan giggled. "Whoever heard of such a thing?"

"I've heard of mail-order brides, so why not mail-order grooms? Heaven knows, we've got enough money. Megan, can't you just picture some man having to cook the meals, do the washing and all those things that women are supposed to do?"

The two women broke out in fits of laughter.

"Not if it's someone like Fargo," Megan added, when she could speak again.

"No," Sara agreed good-naturedly, "I can't picture that either." It felt good to have sisterly talks once again. She hadn't realized how much she'd missed the teasing and even the fights they'd had. Six years was a long time to be lonely.

Hidden by a large boulder, Fargo sat on his horse, watching the two women drive off. He decided to follow unobserved. Perhaps the ladies were off to meet Hawk.

Two hours had passed before Fargo finally settled down for a long ride. The women's direction was now apparent. Though he found it hard to believe, what with Megan riding along, that they were actually going to Tombstone. He had no choice but to follow. He might have reconsidered, had Phew not been with them. They were certainly well armed. He wasn't sure how good a shot Sara was, but Megan could pick off just about anything that crossed her sights.

By the time he reached town, Fargo was tired and dirty and his disposition was sour as hell. He hadn't brought a change of clothes, which meant he'd have to buy some. At least he had money in his pockets, and a line of credit. After getting a room at the Occidental Hotel, he climbed back onto his horse and continued on down Fourth Street to Fremont, dismounting in front of the Summerfield Brothers Drygoods Store.

Later that night, Fargo left the hotel. The bath and fresh clothes had made him feel like a new man. Sara and Megan seemed to have settled in for the night at the Halversons', so there wasn't any need for him to keep watch on them until morning. He was looking forward to a night's entertainment. He deserved it. The first thing that occurred to him was to get roaring drunk. However, the possibility of having to deal with a hangover, come morning, had no appeal. Instead, he decided on a good game of cards at Big Nose Kate's Saloon. He had a hankering to play poker with Kate's boyfriend, Doc Holliday. After all, how many men could say they'd played poker with a legend?

The next morning, Fargo rose early and dressed, thankful that he still had the clothes on his back after last night's losses at the card table. All things considered, he felt good. And after riding by the Halversons' house and seeing the farm wagon still sitting at the side of the carriage house, he even had time to find a place to eat.

Once his appetite had been satisfied, he left the small restaurant in Hop Town feeling content. He glanced up and down the street. Since he was so close to the sheriff's office, he'd decided to take a look at the wanted posters— something he'd done often while living at the San Jose House. He took off down the street. His only interests were the posters with a big reward. Since the sheriff in New

Mexico had said Hawk was so good at his profession, Fargo figured that the bounty hunter would only be attracted to the well-paying jobs.

Fargo was about to leave, when after a quick perusal of the posters, the sheriff stepped out of his office. The five-hundred-dollar reward on the piece of paper he nailed up definitely drew Fargo's attention. He took a long look at the drawing of the wanted man's face before leaving.

After goodbyes had been said, Sara had the farm wagon headed for the feed store. Megan's relief at returning home was evident from the now-relaxed look on her face. It had been obvious to Sara that her sister's discomfort had been increasing. Sara was glad she'd discouraged Rose from sending a message to Penelope last night. The widow would have been too overwhelming for Megan at this time. Maybe next time. All in all, Sara was pleased at how well the visit had gone.

It didn't take long for the men to load the bags of feed and the few other supplies needed into the wagon. Within an hour, Sara had the wagon moving again.

"Megan, I want to stop for just a minute and see Marshall Earp."

"Why?"

"It's nothing to be concerned about. I just want to ask how he's doing at rounding up rustlers."

"I always thought he had a fine mustache."

"That he does."

When Sara pulled up the wagon in front of the marshall's office, Virgil stepped out and tipped his hat. "Morning, ladies. Miss Megan, what a pleasure it is to see you in Tombstone."

Megan managed a nervous smile.

"Have you put anyone in jail for rustling lately?" Sara asked.

"Now, Sara, you know that there is no way I can round up every rustler in these parts."

"I heard that the Clantons and McLaurys have been giving you trouble."

Virgil looked down the street and moved the toothpick from one side of his mouth to the other. "They're wanting control of this town, but it's not going to happen." He handed Sara a wanted poster. "Five-hundred dollars on Lou Duncan's head. I thought Hawk might want to look into this."

Sara held it so that she and Megan could look at the man's picture. "Possibly." She folded the paper and stuck it in her shirt.

Virgil shifted the toothpick again. "You remind Hawk to be careful."

"I will. Well, we have to be heading on. It's a long ride back to the ranch."

When Fargo rode past the Halversons' house and saw the wagon gone, he took off in search of it. He cursed himself for having allowed Sara to get away.

Fargo was about to round a corner when, to his relief, he spotted Sara talking to Virgil. He pulled up his horse and watched. The moment Marshall Earp handed Sara the paper, Fargo's back stiffened. Although he couldn't see what was on the paper, he could have sworn it looked like the poster he'd seen at the sheriff's place. Maybe he was finally going to get a break. He hadn't missed the look Sara had given Megan. He refused to acknowledge the knots he felt in his stomach when Megan stared at the page.

Everything kept pointing to Megan as being Hawk. Maybe that was why he'd started having a hard time accepting it. Hawk had been very careful to keep his identity a secret, and it didn't make sense that he or she would allow something to be so obvious. Also, bounty hunting wasn't an easy job. No, it would take a man to pull off such feats. Once again, he was thinking of Will as a strong possibility. Well, one way or another, he'd find out the truth. Every nerve in his body was telling him Hawk would soon be coming out of hiding.

It wasn't until Sara had the wagon headed along the road toward the Bar C that Fargo chose to let his presence be known. He put his horse into a gallop. At least he'd done something right that morning. He'd paid for his hotel room, and his clothes were in his saddlebags.

Fargo greeted the ladies as he brought his horse up alongside Megan. "What a pleasant surprise. Looks like I'm not going to have to make the trip home by myself after all. I hope you don't mind if I ride along?" The pleased looks on their faces were just what he'd hoped for.

Sara stopped the team, and Fargo tied his horse to the back. Once it was secure, he hopped up beside Megan, who had scooted over.

"Did Rose by chance send some food to eat along the way?" Fargo asked.

Completely at ease in Fargo's presence, Megan laughed. "Unless you get greedy, there is more than enough for three people."

"What were you doing in town?" Sara asked in a friendly tone.

"Ordering supplies. That place I bought is going to need a lot of work to get it in shape. I'm looking for a good bull, maybe even two, to start rebuilding the herd. Do you by chance have one you'd like to sell me, Sara?"

"As a matter of fact, I do."

"Good. I'll be over in a couple of days to take a look at him."

The trip passed in enjoyable companionship. From this point on, Fargo couldn't afford to let either of the Carters out of his sight. The problem was, how did he plan to accomplish that? As worthy as his intentions might be, he still had to eat and sleep.

By the time Fargo had left the women and had his horse headed toward home, he'd made up his mind as to how he'd keep watch on the women. Actually, there really wasn't a choice. He'd have to use his men to help keep watch. The tall hill south of the Carter hacienda had always afforded a perfect place for observation. A small cottonwood grove and some boulders provided a hiding place.

Fargo guided his horse across a wide dry wash, trying to convince himself Hawk wouldn't make a move before he could get a man positioned. If Megan was Hawk, she'd want to rest up before taking off on her quest. Sara had said Will was putting up a line shack at the northern end of the ranch and wouldn't be back to the house until later that week.

Fargo decided that once he had everything ready, he'd get a good night's sleep, then pay Sara a call. When they were returning from town, he'd had a hell of a time keeping control of his desire. Megan wouldn't have been too pleased to see a pair of swollen britches.

It looked like everything was finally beginning to come to an end. Unfortunately, when that happened, he no longer would be able to enjoy Sara's pleasures. He'd have to leave. Besides, she wouldn't want anything to do with him once he'd killed Hawk. Of course, there were always other women to take her place. But in all honesty, he seriously doubted that he would meet another woman the equal of Sara Carter. He had a strong hunch he was going to miss the petite lady with the marvelous green eyes.

Had anyone seen the lantern moving in the dark of night, they would have sworn a ghostly apparition was roaming the Whetstone Mountains. Eventually, the solitary figure disappeared from sight.

The lantern ended up on the ground, and the person, dressed in buckskins, set about saddling a paint horse. When everything was ready, the lantern was extinguished. Then the person mounted the paint and, leading a pack horse, left the small box canyon. A big dog followed.

"Good morning," Megan called when Fargo rode up. She dropped the spade she'd been using to dig up weeds around the small cemetery.

"Doesn't it ever rain in this place?"

"It rained the other day."

"It didn't rain," Fargo said with a smile. "It poured. I expected a flash flood to run right through my house."

Megan laughed.

"Where's Sara?"

"What kind of man are you, Fargo Tucker?" Megan teased gently. "You stop, and instead of talking to me you ask about Sara." Megan dusted the dirt from her skirt. "See this wrought-iron fence?" she asked proudly. "Sara brought it from Mexico. She had it all piled in the back of a ranch wagon, then put it up herself. She wouldn't let a soul help her."

Fargo swung a leg over the horse and dismounted. "That must have been a hard time for both of you."

"I don't know. You'd have to talk to Sara about that. I don't remember much. Some, not much." She looked up at Fargo and flashed him a mischievous smile. "You might as well come to the house and have a cold drink. And you're just going to have to accept my company, because Sara isn't here."

Fargo fell into step. "I can wait."

"Not that I don't enjoy your company, but you'll have to wait quite a while."

"What's she doing? Tending to the cattle? Isn't she fixing to make a shipment soon?"

"Yes, but she's not tending cattle. She went to Elgin. She'll probably be there all week."

Fargo's steps faltered. "Why did she go to Elgin?"

Megan stopped and turned. "You sound concerned. She's just gone to meet the cattle buyer to assure top price and see that there's adequate stock pens for the herd."

"When did she leave?"

"Early this morning."

"How early this morning?"

"I don't know what time. She left before I got up. Now, just what is all this questioning about, Fargo? Since when did Sara start giving you an accounting of everything she does?"

Fargo raised his hands in the air. "Whoa, now, honey. Don't go getting yourself so riled. If you remember, I also have cattle I have to look after. Meeting a buyer and checking out the arrangements in Elgin would be beneficial to me, as well. I'm just wondering if I could catch up with her." He shoved his hat back, looped a finger in his gun belt and looked up at the sky. "Sure wish she'd told me she was going."

Megan nodded. "She didn't even tell me until you'd ridden off yesterday."

"Oh?"

"Now, do you want something cold to drink, or not?"

Fargo's thoughts were darting in every direction. If he only knew whether or not that was a poster Earp had given Sara. "I rode over here because yesterday, when I returned home, I saw a skinny, dark-haired man with a scar across his cheek riding around my house. The minute he saw me, he took off. Could it have been one of your men snooping around?"

"What kind of scar?"

Fargo drew a line down his cheek with his finger.

"No, doesn't sound like any of our men. However, Virgil gave us a poster yesterday of a man that fits that description. It should be in Sara's room. Wait here and I'll go check. You might recognize him."

Megan wasn't gone long. "I didn't find it. Perhaps she took it with her, but I don't know why. Sorry I couldn't be of help."

"Well, it doesn't really matter. I told the boys to watch out for him. Tell you what, Megan, I'll take you up on that drink another time." Fargo flipped the reins over his horse's neck; then, with one hand on the saddle horn, he swung up into the saddle.

"You're going after Sara, aren't you?"

"Well, honey, it's the only way I'm going to find out what I need to know about shipping my cattle. I take it there's a railroad there."

"The Santa Fe. If you don't catch up with Sara, you shouldn't have any trouble finding her. She said there was only one nice hotel in Elgin."

Megan waved at Fargo, but he didn't see her. He already had his horse galloping down the road. She felt a sudden cold chill. She glanced back at the weeds she'd pulled, but was no longer interested in continuing. There was trouble in the air. She could feel it as strongly as if someone had slapped her. But she didn't know what kind of trouble, or where it was coming from. All she could do was wait.

Fargo was interested in seeing if Sara had, indeed, gone to Elgin to attend to business, or if she was delivering the wanted poster to Hawk. Dammit, like it or not, he was jealous at the attention and protection she gave the good-for-nothing bastard. And if she had taken off to deliver news of the reward, that meant he had been wrong about everything. No wonder he couldn't catch Hawk. He didn't even live on the ranch. All his suppositions hadn't even been worth the time he'd spent on them. Like now. He was letting his imagination get the best of him. Maybe she really had gone to Elgin on business.

The first thing Fargo noticed about Elgin was the cottonwood groves spread around town, offering wondrous shade. The second was the railroad yard and the stock pens. There were also plenty of saloons to take care of a traveling man's dry throat. As Fargo rode by, he could hear honky-tonk music and customers' voices coming from inside.

The two-story hotel wasn't hard to find. Now all Fargo could do was hope that Sara hadn't already made contact with Hawk, and that Megan had told the truth. If Sara wasn't in town, he was up the proverbial creek. While signing for a room, Fargo smiled. Sara's signature was several lines above his.

Dressed in a cream-and-lime-green town suit, a small hat perched on top of her head, and carrying a cream-colored parasol to block the sun, Sara crossed the windswept main street of Elgin and headed toward the sheriff's office. She glanced at her lapel watch. Two o'clock. The sheriff had to be back by now.

As Sara stepped onto the wooden walk, she looked ahead at the small building that served as both the jail and the sheriff's office. She came to an abrupt halt and stared in angry disbelief. Fargo Tucker stood in the doorway talking to the lawman! What, by all that was holy, could he be doing here? He had to suspect something. Damn him! Seeing Fargo start to look around, she ducked into the nearest doorway until she could get herself composed.

"Why, Ms. Carter, have you finally decided to take me up on my invitation to supper?" the chubby man seated behind the desk asked as he motioned to Sara to enter his office. His face reddened with anticipation, and he kept cracking his knuckles.

Sara looked at the cattle buyer and cringed. Her hunting instincts had been honed and sharpened over a period of six years. She was here for a purpose, and nothing was going to distract her from her goal. The time had come to use garters and lace for information—a role she knew well. "I have indeed, Mr. Smith. I would consider it an honor to dine with you."

Dusty Smith's bulbous nose turned redder than his face. "Perhaps I'll even be able to persuade you to reconsider my offer for your cattle."

Sara smiled sweetly as she glanced around the cattle buyer's cluttered office. "You never know. But should I choose not to, I think it only fair that I put you in contact with another cattleman. You might find it quite profitable."

"Oh? And who would that gentleman be?"

Sara took him by his ample arm and led him to the doorway. "You see that tall man talking to the sheriff?"

"Yes."

"He just bought a ranch adjacent to mine. He'll be wanting to ship his cattle. Maybe not many this year, but definitely a good-size herd come next year. If you get to him first, he might sell to you."

"Aha! Do you know him?"

"Yes, his name is Fargo Tucker. I'll tell you what I'll do. I'll ask him to dine with us tonight, and you can talk to him."

Dusty's fat jowls sagged a bit. He would have liked to dine alone with Sara, but business was what put money in his pocket. "Excellent idea, my dear. Excellent."

"Then we'll meet in the hotel restaurant, around six-thirty tonight?" Sara blinked her eyelashes a couple of times and wondered if this butterball of a man was going to melt right into the floor. She certainly knew the feeling—just about every time Fargo flashed one of his smiles at her.

Satisfied, Sara left the office and continued down the walk. If luck was on her side, Dusty would dog Fargo's heels for the next few days.

Fargo saw her coming before she reached him.

"Fargo," Sara said, with just the right inflection of surprise. "If I didn't know better, I'd assume you were following me. What are you doing in Elgin?"

"You assumed right. I did come to find you."

The sheriff tipped his hat. "Miss Carter."

"Sheriff," Sara replied. She turned her attention back to Fargo. "You don't seem surprised to see me."

"I'm not. Meg told me I'd find you here."

"I see. Well, pray tell, what have you been bending the sheriff's ear about?"

"I was asking if he knew a bounty hunter who goes by the name Hawk."

His voice was like a caress, and Sara hated the way he could make her feel his presence all the way to her shaking knees. "You don't give up, do you?"

"Nope." Fargo took her by the arm. "Be talking to you, Sheriff," he said as he led Sara away.

"I do have things to do," Sara snapped at Fargo.

"Fine. I'll just tag along."

"Why?" Sara jerked her arm away. "Did you follow me because of your foolish notion that I will contact your mysterious Hawk?"

"You got that right."

Sara stopped dead in her tracks. "I have told you I don't know any such man. I am here for one reason. To get everything ready for my cattle to be shipped. Nothing more."

"Nothing more? Oh, Sara, one should always mix a little pleasure with work." He traced her lips with his thumb. "For instance, are you aware that my hotel room is directly across the hall from yours?"

Now who was the melting butter? Sara reminded herself before she took off walking again. "I want nothing to do with you. You lie. You always lie."

"I haven't lied to you, Sara. In fact, I've made it quite clear what I want."

"You haven't lied? What would you call it?" Smelling the cattle pens up ahead, Sara turned around and headed back in the direction she'd just come from. "You were looking for *me* when you attended the Schieffelin Hall party, not cattlemen. And when I found you, took you in, and nursed you, you didn't bother to say that you'd been roaming my land to find my dog!"

"And speaking of dogs, where is Phew?"

Sara opened her umbrella. Had he not backed away, it would have hit Fargo in the face.

"I left him at a friend's house. I couldn't very well take him to the hotel."

"A friend?" Fargo cocked an eyebrow. "And just where might that friend be?"

Sara pulled up short, her lips forming a big O as she once again closed her umbrella. "Well, I'll be. You think it's Hawk, don't you?"

"That I do, my dear."

"In that case, I wouldn't dream of telling you where Phew is. I like the idea of your imagination running away with itself. You deserve it."

"A decision you may come to regret."

"Is that a threat?"

"Call it what you like, my dear." Fargo took her umbrella in one hand and placed his other hand beneath her arm. "Shall we continue our walk?"

Chapter Eleven

Though the last few days and nights with Fargo had been joyous beyond anything she could ever have imagined, Sara knew the time had come to bring her heaven to an end. As much as she loved Fargo, she wasn't so blind that she couldn't see what he hoped to accomplish. He wanted her to become so enamored of him that she'd tell him anything. Particularly about Hawk. He didn't realize that, even if it meant losing the only man she'd ever loved, Hawk had to remain protected. And with Fargo continually at her side, it had been impossible to collect information on Lou Duncan. She had to find a way of getting Fargo out of Elgin, or at least off her heels. But how?

Sara went to the armoire in her hotel room and opened it. Reaching inside, she pulled the wanted poster from her reticule and stared at it. It was Lou Duncan's picture that had attracted her, not the five-hundred-dollar reward.

The knock on the door startled her. "Just a moment," she called as she stuffed the poster back into the reticule. "I'm coming."

Sara hurried to the door and swung it open. Studying the handsome man standing relaxed with his hand braced against the doorjamb, she momentarily forgot all about Lou Duncan—and even Hawk. Lord, how she loved Fargo

Tucker. There had to be a way for them to find happiness. Surely he couldn't have made love to her all this time without feeling some affection. "Come in," she said softly. "Did anyone see you?"

Fargo closed the door behind him and leaned against it. Sara was a vision of loveliness in her pink diaphanous gown, with her auburn hair free and framing her face. Her full lips, and her eyes . . . Oh, her eyes. Eyes that any man could get lost in.

"Are you going to just stand there without saying a word?" Sara gave him an impish grin. "Or maybe you want me to come to you." She moved forward, but to her surprise he held out his hand, making it clear that he didn't want her to move a step farther. "Is something wrong?"

"No, I was just standing here thinking how you exemplify everything a man could desire in a woman. You're the type to take home and care for. A lady. Yet when we're alone, you're the fire of temptation that could burn a man and make him your slave."

Sara backed away. That cold, calculating look she'd seen in his eyes on other occasions had returned. She tried smiling. "Now you have me totally confused. One minute you're practically calling me a saint, and the next you're calling me a devil."

Fargo's laugh had a hollow ring to it.

Fargo had created an uneasiness within her that Sara didn't understand or know how to handle. She sat on the edge of the bed and threaded her fingers together. "Are you just going to stay leaning against that door?"

"I said a long time ago that if we ever got together, what a pair we would make."

"What is that supposed to mean? And what's made you so brooding?"

Fargo pushed away from the door, strode to where Sara sat and looked down at her. "Sara, we've both known this couldn't continue." He lifted her chin with a crooked finger. "I'm through playing games. Where are you supposed to meet Hawk?"

Sara jerked her chin away from his touch and scooted back on the bed. She couldn't let him know he had succeeded in scaring her. "I don't know what you're talking about."

"You know exactly what I'm talking about. If I remember correctly, you once accused me of telling lies. You were right. But there have been enough lies."

To Sara's relief, he moved back to the middle of the room.

"You asked for truths, so I'll give you truths. At first I suspected Will of being Hawk. Then I thought it was Megan. You needn't look so shocked. Who had a better reason? Plus, she's mighty handy with a gun."

"But I—"

"No, no... By all means, let me continue. I want you to hear all of it. I followed you and Megan into town the other day." He leaned a broad shoulder against the redpapered wall. "When I saw Earp give you the wanted poster, I knew something was fixing to happen. But Megan wasn't the one who left and came to Elgin. In fact, I'm beginning to believe Megan is the one innocent person in the whole group. So, what do we have here? We have one person left, and that person, my dear, is you. Where are you going to meet Hawk? Dammit, Sara, I want some answers."

His voice was low and as smooth as silk brushing against bare skin, and Sara didn't like it. "Oh, please, don't stop there. Do you honestly expect me to believe that you're looking for a particular bounty hunter to collect a particular outlaw? There are bounty hunters everywhere, and every one just as good as, if not better than, Hawk. So why, I ask myself, why Hawk?'' She slid to the edge of the bed and stood. Her hand firmly gripping the bedpost, she looked him straight in the eye. ''Why is Hawk so important to you?''

''Because he murdered my brother.''

Sara's knuckles turned white. Fargo had the look of a man dead set on vengeance. ''Are you saying your brother was innocent?''

''That's exactly what I'm saying, lady.''

''That's a lie! Hawk never killed an innocent man.''

''Well, now, we're finally getting somewhere. The prim Miss Carter has finally admitted that there is a Hawk.''

''Get out of here!'' Sara ordered.

''Not until you tell me who Hawk is.'' He sat on the soft velvet chair and stretched his legs out. ''I envy the man for your loyalty. What is it about him that makes you so protective? He can't be a lover because you were every bit the virgin that you looked when I took you. And he can't be a boyfriend. If he were a boyfriend, you wouldn't have gone to bed with me in the first place. A relative, by chance? A friend that you owe something to? Maybe—''

''Shut up! You don't even know what you're talking about.''

''Well, then, by all means, give me a clue. Am I getting close? Or am I still cold?''

''What was your brother's name?'' Sara whispered.

''Jude Tanner.''

Sara's mouth dropped open, and it was a couple of seconds before she could speak. ''So 'Tucker' was also a lie?''

''That's right.''

''Jude Tanner was as cold-blooded and mean as the men he rode with.''

Fargo sat up in the chair. "That's a damn lie."

"A lie? Have you talked to any of the sheriffs in the area? He liked robbing banks and stages. And what about the houses he burned down and the women he raped?"

Fargo's fury was so strong he didn't dare touch the woman standing in front of him. "I suppose these are things that your friend Hawk told you. Believe me, kitten, I knew my brother. He may have been young, and he may have been wild, but he never would have done anything like that. He had no reason to."

"Maybe he did it simply for the thrill! So why are you here? To revenge his death? To kill the man who, in turn, killed your brother? An eye for an eye? Isn't that the way it goes?"

Fargo rose to his feet. "You're damn right," he snarled. "You stand there defending the bastard, instead of listening to what I'm telling you. Can't you see how he's lied and used you?"

"Used me?" Sara practically screamed the words out. "You, of all people, can make that statement? Use me?" She didn't hold back when she socked him in the chest. "What do you call what you've been doing? And you think you can stand there and cast stones?"

Fargo caught her arm before she landed the next blow. "Do you believe everything he tells you, Sara?"

"Turn me loose. You're hurting my arm!"

"You're a bright woman. Think, Sara, think! Why does he always deliver his captives at night? Why are they always dead? Why doesn't he want anyone to see his face? You told me to ask myself questions. Now you start asking yourself questions, and see what answers you come up with."

"All lies!" Sara protested. "I don't know who's been informing you, but it's all lies! What's wrong with wanting to keep his identity a secret? It's better than having every crook in the country looking for him. As for bringing in dead people all the time, that's another lie. And who are all these people you're talking about? He hasn't brought in that many."

"Maybe you're the one who should go talk to the sheriff. Try the one in Las Cruces, New Mexico. The one that Hawk delivered my brother to."

Tears began to form in Sara's eyes, and she hated her weakness. She rubbed her arm where his strong fingers had been holding her. This wasn't the man she'd fallen in love with, or at least she didn't think so. His convictions were immovable, and he was dead set on murder. Furthermore, he didn't love her. Reality was a hideous thing to behold. It was a destroyer of dreams. "If you don't leave, I'll scream so loud that every man and woman in this town will come running to my rescue."

Fargo went to the door and yanked it open. He turned, his face twisted in fury. "You can be assured that everywhere you go, I'll be right behind you. I don't know how long I'll have to wait, but eventually Hawk is going to make a move, and when that happens, you'd damn well better believe I'll be waiting for him. You might try delivering that message to him. And if your bounty hunter is as worthy as you make him out to be, how come he isn't man enough to meet me face-to-face? Think on that one, Sara." He barged out, not bothering to close the door.

Sara angrily slammed the door shut and turned the key. She tried brushing away tears that had somehow turned into rivers. She fell onto the bed. Will had been right all along about Fargo being dangerous. But she had wanted to know what it was like to be a woman, and she had felt sure she could handle the situation. She hadn't known she was playing a no-win game with the devil. She glanced around her room. She had to get away. Now!

Fifteen minutes later, a small woman stood by the bed, dressed in buckskins. Sara Carter couldn't get out of the room without Fargo following, and she couldn't climb out onto the window ledge dressed as a lady of means. But Hawk could.

Sara pulled the Stetson low over her forehead. With the ability of a person who knew what she was about, she buckled the gun belt just above her rounded hips. She spun the revolver cylinder to make sure there were bullets in all the chambers, then deftly deposited it in the holster. She glanced at the bolted door. Fargo didn't know how close he'd been when he said, "So that leaves you." Hawk had been right under his nose all along. And the proof had been under the very bed they'd made love on.

Sara brushed off the unwanted feeling of sadness and went to the window. She wasn't about to throw away the years she'd spent hunting Dodd Elliot, the man she'd sworn on her parents' grave to kill. It was an obsession that had been with her for so long it had become a part of her. Sara Carter was the one who wore lovely dresses and used her lace garters to procure information. Hawk wore buckskin and spurs, and went after Dodd.

Sara turned out the lantern, then carefully pulled back the heavy drape. Seeing no one below, she slid open the window. The wide ledge made it easy for her to climb out. She carefully made her way two rooms away, leaned over and opened a window. When she jumped inside, a man, in dirty long underwear, boots and a hat, stood staring in disbelief. He never uttered a word.

Sara peeked out his door. Fargo was tying something to the doorknob of her room, which led her to believe that it was a means of alerting him if she left. She opened the door wider, ducked her head and walked down the hallway in the opposite direction. Not until she had started down the stairs did her breathing return to normal.

Once outside, Sara made a beeline for the nearest saloon. The street was quiet and deserted, the only noise coming from inside. She walked up to the hitching rail and untied a horse. A moment later, she rode out of town, headed for Fruitland, where her friends lived. It was five miles away, and she welcomed the time alone.

She kept the horse at an easy gait, and allowed the wind to brush away her tears. She'd known from the start that nothing could ever come of her love for Fargo, but she'd never dreamed it would turn out like this. Fate had been cruel. Strange how they were both motivated by murder. But Fargo hadn't felt the fires of hell, as she had. For six long, unforgiving years, she'd searched for Dodd, waiting to see him suffer a torturous hell for what he'd done to her and her family. And not even her love for Fargo would interfere with her desire to see Dodd's carcass spread across the land.

Now, once again, she had a possible way of finding his whereabouts. Lou Duncan had been with Dodd Elliot the day he had tried to rob the mine payroll. She'd come to Elgin because one of the men she'd captured had said they used to meet Dodd at the Cactus Saloon, just outside of Elgin. She knew she wouldn't find Dodd there, but she might find Lou Duncan. Or at least find out where he'd chosen to hole up. Through Lou, she'd find Dodd.

Fargo paced the floor, the fuse of his temper already lit. He'd been up all night, and never once had the spur that he'd hung on Sara's doorknob jingled. At ten in the morning, she should have long since tried to leave her hotel room. Sara wasn't a late sleeper.

Tired of waiting, Fargo left his room and knocked on Sara's door. Receiving no answer, he knocked harder. Still no answer. He looked up and down the hall, took several steps backward, then reared back and kicked the door with such force that it flew open with a crash. The room was empty. Muttering an oath under his breath, he entered. He glanced around, looking for any kind of a clue as to how she'd escaped. Then his gaze settled on the open window. He had no idea how she'd managed it. Maybe Hawk had helped.

Though he knew she had to have been gone for some time, he still went to the open window and looked up and down the street. He hadn't expected to see her anywhere in sight. She'd outfoxed him, and was probably with Hawk this very minute.

Seeing the armoire door slightly ajar, he went over and opened it wider. She hadn't even bothered to take her clothes with her. He glanced down and saw a piece of paper sticking out of the reticule she'd left sitting at the bottom of the armoire. He pulled the paper out and looked at it for a long moment. No doubt about it. The outlaw Lou Duncan was Fargo's drawing card. If he got to Duncan first, Hawk would walk right into his trap. After all, if Sara had come to Elgin to deliver the news about a five-hundred-dollar reward, he'd be willing to bet that both Lou and Hawk were in the vicinity.

Fargo left. He'd find Duncan, even if it meant searching every saloon in the area. One way or another, he'd find someone who either knew the outlaw or knew where he was hiding.

"I already have enough girls. Now, if you could sing, that would be a whole different bucket of worms." The big, curly-headed owner of the Cactus Saloon leaned against the highly polished bar and glanced across the room. "Always fancied having a singer. That's why I had that little stage built over there."

"Well, why didn't you tell me that to begin with?" Sara gave him a winning smile. "Should I start work tonight?"

"You telling me you can sing?" He looked suspiciously at the small woman dressed in a simple calico dress. Damned if she wasn't a pretty little thing.

"That's exactly what I'm tellin' you. You're gonna be as pleased as if someone had given you a big—a buxom woman to snuggle up to. 'Course, if you don't like my singing, you don't have to pay me." She winked brazenly at him. "But I got a strong hunch I'll be stayin' a spell after tonight. I'll be on my way, and—"

"Oh, no..." He placed a big, restraining hand on her shoulder. "I want to hear you sing first. I've known too many women who said they could sing, but ended up soundin' more like a bullfrog than a nightingale. Well, what are you waiting for? Let's hear you."

"I'd prefer singing on the stage."

Goose Pride waved his hand in that direction, then waited impatiently.

Sara blessed the way long skirts hid women's knees. Hers were shaking so badly that she was surprised she could still walk. She'd played a lot of roles over the past six years, but she'd never been a singer. She tried thinking back to the songs her mother had taught her, and the first one that came to mind was "Daughter of Mine." "I don't know why we can't take care of this tonight," Sara stated, trying to remember the words to the confounded song.

"Are you going to sing or not?" Goose asked, his voice booming across the room.

"Yes, but you needn't yell at me," she stated indignantly. She stepped onto the stage, still trying to remember the song. When she felt she was ready, she faced the saloon owner.

As Sara started her song, she could clearly hear a quiver in her already weak voice. She had to force herself to sing louder, and at the same time she began applying emotion. When she sang of the mother's death, she clasped her hands to her breast, cast bereaved eyes to the ceiling, all the while batting her lashes. At the part about the little girl being orphaned, she returned her gaze to big Goose Pride, and was shocked to see a tear glide down his cheek. It encouraged her to show even more emotion, even though she wasn't sure if his tears were a good or bad sign. When she finished her song, she didn't know what to say or do. There was dead silence. None of the few customers said a word. She watched Goose down a double shot of whiskey in one gulp. "Damned if that wasn't the prettiest song these ears have ever heard. What's your name?"

Sara shrugged her shoulders. "How about Cactus Queen?"

Goose nodded. "You're hired." He marched to the back of the saloon and sat at one of the empty tables.

Sara stared in disbelief as other men wiped the tears from their eyes. There were several loud snorts as some blew their noses. Sara knew she could carry a tune, but she hadn't thought she was that good.

Not wanting to give Goose a chance to change his mind, Sara hurried out through the swinging doors. She inhaled deeply, drawing fresh air into her lungs. A smile tickled the corners of her mouth. She must have been pretty darn good! She would need to use a lot of paint on her face to make sure no one recognized her. Once again she had accomplished what she had set out to do. The saloon was a popular haunt of the railroad men and cowboys. And, she

hoped, this would be where she'd find out about Lou
Duncan.

That night, Sara returned to the saloon. This time, she
wore a red dress with lots of ruffles around the neck and
the bottom. The skirt was slit up the side, showing a
fetching length of leg and a bright green garter. She had
piled her hair on her head in a mishmash of disarray, and
a red bow had been pinned on the top.

This time when Sara had finished her song, practically
every man in the saloon was in tears. Had she known the
effect her singing would have, she would have used it a
long time ago.

News of Sara's voice spread quickly. Each night there
were more customers, much to Goose's delight. Yet every
time Sara sang, he stood off to himself, listening. Afterward, he always came forward and told Sara what a wonderful voice she had. She became quite fond of the big,
tender-hearted man.

Sara didn't like drawing attention to herself, but there
seemed to be nothing she could do to stop it, short of
quitting her job. She constantly worried that Fargo would
hear about her and show up one night. She began keeping
an eye on the door.

But Sara's luck held. By the fifth night, she was being
toasted as the queen of Elgin. Men offered unbelievable
amounts of money just to have her toss her garter in their
direction. Sara's nervousness had passed after the first day,
when she'd auditioned for Goose. Having worked in more
than one saloon, she was now on home turf. Years ago
when she'd first started working in saloons she had quickly
learned how to use her feminine attributes to get needed
information while, at the same time, keeping the men at a
distance. This way she didn't make the other girls angry at
her. Sara had learned the hard way that if she didn't make

friends with the saloon girls they could get real nasty. As the girls came to realize Sara wasn't trying to take money from their pockets, they became friendlier. They also spoke more freely around her. Exactly what Sara had counted on.

On the sixth night, Sara was painting her face when she overheard a conversation between Lola and Bets.

"I don't know why you keep Lou around." Bets checked herself in the mirror. "I'll take a good railroad man to an outlaw anytime."

"Don't go makin' them kind of statements until you find out what you're missin'," Lola replied. "He may be in hidin', but that don't mean he can't pleasure me. He's got a fine-lookin' redheaded feller hiding out with him. How about you joining us when I go see him next Sunday afternoon? They pay well, too. Afterward, we'll see what kind of song you sing about those railroad men."

"You daring me? All right, I'll give your outlaw a tussle he'll never forget. But I'm tellin' you, Lola, don't come cryin' on my shoulder when Lou ups and leaves you. Now where's the cabin located? I'll meet you there."

Sara wanted to kiss Bets for asking. A few minutes later, she had the exact location of Lou's cabin. Having acquired the information she needed, Sara could see no reason to stay at the saloon. She'd accomplished what she'd come to do. But then she thought about Goose, and decided to stay this one last night. Besides, if for some reason Lou took off for a spell, she needed to be able to keep an eye on Lola. If Lou cared as much for the chubby brunette as she claimed, he'd probably keep in touch.

An unwanted scene suddenly flashed in Sara's mind. She'd found all of her family dead, all except Megan. She'd sat down on the ground and pulled her frightened sister into her arms. She'd sat there for a long time, rocking Megan. "They're not going to get away with this," Sara had promised.

Sara batted her eyelashes to fight back the tears. Six years. She had kept the vow she'd made that day.

When Sara had finished her last song, she started to leave the saloon, but Goose pulled her aside, saying he wanted to talk to her. They sat at a table in the back, and he proceeded to tell her about his plans to build another saloon. A much bigger one. And he'd give her a percentage if she'd stay on. Sara felt guilty for leading him on. She knew then that this would have to be her last night.

Sara was telling Goose why she had to leave when Fargo entered through the swinging doors, looking handsome, dark, and dangerous. For once, she blessed the crowd. Fargo hadn't seen her. After a quick farewell to Goose, she cautiously weaved her way through the men, each of whom wanted to have a word with her. Fargo had started looking around the large room. Her progress seemed to take forever. Dampness had already formed on her brow. Finally, she made it to the back entrance.

At dusk the following evening, Sara tied her paint horse to a tree about a quarter of a mile from where Lola had said Lou's cabin stood. Dressed in buckskins and a hat pulled low, she covered her nose and the lower part of her face with a bandanna, tying it in the back. Her revolver rested loosely in her holster, ready for a quick draw. She tucked her rifle beneath her arm, and silently neared the cabin, Phew following close behind.

By the time Sara found a hiding place that allowed her a good view of the cabin, it had turned dark. She squatted down, ready for a long wait. It being a hazy night, she could smell the smoke coming out of the chimney. There were at least two men inside, because each one had come out to relieve himself. She doubted there were others because no one else had come out or passed by the window. But she couldn't be sure. Someone could be lying on the bed. She decided to go in after they were asleep. It would give her the element of surprise.

It had turned pitch black when Fargo rode into the area. Buying drinks and being friendly to a girl named Bets had finally produced the information he'd been looking for. It more than made up for him missing Cactus Queen's performance. The lady had developed quite a reputation.

He had almost made a wide circle of the cabin when he spotted the paint horse. Even with the moon not up yet, it would have been hard to miss the white markings. At last, he and Hawk were going to meet. Fargo didn't give a damn about Lou or the money. He just wanted to settle up with Hawk and get back to Texas.

Having secured his horse, Fargo carefully worked his way toward the cabin. At this point, he could do nothing. Hawk might be waiting nearby to make his move, and Fargo didn't want anything to alert the bounty man to his presence. The light coming from the one window in the cabin meant the men were still awake. Hawk might be inside right now. If so, Fargo would catch him when he came out. If he hadn't made his move yet, Fargo would wait until he did. One way or another, after tonight, the bastard would never again see the light of day.

At midnight, the light in the cabin was extinguished. Sara continued to wait another hour, wanting to be sure the men were fast asleep. Then she'd make her move.

The hour passed, and Sara finally motioned to Phew to head toward the back door. The dog had almost reached his position when Sara rose from her hiding place. She took a couple of steps, then stopped dead in her tracks.

Something had moved in the shadows up ahead. Apparently, someone else was in search of a reward.

With the agility of a cat, she silently moved forward. The other bounty hunter had shifted his position, but remained hunched over. Phew had drawn his attention. As his gaze followed the dog around to the back, Sara was able to see his profile. Fargo! She cut off a curse word just before it escaped her throat. How had he found out about the cabin? He'd probably seen her horse, as well! She not only had to keep him from seeing her, she also had to keep him from making any noise and ruining her chance to catch Lou. She drew her gun, and stealthily moved forward. She was practically on top of him when a twig snapped. He jerked his head around—too late. Sara brought the butt end of her revolver down hard on his head. He slumped to the ground, knocked out cold.

With her time now limited, Sara continued on to the cabin. The door hadn't been bolted. She opened it slowly, waiting for it to creak. But no sound broke the silence. Inside, it was too dark to see anything. Knowing Fargo could come to anytime, she had to take a chance. She reached into her pants pocket and pulled out a match. One strike against the door provided a large enough flame to see by. To Sara's amazement, the two men lying on cots didn't even stir. She quickly glanced around the room and spotted a candle. A moment later she had it lit and standing in its own wax. Sara aimed the muzzle of her gun at the floor and pulled the trigger. The loud shot brought the men to their feet. "What the hell's going on?" Lou demanded.

The other man reached for his gun, but Sara shot it out of his hand. Lou made a dive to the floor, and the other man ran to the back door. Another shot convinced Lou that he had best stay put. A minute later, the second man returned, with a snarling Phew behind him.

"Who the hell are you?" Lou demanded again.

"I've been called Hawk."

"Shit!" Lou expelled a heavy sigh. "I don't know where the hell Dodd is, so you've gone to a lot of trouble for nothing."

"You rode with him. You must know where he's hiding out."

Lou slowly climbed to his feet. "I told that bastard after the payroll heist I didn't want to see his face again until he got you off his ass. And he knew I meant it."

"You didn't tell him soon enough, Lou. I wouldn't have known about you if you hadn't been on that payroll job. Now you're going to end up in prison."

"What the hell do you wanna put me in prison for? I ain't done nothin' to you."

"The hell you didn't! You and your men's bullets allowed Dodd to get away that day." Sara stepped back. "Let's get going, boys. And don't try anything. If I don't get you, my dog will." Her voice lowered to nearly a whisper. "Do you really expect me to believe that you don't know where Dodd is, Lou?" She motioned them with her gun to go out the door.

"Hell," the second man said, "we ain't got on nothin' but our underwear."

"I told you, I don't know where Dodd is," Lou insisted as he stood in the doorway.

"That's too bad. It might have saved you from Yuma." When she received no reply, she knew Lou had, unfortunately, told the truth. He had no information to give her.

After she had the prune-faced man tie Lou's hands behind his back and help him onto his horse, Sara tied the second man's hands and helped him onto his horse. Before long, Sara had her prisoners well away from the cabin.

* * *

Fargo kicked the chair, which sent it flying across the room. The cabin was empty. Hawk had bested him and had gotten away with Lou Duncan. They couldn't have been gone too long, because the stub of a candle still burned on the table. To his surprise, he found no blood-stains. If Hawk had shot either of them, it certainly hadn't been in here. He rushed back outside and stood listening in the quiet night. Then he heard what he'd been listening for: the sound of horses' hooves. Hawk was taking his captives away.

Fargo ran to where he'd left his horse tied. His horse was gone. He should have known Hawk wouldn't leave him any means to follow, and there wasn't a damn thing he could do about it. Hands on hips, he stood listening as the retreating sounds faded into the night. He and Hawk would meet again—and next time he wouldn't be so care-less.

Chapter Twelve

The sun was just spreading its rays over the Mustang Mountains as Sara neared the fort. The troopers were already throwing saddles onto snorting mounts and jamming rifles into scabbards as they prepared to go out on Indian patrol. But there had to be a few men left in the long three-story barracks.

Remaining out of sight, Sara brought her horse to a halt. She had said nothing to her prisoners, whose horses continued on toward the parade grounds of Fort Huachuca. She had tied a sign around Lou's neck stating that he was a wanted man. The hungry and tired horses knew where they were headed.

Sara turned her horse around and rode off, Phew trotting along beside her. She had mixed feelings about the fort. These were the patrols that watched the Apacheria land. The troopers were very familiar with such names as Magnus Colorado, Victoria, Cochise, and now Geronimo.

As Sara headed north toward home, she wondered how long it would take for the soldiers to flush out the Apache from their stronghold in the Sonora Mountains of Mexico. She assured herself that it had nothing to do with her having Indian blood, but part of her pulled for the Indians while the other part pulled for the white man. She was so divided.

Tired of trying to rationalize things that she had no control over, Sara kicked her horse into a gallop. She had a long ride ahead of her. She also had to decide what she was going to do about Fargo. There was no doubt in her mind that he'd come to the ranch looking for her.

By the time Sara had changed clothes, had her paint horse settled in the hidden boxed canyon and was approaching the hacienda, she was worn out. Her body kept reminding her that she hadn't slept in two days. All she could think of was her bed and how good it would feel.

When Sara entered the house and saw Penelope standing in the foyer, Sara knew any thoughts of sleep would have to wait.

"Sara!" Penelope gushed as she rushed forward. "I had begun to think you'd never return home!"

"What a pleasant surprise." Sara didn't bother to hide her yawn. Surely Penelope would get the hint. She entered the parlor and sank into a chair. "How long have you been here, Penelope?" Sara tried to sound interested.

"Only since yesterday. I even considered going to Elgin to find you. Oh, Sara, I just have to tell you the horrible news."

Carla came in carrying a tray with a pitcher of lemonade and glasses. Because Penelope had always had a tendency to get overexcited about things, the woman's words had little effect on Sara. She was more interested in the glass of lemonade that Carla handed her. After several swallows, Sara felt a bit more refreshed, and she looked at her friend. "All right, Penelope, what's happened this time?"

"Rose has been stolen."

"Oh, be serious, Penelope. Who would want to steal Rose?"

Penelope went to the small corner table, where someone had set the liquor decanter, and poured a generous shot of whiskey into her lemonade. "It's a horrible story." She placed a delicate hand over her heart as she took a sip of her drink. "As I heard it, there was another shooting at the Bird Cage Theater. All of a sudden, there were two men lying dead with their heads resting on the poker table, and one man standing with a gun in his hand. Anyway, he rushed out of that horrible place, jumped on his horse, racing down Sixth Street, then turning right on Toughnut."

"Please, Penelope, just get on with the story."

Penelope took another drink. "It seems Rose was crossing Toughnut Street when the gunman rode by. A witness said the man just leaned over in the saddle, reached out, and swooped Rose right off her feet. Norma Stanislaus, who witnessed the whole thing, said she could actually hear the man laughing as he rode by her."

Sara was astounded. "How did she manage to get back to town after he turned her loose? Is she all right?"

Penelope finished the drink and poured herself a straight shot before going back to the sofa. Taking her time, she sat down, smoothed her skirts, then looked soulfully at her friend. "That's the problem. Rose hasn't returned."

Sara jumped to her feet. "How terrible! Cyrus must be out of his mind with worry."

"I don't know about Cyrus, but I certainly was—at the time."

"Is Virgil looking into this?"

"Not only Virgil, but Cyrus rounded up every man he could find, which wasn't many."

"When did this happen?"

"Three days ago."

"Poor Rose. What she must be going through! Do you think it would help if I gathered my men and went in search?"

"I doubt there's anything you can do at this time. But you do need to talk to Megan."

"Why Megan?"

"I was so stupid. When I told her about what happened to Rose, I just…I just didn't think about what you and she had gone through in the past."

"She was upset?"

"Yes. She and Will are out on the patio talking."

"I'd better go to her."

Sara didn't find Megan in the courtyard. She found her out by the corral fence, feeding her horse a carrot. She stepped up beside her and, like Megan, watched the horse munch on the tasty tidbit. "I heard Penelope told you about Rose. I'm concerned about you."

"I'm fine." Megan turned and looked at her sister. "Though I have to admit that when I heard the news I didn't take it well. Oh, Sara, do you think Rose will be killed?"

"I don't know," Sara replied sadly. "But I do know that not all men are like Dodd and his bunch, Megan. Hopefully this one is from an entirely different kettle." Sara looked toward the house. "I'm sorry about Penelope. Unfortunately, she tends to speak before she thinks."

"It's something I'm going to have to get used to. Sara, I know the world isn't all made up of angel cake. I'll be fine. Oh, Will said he needed to talk to you as soon as you returned. He's in the old barn. When do you plan to get some rest? You look worn out."

"After I talk to Will. Penelope is just going to have to entertain herself." She laughed. "Something she's not going to find difficult if she stays near the whiskey decanter.''

When Sara reached the barn, she hesitated about going inside. Though there were four different barns surrounding the compound, this was the one she'd been in when Dodd and his men arrived. Somehow that inner fear and deep hatred had never left. They're only memories, she tried telling herself. Nevertheless, the first few steps inside were always hard.

''Will? Will, where are you?'' Sara walked slowly toward the back, but the barn appeared to be empty. When she came to the ladder going to the loft, she automatically looked up, as if expecting someone to be waiting for her up there.

''Sara!''

Sara managed to prevent a scream just in time. She turned and watched Will walk toward her.

''Didn't you hear me calling your name?'' Will asked.

''No...no, I didn't....''

''Sara, is something wrong?''

She crossed her arms to ward off a sudden chill. ''I found Lou Duncan,'' she said, wanting to get her mind onto other things. ''Dodd wasn't with him.''

''Megan told me Fargo had taken off to Elgin after you.''

Sara watched a hen pecking its way around the barn floor. ''I ended up having to knock him out with the butt of my gun so I could get the job done.''

''Damn, Sara!'' Will tossed his hands in the air. ''What is it going to take to make you quit all this? I certainly don't know the answer. For three long years I've done everything in my power to get you to stop. It could have been six, had I learned sooner what you were up to when you took those trips. Don't you realize that killing Dodd is not going to solve your problems? You've been doing this too long. When and if you catch him, and kill him, you're just going to find other excuses to search out men who are his type. Why? Because you can't forgive. You can't accept that what happened is over with and get on with your life!''

"What would you have me do? Let Dodd get away with all his murders? It's not just my family, you know. There have been others."

"And what if he kills you instead? Is someone going to take up where you left off? Hell, no!''

"I don't want to talk about this."

"You never do." Will started to leave, then changed his mind. "I suppose that you're also going to go looking for Rose?''

"I've thought about it," Sara admitted. "But I won't be much good for anything until I get some sleep."

"Great. You always have thought you were better than the law. Hell, they've got every available man out searching for her. Oh, but what difference does that make? The great Hawk can do anything. Have you thought about how Megan's going to feel when she finds out you're Hawk?''

"She won't."

"She's changed a lot lately, and things aren't going to slip by her like they used to. So now we have Dodd looking for you, Megan, who is going to start wondering what her sister *really* does when she goes on trips—oh, and let's not forget Fargo. I'd give twenty dollars to know what he wants with Hawk."

Sara looked down at the ground. "I know what he wants."

"And how did you find that out?''

Sara studied Will for a long moment. "He was with me in Elgin. He wants to know who Hawk is so that he can kill him. He thinks Hawk murdered his brother."

Will groaned as if he were in pain. "Oh, hell, Sara. Can't you see how tight that noose is getting around your neck?" He headed for the barn door. "I don't know why I even bother," he said in disgust.

"Will?"

Will turned and looked at her.

"When I was in Elgin, I had to sneak out the hotel window to get away from Fargo. There's no doubt in my mind he's going to come looking for me. When he does, you tell him I'm not home. I don't want to ever see him again."

"Oh? Why is that? Could it be that you've finally come to agree with me about playing with fire?"

"I don't need this," Sara replied. "You know how I feel about Dodd, and nothing you can do or say is going to change that. You should know that by now. As for Fargo, I don't think I owe you an explanation."

Will backed away and made a bow. "Whatever you say, boss."

For three days, Sara partly slept, partly paced and mostly worried. Her two biggest concerns were Rose and Fargo, neither having anything to do with the other. Though she hated to do so, she had to agree with Will. Finding Rose at this point would be an impossibility. There was nothing she could do but sit and wait, like Penelope. Once she'd accepted that, her thoughts had turned to Fargo. It bothered her that he hadn't shown up. She hadn't hit him *that* hard over the head.

When Sara entered the kitchen for breakfast on the fourth day, she felt considerably more rested, despite her concerns. Penelope arrived while Sara was in the middle of her meal. "Carla," Sara called, "please fix Penelope some breakfast."

"No, no. I've already eaten. Sara, I'm going to have to return home."

Sara swallowed a bite of scrambled eggs. "I'm sorry I haven't been better company, Penelope."

"Oh, it has nothing to do with that. Megan has been a perfect hostess. But I realized that if Cyrus and his men find Rose, it might take forever for someone to think to inform us." She pulled out a chair and joined Sara at the table.

Sara noticed how Penelope's blond hair was coiffed to perfection. Even the white dress she wore, with accents of blue, looked fresh from the dressmaker's. "I never asked you, Penelope, how did you get to the ranch? I certainly can't see you driving all this distance by yourself."

"Heavens, no. I wasn't about to do such a foolish thing, what with all the Indians and the renegades, plus someone carrying Rose off. I saw some of your men at the feed store, and I traveled back with them."

"How did you know they were my men?"

Penelope took a slice of toast from Sara's plate, examined it, then took a bite. "Will was with them," Penelope replied after she had swallowed. "Surely you can spare a couple of men to take me back."

"Will?"

Penelope gave her one of those kittenish grins.

Sara broke out laughing. "No wonder you were in no hurry to leave." Sara shoved her plate away.

"I can't believe he's been under your nose all this time and you haven't even seen what you've been missing."

"Penelope, Will is like a brother to me. I'm sure he's informed you that we're starting our roundup. He's not going to like me taking several of the men away. Still, I, too, would like to know if Rose has been found, and I want to have a few men along."

"But you ride to town by yourself all the time, so why take any men this time?"

Sara placed her elbows on the table, wondering how much she should tell Penelope. Friends or not, there were some things she preferred to keep to herself. "While I was in Elgin, Fargo was also there."

Penelope leaned forward, her eyes alight with interest.

"Fargo and I had a fight, and I know he's going to come looking for me. I don't know when he'll find me or what he'll do when he does, so I intend to be prepared."

"Whatever for? I would think you'd like to be alone with a man like that."

"You see, Penelope, that's the big part of the problem. I do not want to see or ever talk to Fargo again."

"It must have been *some* argument. What was it about?"

"It was a senseless argument over some man Fargo is hunting for. He thinks I know him."

"That's it? That's all there is to it?"

"That's it."

Penelope leaned back in the chair, the tips of her fingers drumming on the table. "No, no, no. There is far more to it than that. You just don't want to tell me. Nevertheless, I'll find out in time. Why can't Will go with us?"

"That's a positive no. I need him here to watch over everything."

"Too bad." Penelope sighed. "When can we leave?"

"How about first thing in the morning?"

"Perfect." Penelope rose from her chair. "I must do my packing."

As soon as Penelope left, Sara's thoughts jumped immediately to Fargo. She probably never would have thought about him trying to kidnap her had it not been for what had happened to Rose. Somehow that seemed just the sort of stunt Fargo would try to pull.

Carla waddled over and picked up Sara's plate. "Maybe you should have let him die."

Looking up, Sara returned Carla's broad smile. "Maybe I should have."

The following morning, Sara and Penelope sat side by side in Penelope's buggy. Sara's saddled horse had been tied to the back, and three men followed along behind. Like Sara, they were well armed.

The five-hour ride to town proved uneventful, and Sara knew she should kick herself for taking needed men away from the roundup. Fargo had her running scared, and she'd let her imagination go crazy. He wasn't within miles, and why, by all that was holy, would he want to kidnap her, anyway? What would that accomplish? He had no way of knowing that she was going to Tombstone, or when she intended to return.

But Sara knew that for the first time in her life she was frightened. Chasing Dodd was like going after a bull that had just one thought in its mind. Fargo was different. Besides being physically dangerous, he also had a clever mind and knew how to use it. That was perhaps the most frightening thing of all. From this time on, he would do everything he could to outsmart her.

When they arrived in Tombstone, Penelope drove straight to the mercantile store. The young male clerk informed them that Cyrus hadn't returned since going after Rose, nearly a week ago.

"So you haven't heard anything?" Penelope asked.

"No, ma'am, not a thing."

"This must have been such a blow to Cyrus," Sara commented.

The red-cheeked man shook his head. "I don't think so."

Sara noted the touch of bitterness in the clerk's attitude. "Why do you say that?"

"Well, it's none of my business, but he didn't seem the least bit concerned about his wife's well-being."

They had both noted the clerk's inordinate concern for Rose.

"He seemed more interested in having a hanging," the young man continued. "Something Cyrus has always enjoyed watching. Mrs. Halverson was another one of Mr. Halverson's possessions, if you know what I mean. For as long as I can remember, he never could stand having anything he owned taken away from him."

Both Penelope and Sara stood staring at the clerk.

"Are you saying that he is treating this more like an outing?" Penelope asked.

"I would say exactly that, though it's probably going to cost me my job."

"You needn't worry about a thing," Sara said. "We'll say nothing."

"Oh, it really doesn't matter. Cyrus and I never got along. I'm sure you don't know that I'm his cousin. I don't think the man has an honest emotion in him. But this takes precedence over anything in the past. I'll never be able to forgive him for his attitude in this matter."

Sara and Penelope looked at each other, both of them thinking the same thing. The prissy clerk had an attraction toward Rose. A most profound turn of events.

"Thank you for the information, Mr. Pitt." Penelope smiled charmingly at the frail man, praising herself for remembering his name. "We really must be on our way."

When the women were back outside, neither could say a word. They were both in a state of shock over this new information about Cyrus. It wasn't until they were in Penelope's house that both women started talking, almost at the same time.

"I never dreamed—"

"Rose had complained to me," Sara butted in, "but I had no idea that the situation was so bad."

Both women collapsed onto the brocade sofa.

"How could Cyrus be so uncaring?" Penelope asked. "Why, he couldn't ask for a sweeter wife than Rose."

"Have you ever noticed the way he belittles her at times?"

Penelope sat up straight. "Yes, as a matter of fact, I have."

For the next two hours, Sara and Penelope picked at everything they could think of that was wrong with the Halversons' marriage.

"Maybe she's better off with the outlaw," Penelope commented when the two women went upstairs.

"Penelope, that's a terrible thing to say."

"It may be terrible, but I'll bet it's the truth. Sara, after the concerns you expressed about Fargo, do you think it was wise to send your men back?"

"Fargo has no idea where I am," Sara said as they reached the landing. "Besides, Will needs every man he can get, and I want to stay here at least a couple more days in case Rose shows up."

The following day, three dirty, worn-out men returned to town. They were the only men left alive from Cyrus's search party. They had been attacked by Indians. The men had barely escaped with their lives, and had been forced to leave the dead men behind. Cyrus was one who had been left behind. If and when Rose returned, she would discover she was now a widow.

Though there was no body, Sara felt obligated to have a funeral service for Cyrus. Few people attended. Sara and Penelope couldn't believe that they had been the last to discover Cyrus wasn't particularly well liked in Tombstone.

Chapter Thirteen

After Penelope promised to contact her immediately if Rose returned, Sara left town and headed for home. As one mile followed another, she began to relax and enjoy the solitude—something she hadn't had for what seemed like an eternity. But why would she want solitude? She'd always felt as though she'd been cheated of normal pleasures, and pleasures are generally shared with others. Fargo was simply an extension of everything she'd missed out on. Knowing he would never be a permanent part of her life was unquestionably devastating. If only she could have foreseen the future. On the other hand, would she be willing to give up the wonderful memories of being held in his arms? At least she hadn't allowed her pain to show or openly wallowed in it. She couldn't have withstood the unwanted comments from others.

It was all so unfair! She hadn't killed Jude Tanner, but Fargo wouldn't believe her, even if she told him the truth. His determination to kill Hawk left no hope of them ever being able to share a future together.

Sara sighed. Fargo. She could clearly remember the first moment she'd laid eyes on him. He'd been standing behind Doc, and her heart had leapt into her throat. Oh, she'd denied it to Rose and Penelope, because she hadn't wanted to appear the fool. Then he'd started toward her—to ask her to dance—and everything and everyone had faded from view. Their relationship moved so fast that now she seemed incapable of resisting the physical desire he ignited. And he knew it. He not only knew it, he used it to his advantage! It was as if she were being pulled into a mass of quicksand.

She passed the two-mile post that had been driven into the ground years ago. Soon she'd be home. Suddenly a bevy of complaining birds took flight from a stand of cottonwoods up ahead. Sara took up the slack in the reins, then turned her horse to the right—away from the road and the trees. A solid kick sent her gelding lunging forward.

Within minutes, Sara heard the steady cadence of hoofbeats coming from behind. She turned in the saddle to discern her pursuer.

Somehow it didn't come as a surprise to see that it was Fargo who was chasing her.

The hard, determined look on his face was something she chose not to deal with. She drew her revolver and landed a couple of shots in the ground as a warning, but the horse and rider kept coming.

Fargo was quickly gaining on her.

Sara holstered her gun, then flicked the end of the reins against her horse's neck, pushing him to a faster speed. Unfortunately, the sorrel didn't have the speed or power of her paint. Again Sara took a quick look behind.

Fargo was almost on top of her.

Sara slowed her horse the slightest bit, waiting for Fargo to pull alongside. The moment he drew close enough, she drove her sorrel into the gray, intending to dump the other horse and rider to the ground.

It didn't work.

She couldn't believe Fargo had managed to stay in the saddle. But it had slowed him down, and he was now well behind her. Sara seized the opportunity to escape. As the sorrel's legs again stretched out, she leaned down low over the horse's neck, helping him to move faster. She had no intention of letting Fargo get his hands on her. Her auburn hair had started to come loose from its confinement, and it whipped across her face, making it difficult to see.

Again Sara heard the thud of the gray's hooves closing the distance. Fargo's horse was fast, and she knew she had no chance of making it to the house or to her men—unless she did something.

Left without a choice, she drew her gun again, this time ready to shoot Fargo or his horse. She turned and tried to aim, but her hair impeded her view. In that brief moment, Fargo managed to move his mount alongside. He was too close for Sara to shoot without causing serious damage.

Expecting him to try to lift her from the saddle, Sara hunched down and leaned away. But instead he grabbed hold of the reins by the horse's bit, bringing the sorrel to an abrupt halt, and jerking Sara off balance. In the process of trying to keep her seat, she lost her revolver. She was defenseless.

"What do you think you're doing?" Sara demanded.

"Now, is that any way to greet your lover?" His voice was as cold as a mountain stream. "Or can I assume that after escaping out a window and trying to kill me, our affair has ended? I'm fortunate in that you're not as good a shot as your sister. I would have been ready for Boot Hill."

His face showed every bit of his anger, but Sara refused to let him see how he intimidated her. "I wasn't trying to shoot you, I was trying to make you leave me alone. Now that we've gone through all this, I'd like to know why you won't. And make it quick, so I can be on my way."

"You won't be going home. I have other plans for you, my dear."

"Other plans? Like what?"

"Get off your horse," Fargo ordered.

"What do you mean?"

"Just what I said, Miss Carter. Get off that damn horse!"

Sara had been watching him closely, waiting for him to relax. As he reached out to grab her arm, she jerked her horse's head away and sank her heels into its sides. Again the horse bolted forward, pulling the reins from Fargo's loose grasp.

With the steed once again at a full gallop, Sara reached down and pulled her rifle from the saddle scabbard. This time she wouldn't hesitate. But she didn't get as much of a lead as she'd thought. Before she could even swing the barrel around, she felt herself being yanked from the saddle, a powerful arm the only thing that prevented her from falling beneath the horses' hooves. When Fargo lowered her to the ground, then rode off after her horse, Sara was totally confused as to the purpose of all this.

"Whoa, boy," Fargo said to her horse, which continued to trot nervously about. "Easy boy."

Sara at least had one answer. Fargo didn't want the sorrel to return to the house. It would alert her men, and they'd come looking for her. She rushed forward. Her men were busy with the roundup, and they hadn't the foggiest notion when she planned to leave Tombstone.

As she drew near her horse, Sara jumped, yelled and waved her arms, but the impossible beast only shied away. Angrily, she shoved her hair from her face and released a loud, high-pitched scream.

At last! The horse finally started to take off. Unfortunately, Fargo was now close enough to grab the reins.

Sara spun around and ran toward the rifle she'd dropped. She should have thought of that first. Just as she leaned down to grab it, a bullet hit the ground only inches from her hand. She tried again. Again a bullet struck the ground, this time even closer.

Frustration changed to fury as Sara raised up and stared with indignation at her nemesis. She wanted to knock that lopsided smile off his face. It infuriated her even more that he took his time dismounting, appearing not to have a care in the world. "What do you think you're doing?" she spit out. "You could have hit me."

"If I'd wanted to do that, I wouldn't have missed. What, may I ask, were you planning to do with that rifle?"

"Shoot you."

"Well, at least you're not going to mince words." With the horse's reins still firmly clutched in one hand, he walked over and kicked the rifle away.

"What gawd-awful reason do you have for doing this?" Sara demanded. "Why can't you leave me alone? I never want to see you again."

"You once told me you were a good rider. I should have listened. Start walking."

"I have no intention of going anywhere. Whatever you have to say can be said right here." She twisted the waist of her black riding skirt around until the seam hung in the right place.

"I said, start walking."

"No." Sara stubbornly tilted her chin. "If you're going to shoot me, you might as well get it over with. But you can't do that, can you? How would you ever find Hawk?"

"Either you walk, or I'll carry you."

"Why can't you go ahead and say what's on your mind? And where do you expect me go? Now, if you're smart, you'll let me get back on my horse and leave. You needn't worry that I'll say anything about this. It would be too embarrassing. You might like to know that *I* keep my word. On the other hand, if you don't give me my horse back, I'll have every man on my ranch hunting you down."

"How do you expect to accomplish that? Who is going to know what happened? Tsk, tsk. Such big threats from such a little woman. But you're right. We can end this right here. Just tell me where I can find Hawk."

"Haven't you realized yet that I'm not going to tell you anything? Do you understand me? Nothing! Not about Hawk, not about anything!" She placed her curled fist at her side to keep from shaking it at him. "Now, what do you think you're going to do with me?" she asked calmly. "Shoot me? Kill me? Like I said, I have no intention of going anywhere." She sat on the ground and folded her arms across her chest.

"Well, I guess we'll have to see about that." Fargo reached down and wrapped an arm around her waist. He scooped her up off the ground, then rested her on his hip. With her head and feet pointed at the ground, he took off walking.

"You let me down, Fargo Tanner!" Sara kicked and flayed him with her fists, but nothing seemed to have any effect. He continued on. "You're hurting me!" No reaction. Her hair was dragging on the ground and picking up dirt and small twigs. "You overgrown coward!" Talking was becoming increasingly difficult. "You only beat up defenseless women! You wouldn't have—" She had to catch her breath. "You wouldn't have fought Ocha if I—" Watching the ground moving beneath her, plus being jarred like a sack of grain, was making her nauseous. "Okay! I'll walk!"

Fargo stood her on her feet.

"I just want to know one thing," Sara said as soon as she caught her breath. "How did you know I'd be coming from Tombstone?"

"For quite some time I've had a man staked out on that big hill south of your place. I pulled one of your stunts, my dear. You were followed to town. When you left, my man hightailed it back to let me know."

The importance of what he said struck Sara like a lightning bolt. For a change, luck had been on her side. Had something come up about Dodd, one of Fargo's men would have seen her leaving the house, mounted on the paint. Fargo would have discovered the truth.

Fargo climbed back in the saddle. "Get going."

"But . . . why can't I ride?"

"You can. Just as soon as you tell me where Hawk is."

Sara pushed her hair away from her face, tilted her chin up and headed south. "Any particular direction?" she called angrily over her shoulder.

"You're doing just fine."

"Are we headed for a particular place?"

"Nope."

Sara spun around and stared at him in disbelief. "You're not serious!"

"I'm quite serious."

"What do you expect to accomplish by this?"

"That shouldn't be hard to figure out."

"I told you, I won't tell you where Hawk is."

"Then get moving. I'm beginning to lose my patience real fast."

"Oh, how I wish I were a man!" Sara turned in a wide circle. "You're telling me I'm going to be walking to no place in particular? Is there a time limit?"

"Maybe a day. Maybe three days. Maybe three weeks. It all depends on you."

Sara didn't believe his threat for a minute. Three weeks, indeed! And he honestly thought that this would make her tell him about Hawk? Poor planning. Again she took off, quite proud of her jaunty step. As she walked, she worked at pulling the dead leaves and other rubble from the ends of her hair.

Sara experienced total relief when Fargo said in a clipped voice, "Stay put. I'll be back shortly." This was the first rest she'd had since starting out over an hour ago.

As soon as he'd disappeared from view, Sara's pace picked up. But instead of continuing on, she turned and headed back in the direction she'd come from. She knew her exact position. All she had to do was line up with the Whetstone Mountains.

Another fifteen minutes passed. Fargo still hadn't returned. Suspicion began eating at Sara. Why would he go to all this trouble, then let her go? He had to be up to something. On the other hand, perhaps he'd only been trying to scare her, and he'd finally realized his plan hadn't worked. Either way, she had no intention of taking the time to figure it out.

Her confidence growing, Sara ignored her already worn-out condition and began to trot. Her white shirt clung to her damp body, and her skirt became heavier with each step she took. Still, she pushed on until she could go no farther. Gasping for breath, she fell to the ground, then rested her head on a raised knee. Her heart pounded unmercifully from overexertion.

As her breathing slowly returned to normal, Sara realized she should have looked for a place to hide, just in case Fargo decided to return. She took a quick glance at the terrain before turning to see if he was anywhere in sight. She sucked in her breath as she scrambled to her feet. No more than fifteen feet away, Fargo sat on his horse, silently watching her. He no longer had her horse. He'd replaced it with a pack mule that looked well provisioned. For the first time, Sara realized that this had not been a spur-of-the-moment decision.

Sara took several gulps to prevent panic from taking over. There were times when Fargo scared her. This was one of them. His face looked as though it had been molded of steel. Cold, mean and ungiving. She wanted to yell and call him every name she could think of, but she'd tried all that before, and it hadn't gained her a thing. But Fargo had a vulnerability. He felt the need to protect helpless women. It was something she could use to her advantage. It might also give her an opportunity to get to his revolver—and her freedom.

Sara smiled sweetly. "Am I going in the right direction?"

"Not hardly, since you turned. I believe I told you to stay put. Now that you've had your jaunt, you can head back the other way."

Sara gritted her teeth. Being sweet and ladylike was not going to be easy. "Whatever you say, but surely I'll be allowed to have a little rest?"

"You just had a rest, but it would've been a lot longer if you'd stayed put, like I told you. It's time to get going."

Sara gave him a come-hither look, but his face remained stoic. "I was thinking of a different kind of rest." She ran the tip of her tongue across her lips. "Actually, I wasn't thinking of resting at all. Let's not fight, Fargo. I'd much rather make love.''

"One more time, Sara. Pick those feet up and walk."

Sara pouted her lips and began unbuttoning the top of her blouse. "Now, Fargo, let's look at this sensibly. How are you going to make me walk? Oh, you can carry me, but that would defeat your purpose, wouldn't it? And how long and how far could you carry me?''

"But, Sara, sweetheart, you just got through saying you'd do anything I wanted you to."

"With limitations, my dearest.'' She pulled her shirttail from the waist of her riding skirt. Fargo slowly dismounted, and she knew she'd won the battle of wills. She had just lowered her blouse over her shoulders when he released the rope from his saddle. "What are you doing?''

"As I see it, you haven't left me much choice. I'm going to tie your wrists and pull you behind my horse. Just like the Indians did to me."

Sara yanked her blouse back up over her shoulders. "You can't do that!''

With the rope still clasped in one hand, Fargo tipped his hat back and stared at her. "You seem to be having a hard time understanding what I'm about. I'll explain it to you one more time. One way or another, you'll keep going until you finally spit out where I can find Hawk. I have more than one matter to settle with him. I mean business, Sara, and nothing—not your feminine ways, or anything else— is going to get you out of this. I suggest you button your shirt, because if you don't, you're going to get sunburned as hell."

"You wouldn't really pull me behind your horse, would you?" Sara asked as she frantically buttoned her shirt. She didn't like the way Fargo's eyes had narrowed or the way the muscles in his jaw were twitching. When she had her shirt tucked back into her waistband, Fargo reached for her hands. She jerked them away.

"We can do this the easy way or the hard way. Which is it going to be?"

Sara thrust her shoulders back and stomped away. "You just point the way," she said with a snarl.

"I'll do better than that." Fargo swung back into the saddle. "I'll lead the way. All you have to do is follow."

An hour later, Sara was already questioning how much farther she could go. She wasn't used to walking. She'd started out determined to prove to Fargo that he couldn't get the better of her. It didn't seem to be working that way. Her skin was sticky, her face felt as if it had two layers of dirt clinging to it, and each hill seemed to get higher and higher. And never once did Fargo look back. Still, she had an eerie feeling that if she stopped he'd know immediately. It was as though he had eyes in the back of his head. Besides, she didn't want to give him the consolation of knowing his plan was working. At least the sun had started to set, and the heat had decreased somewhat. Surely Fargo would stop soon.

But Fargo didn't stop until it was so dark that Sara couldn't see where to plant her feet. She half expected him to tell her to make camp and cook their meal, but to her relief, he took care of everything. He hadn't talked to her since their confrontation that afternoon. He'd said what he had to say. Now he waited for her reply.

Fargo had brought two bedrolls, and when he stripped the pack mule, Sara grabbed one and went off a ways. Convinced she'd never be able to move again, she rolled it out and lay down.

Sara didn't know when she'd fallen asleep, but she awoke to the tantalizing aroma of food cooking. It certainly smelled better than she did after all the perspiring she'd done.

Fargo had made a small campfire, and he even had the hooks to hang the pots over it. The aroma of cooking food already had her salivating. She sat up, and a moment later Fargo shoved a tin plate into her hand.

The savory stew proved to be every bit as good it smelled. Sara wondered where Fargo had learned to cook so well, but she was determined not to ask. They ate in silence, then went to bed in silence.

Sara had it in her mind to run away in the middle of the night, but she didn't have the strength. Maybe tomorrow night. Hopefully, before that happened, the stubborn bull would realize this was a waste of time.

On the fourth day, Fargo again had them on the move before the sun appeared over the horizon. Sara had reached the end of her endurance. Everything about her was either filthy or smelly—or both. She needed a bath, or at least something she could use to bathe! Never once had Fargo offered her water from the canteens to bathe with. Her aching muscles and joints added fuel to her fury at the way she was being treated. Having been in good physical condition all her life, she had never realized how sore a body could get. And, since that first day, Fargo had maintained that damn silence. She had no idea where they were or where they were headed, other than that they traveled south or southwest most of the time. At the rate they were going, they'd soon be in Mexico. Maybe they already were.

At first, Sara had been certain that they would meet up with the cavalry or the Apache. Today she still longed for the cavalry, but she'd changed her mind about meeting a band of Apache. There were an awful lot of Chiricahua who had no idea who she was.

As the sun continued to rise in the sky, so did the heat. By noon, Sara had had enough of everything. She was tired of Fargo's silence, tired of the way he led without turning to make sure she wasn't hurt or unable to follow, and tired of trying to prove that he couldn't get the best of her. He was succeeding at what he'd set out to do. With each passing day, she gave more consideration to telling him the truth. But he wouldn't believe her. And if he did, she couldn't be sure he wouldn't kill her. The man seemed to be devoid of feelings. He didn't have to say anything. It was in his eyes. Those cold blue eyes that not only accused, but also waited for her to break down. This was a man driven. A man she hadn't known existed.

Will had seen it, or he wouldn't have been so worried about her. But he knew she could take care of herself. Or at least he thought she could. After all, she'd done a good job of it for six years. Will had been right all along about her playing a dangerous game. She'd been too blind to see what a cold-blooded man she'd fallen in love with. But, in all fairness to herself, Fargo had kept it well hidden.

Will had seen the danger when she'd brought the nearly dead man to the house. She'd seen a glimpse of it during the knife fight with Ocha. Fargo's cold hate and determination were frightening to behold. But, as she continued to move one foot in front of the other, Sara had long since passed the point of either concern. She didn't care what he did. And, by golly, one way or another, she'd prove she could be every bit as stubborn as he. This had become a war of wills!

Sara had to relieve herself. Still determined not to be the one to break the silence, she began watching the ground for a rock. She'd get the mighty man's attention in another way!

Spotting a small rock, Sara leaned down and scooped it up in her hand. Without missing a step, she tried judging how hard she'd have to throw it. The rock wasn't large enough for what she wanted. She dropped it and continued her search. When she hit Fargo in the back, she wanted it to be a damn hard smack. Hopefully it would hurt for weeks.

A bit later, Sara smiled as she picked up another stone. Perfect! She stopped, again judged the distance, then sent it sailing through the air. The rock whizzed past the pack mule's head and struck the rump of Fargo's horse with a hard thud. The mule jerked back on the lead rope.

Sara watched in astonishment as Fargo's horse began bucking, while the pack mule reared and threw his head back and forth to get free. She gasped as Fargo flew through the air and landed on the ground to the right, while the horse and mule took off to the left. Sara had to give Fargo credit. He'd done everything he could to remain in the saddle and keep hold of the pack mule. But he'd been relaxed and hadn't expected the chaos that broke loose.

Coming out of her stupor, Sara tried to catch one of the animals as it galloped by. She missed. After they'd disappeared behind a cloud of dust, she glanced back at Fargo. The look on his face would have made an oncoming storm pale in comparison.

"Appears I'm not the only one who's going to be traveling by foot." Her try at sarcasm came out a strained whisper.

As Fargo stood, Sara began backing away. Now they had no supplies or water. Although she wouldn't blame him if he wanted to wring her neck, she wasn't about to let it happen.

Fargo moved forward, vivid fury glittering in his eyes.

Gripped by icy fear, Sara stumbled on something, but managed to keep her footing. She tried thinking of a way to defend herself. In desperation, she raised her fists, but to her surprise, Fargo went right past her and continued on in the direction the horses had gone. Relieved at her narrow escape, Sara plopped onto the ground. As she enjoyed her wonderful bed of grass, Sara was determined that neither man nor beast would ever make her move another inch—at least not until she took a deserved rest.

But as the distance between her and Fargo grew, a sense of uneasiness settled over Sara. She had no gun, no horse, no Phew. And, she might also add, a serious lack of provisions. Fargo was her only protection. She slowly got to her feet.

"Are you planning to come back this way?" she hollered.

Fargo didn't even give her the courtesy of a reply.

Considering self-preservation to be the better part of valor, Sara took off after him. But this time she couldn't keep to her regular pace. Fargo's legs were much longer than hers, and he wasn't moving slowly. The distance between them continued to grow. Sara started to run, but her boots were a hindrance. She had sore spots on her feet—blisters, undoubtedly.

Sara's running slowed to a walk, then a shuffle, then a slow limp. She looked ahead, and, just like the horses, Fargo had disappeared. She finally stopped and sat on the ground. She couldn't even hope to catch up with any of them. She could do nothing but wait. The animals had to come to a halt eventually. Perhaps Fargo would catch one of them and come back for her.

For the first time in days, Sara took a good look at the terrain. They were in the foothills of a mountain, but she had no idea which mountain range. The ground and grass were parched from the summer heat. All the shrubs were low, and, from where she sat, there were no trees in sight. Or water. Over the past few days, she had divided her time between feeling sorry for herself and planning how she would get even with Fargo. She had honestly believed that help would eventually come. Now, she wasn't sure anyone would ever find her.

Hearing noises, Sara looked up at the sky. Buzzards? Certainly they couldn't be circling her. She had a long way to go before they'd feast on her bones! Finally, she realized their meal had to be in the hills. Had she and Fargo continued on, they probably would have seen whatever lay dead.

Chapter Fourteen

After another hour had passed, Sara contemplated the unpleasant but strong possibility that she'd been abandoned. It would serve Fargo right if he couldn't catch the horses and he ended up stranded in the middle of nowhere!

Sara stood. Concern rode heavily on her shoulders, but she knew that to give in to it was the worst thing she could do. Her first priority was water. She looked to the north, searching for birds. She'd heard Indians used them to locate water. Unfortunately, searching for water was one thing her father hadn't gone into detail about. She didn't know what kind of birds to look for. One thing was certain. She'd never get anywhere if she didn't get a move on. And there was no need to worry. It wouldn't solve anything. This wasn't the first time she'd had to get herself out of trouble, and it probably wouldn't be the last.

She picked up a small stone and cleaned it off as best she could on her skirt. Satisfied, she placed it under her tongue to help ward off thirst. That was one Indian trick she did know.

Once again she took off walking. When she arrived home, she'd ride a horse everywhere. Even to the graveyard. Even to the well!

Sara hadn't gone far when she saw something coming over the next hill. Perhaps some outlaw. She stopped. Her breathing became shallow, and her eyes were fixed on whatever it was. First a hat, then a head, came into view. It had to be Fargo. He'd returned for her! She had to spit out the stone for fear of swallowing it in her excitement. Finally a body. Even though Fargo was still nothing more than a silhouette against the sun, she knew no one else could look like that. Her relief and delight spewed forth in the form of laughter. She couldn't remember ever having known a happier moment. Fargo had come back for her. How could he act like a mercenary, then turn right around and be concerned about her?

The laughter faded. No horse or mule followed behind Fargo, and she didn't have to see his face to know he was furious. Especially after not catching at least one of the contrary beasts. Now that she could see him from head to toe, he seemed to be walking a bit stiffer than usual. Another indication of his sour mood. She didn't care. He had returned for her and that's all that mattered!

Fargo waved his hand, and Sara didn't need a second invitation to run in his direction. Having already relieved herself and rested, she had no trouble making it up the hill. By the time she reached the top, Fargo had nearly reached the bottom on the other side. She hurried forward, not daring to say a word. She had a strong hunch that, at this point, silence would be a wise choice.

They traveled on, still with no words exchanged. Sara kept her arms swinging and her feet moving as she savored her contentment. Feeling considerably safer with Fargo by her side, she now deemed it only right that he pay for what he'd put her through after these many days. At last he'd find out what it was like to have blisters on *his* feet and to be so bone-tired at night he couldn't be sure he could sleep. He deserved everything he received. And she had the advantage. She'd become used to walking. He hadn't!

By three in the afternoon, Sara's feet were already starting to drag because of Fargo's fast pace. Surely he'd stop soon for a rest. She checked the direction in which they were heading. Not far away were clusters of trees and lots of green shrubbery. There had to be water! Her feet began moving faster, and all thoughts of being tired immediately disappeared. For some unknown reason, she suddenly wondered if it was lack of water that drove a man out of his head, or the knowledge that there was no water to be had?

As soon as the large pond come into view, Sara headed straight for it. She didn't bother to stop. She walked straight in, clothes and all, then sat down. Nothing had ever felt so glorious. However, in her eagerness, she'd stirred up the bottom, and the water was now murky. She sat very still, licking her dry lips in anticipation.

Finally the water cleared enough for Sara to skim the top with her hands. From the corner of her eye she could see Fargo kneeling at the water's edge, but she was only interested in quenching her own thirst.

After drinking her fill, Sara fell backward, submerging her body in the water. Glorious, glorious water. She had no idea how long she remained that way before she finally raised up, soaking wet and feeling as if she could conquer the world. She finally looked to see where Fargo had gone. He stood at the water's edge, watching her.

"Aren't you coming in?"

Fargo hesitated a moment, then unbuckled his gun belt and let it fall to the ground. "Why not? We aren't going to be able to leave anytime soon," he grumbled. "We'll have to wait until your ankle jacks dry, and we have no horses.

You took care of that. Now we've got one hell of a walk in front of us." He sat down on the bank and pulled off his boots.

Sara was furious at herself for being so stupid! She'd become so excited about seeing water, she hadn't thought about anything else. Including boots. She tugged at one, but it didn't want to come off. She tried the other one and had the same results. Hearing the water splash, she looked up. Fargo hadn't bothered to remove his clothes, either. When he reached her, he leaned over and pulled up her foot. A few minutes later, both her boots were on the bank where he'd tossed them.

Fargo splashed water over both of them as he joined her and stared at the open span of land stretched out in front of them.

It occurred to Sara that Fargo had actually spoken to her. Sarcastically, perhaps, but nevertheless, he had spoken. "Aren't you worried that I'll find some way to get to that gun and use it on you?" she asked, wondering if he'd grant her an answer.

"What good would it do you? The way you shoot, you'd end up missing me. Maybe you should get Megan to give you lessons."

It was extremely tempting to inform Mr. Tanner that she was the one who had taught Megan, but it worked out better to leave him with his convictions. Still, she couldn't resist saying, "You may be surprised at what I can do with a gun."

"Then by all means, help yourself. But you know as well as I do that you have a better chance of returning to civilization with me than without me." He washed his face. "I don't know what you thought you would accomplish by getting us stranded like this."

"Me?" Sara angrily pulled out what few pins she had left in her hair. "If I recall, you were the one who came up with the harebrained notion of making me walk to who knows where. And, if you'd minded your own business in the first place, we wouldn't be out here."

"Well, if you want to split hairs, why don't you think about how none of this would have happened if you'd told me about Hawk instead of being so damn stubborn? But no, you want to protect that no-account coward—"

"No-account?" Sara screeched. "Well, if you want to take a look at no-accounts, take a look at yourself."

"At least I'm a hell of a lot better—"

"Don't you dare say it!"

"Than Hawk."

"You're better? Think again, Mr. Tanner. Because of you, my feet will never be the same. You had no right to put me through all this."

"Well, hang in there, Sara, because this is only the beginning. You're not going to see home until you tell me exactly what I want to know. I've tried asking nicely, sweetly, and even threateningly. I'm at the end of my patience."

"You mark my word, someway, somehow, I'll get even." She hated Fargo. Absolutely despised him. "And then, to top it off, you have the audacity to turn around and blame me for this!" How was it possible to hate, love and desire someone all at the same time? "If I ever get home, I want you out of my life permanently." If he wouldn't, she would surely lose her mind.

"I can do that now if you say the right words."

She couldn't take the constant pressure he put on her, demanding to know who Hawk was. She had to find a way to get him off her back. "You can squirm in hell!" was all her poor mind could come up with.

"Such strong words from a lady. Well, honey, you might as well—"

The sound of a man clearing his throat caught the attention of the squabbling pair. They looked up. At the edge of the pond were some of the filthiest and meanest-looking men Sara had seen in a long time. There had to be at least thirty of them. They were all smiling, revealing a combination of missing, blackened or yellowed teeth. As dusty as their clothes and mounts were, they appeared to have been chased for miles by the devil himself.

"Well, would ya look what we have here?" a man with yellowed buckteeth said.

The others laughed.

"I think maybe I got me a woman for the night."

Fargo watched the bushy-faced man nudge his horse into the water. When the man reached Sara's side and leaned over to pull her up, Fargo grabbed the bandit's arm and yanked him from his saddle. Fargo pushed the man beneath the water's surface and held him there until his eyes bulged. When Fargo brought him back up, the outlaw was gasping for air. And not just from being submerged. Fargo had an arm wrapped tightly around his throat.

"Back off," Fargo warned the others, "or I'll break his neck."

"Go right ahead," another man called calmly. "I don't think any of us will miss him."

The man rode into view. He appeared to be much younger than the others. Though equally dirty, his long blond hair was neatly tied back, and his beard and mustache were well trimmed. But it was his eyes that drew Fargo's attention. They were a pale, crystalline blue. Fargo had once heard that most gunfighters had blue eyes—a fact that he'd found interesting since his eyes were also blue, though much darker than the man's.

Fargo knew he'd made a mistake. Because the buck-toothed one had done all the talking, he'd assumed he was the leader.

"I don't know what you think you're going to accomplish," the blue-eyed man stated in a thick southern drawl. "All I have to do is to tell my men to shoot, and you and your lady are dead. If Hector gets caught in the fire, it will simply be his punishment for doing something so stupid."

Fargo thrust his prisoner aside as if he were a piece of driftwood, then stood. He reached down and helped Sara up.

"Good choice, my friend." The gentleman gave Fargo a friendly smile. "I find myself in a bit of a predicament. We have the cavalry on our tail, and there's a strong possibility we have Indians ahead of us. A small wagon train was attacked in the foothills, two, maybe three days ago. Terrible mess. Everyone slaughtered. Now, I don't know about the Apache, but a couple of hostages would certainly help my situation with the cavalry. If the two of you come along peacefully, I can assure you that nothing will happen. At least not from my men. I can't speak for the cavalry. Now, sir, I'll give you one minute to make up your mind."

Sara thought about the buzzards she'd seen circling. Now she knew why.

"Apparently we have no choice," Fargo answered.

"You're right. Bring his horse," the leader ordered one of the men.

The animal brought forward was Fargo's gray. "I suppose you also found the pack mule."

The leader laughed. "As a matter of fact, we did." He studied the pair, who were still standing knee-deep in water. "I must ask you to be hasty, as we haven't time to fool around. There are no extra horses, so you'll have to ride double. Please excuse my ill manners, mister, but I'm afraid your hands must be tied behind your back." He looked at Sara. "I suggest you don't try untying him, my dear."

Fargo left the water and stood on the bank. Mud formed around his bare feet as water drained from his clothes. "Will we be allowed to put our boots on?"

"I think not. I'm sure you can understand my position in this matter. You would do the same if you were in my shoes. What might your name be, sir?"

"Fargo. Fargo Tanner."

The other man's blue eyes lit up with interest. "I've heard of you. From over Texas way, I believe." He glanced around at his men. "*Compadres,* we have a rather famous gentleman in our midst. He's not only known for his conquests with women, he's also known to be a fast gun."

"I'll bet he ain't as fast as Hector," one of the men called.

"Nobody's as fast as Hector," another one replied.

The blond man smiled. "Well, maybe we'll have an opportunity to find out."

"And you can be none other than Gentleman John," Fargo commented as he placed his hands behind him to be tied.

"So, you've heard of me, as well."

Seemingly from nowhere, a big fist landed hard on Fargo's jaw, causing him to stagger backward. He shook his head and looked for the man who had delivered the blow. It was the one he'd pulled into the water. Fargo smiled. "You look a lot better now that you've had a bath."

The man would have charged Fargo if Gentleman John hadn't moved his horse between the two men. "You'll get your chance, Hector," John said sharply. "Now catch your horse, so we can be on our way."

Seeing the men staring past him, Fargo glanced back at the pond. Sara still stood in the water, looking like a forlorn child. Her wet, straggly hair almost hid her mud-streaked face. But it was the way her shirt molded to her body, showing taut, inviting nipples, that drew his and the other men's attention. Fargo looked at the mangy gang, tempted to take them all on for not looking the other way. "Could I have a private talk with you, Gentleman John? It will only take a minute."

As the two men talked, Sara was trying to decide what to do. She didn't like the way the bandits were ogling her—including Gentleman John. To remain in the water was ridiculous. She left the pond with as much dignity as she could muster. Nothing, absolutely nothing, had gone right since the day she'd met Fargo Tanner. How could she have allowed herself to be deceived by his charm? If she'd opened her eyes, she would have seen he was nothing more than a no-good, low-down snake in the grass.

Sara watched the two men move away from the others. The sharply dressed but dusty outlaw sat straight and proud atop his horse, while Fargo's feet gathered more mud with each step. As the two men entered the sunlight, Sara could see Fargo's back muscles flex as he walked. Even though he was a soggy mess, there was that odd kind of grace—a strange combination of the magnetic and the lethal. Her curiosity was getting the better of her. What could Fargo possibly want to discuss with Gentleman John? Was he trying to wheedle for their freedom?

When Fargo returned, he walked straight to the gray, stuck his foot in the stirrup, then swung his other leg up and over. He kicked the stirrup free so that Sara could use it to mount up behind him. She placed her arms around his waist to keep from sliding off, then adjusted her bottom until she was as comfortable as it was possible to get on a horse's rump. Another rider held the gray's reins, and the group departed, Sara and Fargo bringing up the rear.

Sara leaned over Fargo's shoulder. "What were you and Gentleman John talking about?"

"I told him you were my woman, and if he made sure everyone kept their hands off you, we wouldn't cause him any trouble."

Sara felt delightfully light-headed. It was a feeling she hadn't known for some time. Fargo had actually proclaimed her as being his! Of course, he hadn't meant it. He'd just wanted to protect her. Would she ever understand the man? He could force her to walk for days, but he was going to make sure no one else harmed her. But she liked the idea of being called his woman, and it gave her something to fantasize about. "Who is Gentleman John? I've never heard of him."

"He spent a lot of time in Texas. Word is, his family lost their plantation during the war. His father went berserk, and his mother killed herself. He chose to become an outlaw. He can't be as young as he looks. I've heard he enjoys killing, and that it takes very little to set him off. So don't try messing around with him, Sara."

Sara wasn't sure whether to believe Fargo. Again she leaned forward. "You have a reputation with women, and you're a fast draw?"

Fargo made no reply.

"You didn't tell me."

"There's a lot of things you don't know about me. We haven't exactly swapped life stories, now have we?"

"No, I don't guess we have."

For the rest of the day, Gentleman John pushed his group as hard as they could travel. There was no sign of the cavalry. Even so, that night, fires weren't allowed, so everyone ate hardtack. After the small meal, Sara and Fargo's wrists were bound. They were forced to lie down, their arms were stretched over their heads, and the ropes tied to a stake. The night guard kept an eye on them.

The men were no sooner on their bedrolls than loud snoring could be heard throughout the camp. Although she no longer had had to walk, Sara's exhaustion had grown. She, too, quickly fell asleep. Fargo lay awake for some time, trying to figure out what he could do to get them out of this mess. There were just too many men in the gang for him to try to befriend one of them. Having Sara untie him while they rode the horse wasn't the answer, either. They'd never get away. For now, Gentleman John had the upper hand. Fargo had no choice but to wait and see what happened next. Perhaps, once they reached their destination, an opportunity to escape would present itself. At least, they had food and water—for now.

For five days they pushed on. As each day passed, their pace became slower. Gentleman John had apparently decided they were safe from the cavalry.

Fargo had heard the men discussing a town in Mexico where they'd relax and enjoy themselves and split the loot from several big bank jobs they'd pulled. Though none of the men had tried to force themselves on Sara, they certainly had no problem with leering at her—something he still found hard to swallow. Though Sara didn't complain, each day she spoke less, and an occasional groan escaped her lip. But he offered her no sympathy. Instead, he forced himself to think of Jude, waiting to go home.

Each night, he tried using their circumstances to his advantage. Before Sara fell asleep, Fargo would say, "Tell me where I can find Hawk, and I'll get you out of this mess.

Otherwise, I can assure you that when I leave I'll leave alone. This is a pretty hungry looking bunch of men.''

Her response never varied. Dead silence. Unfortunately, he would not have many more opportunities to wear her down. They were well into Mexico, and the village they were headed for couldn't be far off.

The following day, Fargo heard one of the Mexicans in the band holler to another that tomorrow he would be seeing his Marguerita. That night, knowing he had reached the end of his rope, Fargo changed his approach. After being tied to their post, as usual, he said softly, ''Do these men appeal to you, Sara? Do you wish you could be around them all the time?''

''Of course not,'' she replied angrily. ''I'm not up to answering foolish questions, Fargo.''

''Have you listened to them bragging about the men they've killed? Or the women they've enjoyed? Think about it, Sara. If these aren't the kind of men you like to be around, then why the hell are you protecting Hawk? He's no better. Sending him to Boot Hill would be a good riddance.''

Sara turned her back to him. Each day she dreaded the coming night. Fargo's words and threats were tearing her apart. More than once she'd opened her mouth to spew out the truth, but the words never came out. What a grave she'd dug for herself. All because a man had crossed a ballroom floor to ask her to dance, and she'd wanted him more than she'd ever thought possible. It wasn't easy being next to Fargo each night, wanting him, yet having to listen to his cruel words. She wanted to cuddle up next to him and draw strength from his warmth. Having to sleep on the hard ground, with her arms pulled over her head and tied to the stake, didn't help matters. She was tired. Worn out would be a better term. Worn out from traveling. Worn out from lack of sleep, and worn out from listening to Fargo doing everything in his power to get her to tell him Hawk's location. How could she make him understand that he was wrong? She knew he felt justified in everything he'd done. Didn't she feel the same way toward Dodd?

Yet, even with Fargo's hounding, and everything else, she felt safe as long as he was near. And, for the first time in her life, she needed that assurance. For some unexplainable reason, she honestly didn't believe he'd allow anything to happen to her. Why hadn't she come to that realization when he had her walking across the world! Why he was protecting her was anyone's guess. He did it either because she was his means of getting to Hawk, or because he cared for her. No matter what he said or did, Sara knew in her heart that in many ways Fargo loved her. She also believed that he'd eventually get out of this mess, but for the life of her she didn't know how. The biggest question was, when he rode away, would he take her with him?

They arrived in the small, dusty village the next day. There were no trees, no plants, nothing that could offer shade. Even the adobe buildings were flat-faced. As long as they'd been on the road, Sara had felt safe. Now she didn't know what to feel. Mexican women were standing around the well in the center of the pueblo, and others were walking away with pots on top of their heads. They all laughed and waved at the men. Old men sat on chairs in front of the adobe buildings, watching with interest as the men rode down the street. A goat scurried out of the way, some chickens took flight, and several dogs started barking and charging toward the horses. Then, at the last minute, the dogs changed their minds and returned to their sleepy positions.

For a place this small, there were quite a few stores. There was one cantina, with a painted sign across the top reading Gentleman John. As the men brought their horses to a halt, women ran from inside, their clothes bright and their dark faces lit with laughter. The men quickly dismounted and threw their arms around the soft, female bodies.

The last woman to leave the cantina was different. She was tall and beautiful, with coal-black hair slicked back into a tight bun at the nape of her neck. Her clothes were simple, her demeanor proud. She stood and waited for Gentleman John to come to her.

Sara felt someone touch her arm. She looked down and saw the bandit leader's extended hand. After traveling so long, Sara felt like anything but a lady, and the gentlemanly gesture was appreciatively accepted. She placed her hand in his, and he lifted her from the horse's rump. When her feet touched the ground, his hands lingered on her arms. It was another compliment, and made her feel more than just a smelly piece of human flesh. Fargo certainly hadn't gone to any trouble to point out her feminine attributes.

"Angelica, my dear, I have brought us guests."

In a fraction of a second, Sara knew that being around this woman could be dangerous. Angelica wrapped her arm about Gentleman John's, making it clear he belonged to her. Sara hadn't missed the cunning look the woman had given her, and Sara had the distinct feeling that not only was Angelica possessive of her man, she could also be extremely jealous.

"How sweet of you, my darling," Angelica told Gentleman John in a strong Mexican accent. "But why not give her to one of the other women as a servant? However, I would be more than happy to take care of the man."

Sara didn't like the sarcasm in the dark beauty's voice. But she knew that being drenched in a pond, being forced to ride at the back of the gang amid the cloud of dust the horses kicked up and being roped to a stake or the ground all night had all combined to make her look a disheveled mess. Angelica, no doubt, assumed she was a whore. But she could put up with all that. The way Angelica looked at Fargo bothered her a lot more. What made the hussy think she could claim any man who pleased her eye?

Sara stepped forward. "The man is mine."

Angelica leaned over and said something in Spanish to John. He turned and looked at Fargo, then at Sara. He replied in Spanish. Sara had no idea what they were saying.

Angelica laughed and again looked Fargo over. Sara wondered if she'd been mistaken about the woman. She had heard of women who required more than one lover.

"If you're talking about me, I'd appreciate your speaking English so I can understand." Sara lifted her chin and stared at them defiantly.

Gentleman John led Angelica into the cantina, leaving Sara and Fargo alone.

"Turn around so I can untie your wrists." Sara glanced back at the cantina. "Then I'll grab another horse and we can get out of here."

Fargo swung his leg over the saddle, then slid to the ground. "We won't get far," he stated simply, nodding toward the building across the street.

Sara looked up and saw a man on the roof, holding a rifle. "Well, what are we supposed to do? Just stand here? Judging by the noise coming from inside, the men must be having a good time."

Sara had no sooner spoken the words than one of the girls came back out of the saloon. She cut the rope from

Fargo's wrists, smiled seductively, then pointed him toward the saloon. As he walked inside, the girl pushed Sara down the dusty street.

The woman led her into what appeared to be a bathhouse. She'd heard of such places, but she'd never seen one. There were four round tubs, all of which had some water in them. Sara wondered how many people bathed in them before the water was changed. Maybe it never got changed. Several young women stood about in nothing more than chemises and pantalettes, looking bored as they waited for customers. If the customers were the men who had ridden into town, they were in for a long wait.

The girls seemed to find the idea of Sara being brought to them extremely funny. Giggling abounded. They spoke only Spanish. One of them raised a strand of Sara's hair and then dropped it as if it were full of maggots. No one seemed particularly eager to touch her clothes, either. It soon became apparent to Sara what they were talking about.

Refusing to allow them to look down on her, Sara undressed herself. Finally down to her chemise and pantalettes, she started to step into the tub. This raised all kinds of hell. Apparently the young ladies wanted her all the way down to the bare skin. As Sara glanced around, she prayed no men would enter. Because there was so little water in each tub, she had nothing to hide beneath, should others enter.

Stripped of her clothes and her dignity, Sara again moved to step into a tub. This time they let her. As Sara wondered just who had arranged all this, most of the girls hurried away. A moment later, they returned with buckets, soap, and anything else possibly needed to clean the body. Without any warning, one of the girls lifted a barrel over Sara's head and dumped new—and hopefully fresh—

water over her. Another one followed, then another, until
Sara felt absolutely drenched. She sputtered, but the
women paid no attention.

They scrubbed every inch of her body, until Sara seriously doubted she had any skin left. Then the bucket bri-
gade and the sputtering started all again. By the time Sara
climbed out of the tub, there was no question as to her
cleanliness.

Oddly enough, the girls now appeared to be enjoying
themselves. They wrapped Sara in a large linen towel, then
led her into another room that contained a bed, a mirror,
a dressing table and two high-backed wooden chairs. Sara
found it to be a questionable combination. Why would
there be such rooms in a bath house? Was this also a bor-
dello? Should she be thanking Angelica, or Gentleman
John for the wonderful bath?

After being dried, she slipped into some coarse peasant
clothing that seemed to have appeared out of nowhere.
Sara rather liked the way her skirt ended at her ankles.
There wasn't any chance of a heel getting caught in the
hem.

The girls placed her in a chair, then proceeded to attack
her hair. For the next hour, Sara groaned, screamed, yelled
and threatened as tangles were removed and the hair was
eventually combed smooth. One of the younger women
took great pride in plaiting her glossy auburn hair. When
she had finished, a long braid hung down Sara's back, the
end tied with a bright green ribbon.

When all was completed, the girls gathered, stared and
jabbered at each other, obviously pleased with their hand-
iwork. Sara stood and went to the mirror. She didn't recognize the person staring back at her. Her skin had
darkened from having spent so much time in the sun.
Though the effect was decidedly unfashionable, she liked

it. There was even a rosiness to her cheeks that she'd never seen before. She'd lost weight, but the result was not unpleasing. Or maybe her weight had been redistributed by all the walking she'd done. Whatever had happened, she couldn't remember ever having looked better. Sara hugged and thanked each of the girls. Their wide smiles showed their delight.

After taking Sarah to a different room, the women served her a meal fit for a queen. By the time she'd finished, Sara discovered she'd been left alone. She looked longingly at the bed against the wall. She could hardly keep her eyes open. How long had it been since she'd slept on a mattress? Surely a short nap wouldn't do any harm.

Chapter Fifteen

When Sara awoke from a deep sleep, she felt completely disoriented. Nothing looked familiar. It took several minutes before she remembered the girls and how she had ended up in the small room. How long had she been asleep? She sat on the edge of the bed. In the middle of a long stretch, she spied an old woman sitting quietly in the corner.

"Could you tell me—?"

The woman gave her a toothless grin, then stood and left the room, closing the door behind her.

From the way she felt, Sara found it hard to believe she'd been asleep only for a few minutes. Yet sunlight was still flooding in through the high, narrow windows. And what had Fargo been doing all this time? Accommodating Angelica?

Sara clenched her teeth as she stood. How dare he be with that hussy? She looked toward the door. Had the woman locked it? Again she wondered who had arranged the bath, clothes and food for her. Maybe Gentleman John?

She straightened her blouse and skirt, then started toward the door. It suddenly swung open, and the pitiful old woman returned, this time carrying food. She gave Sara another toothless smile before placing the food on the table. The task completed, she resumed her place in the corner.

Sara debated whether she should rush out the door—or eat. The food won. Besides, once she made it outside, what then? She had no horse, and she had no gun.

Not until the woman had left with the empty plates did Sara decide it was time to get out of there. The door again opened. But this time it wasn't the old woman who walked into the room, it was a blond southern gentleman, who had also bathed and changed clothes. His mustache and hair had been properly trimmed, and he wore tan trousers, a ruffled, pristine shirt and a blue satin vest with silver thread running through it. Sara had to admit the transformed Gentleman John presented a striking figure.

"Well, my dear, I must say this is quite an unexpected change. I knew you were a beauty, but I had no idea— You look nothing like the wild urchin I saw at the pond. Yes sir, a rare beauty."

"Do you always walk in unannounced?"

"Yes, I seem to have a tendency to do that. Fargo told me you're a lady. The man knew what he spoke of. I hope you enjoyed your long rest."

"I couldn't have slept long. Sunlight is still coming through the windows."

"Approximately twenty-four hours."

Sara started to sit back down on the bed, then suddenly thought better of it. She chose a high-backed wooden chair instead. She sat with her back straight and her hands properly folded in her lap. "I had no idea. I thought I'd rested only minutes. Why have you gone to all this trouble for me?"

"That's very simple. I desire you and look forward to our becoming better acquainted." He smiled.

"I don't think Angelica would like that."

"Angelica was no different than the other peons in the village until I made her what she is. She can easily be replaced. To have a real lady as a mistress would be much more to my liking. I'm tired of constantly having to be around rabble."

Sara rose angrily to her feet. "I'm not one of your whores."

"My dear, I never implied such."

Sara suddenly realized that Gentleman John had given her a tool that would help to keep him at a distance—perhaps until she could escape. He wanted a lady, and a lady was exactly what he would get. She sat back down and gave him just the faintest hint of a smile. "I apologize for my crude words. But you must realize that for two weeks I have been tested nearly to the breaking point. I'm not used to such treatment, sir." She smoothed her skirt. "Just what reason did Fargo give you for having me in tow? That I was his woman?"

John leaned against the tall back of the other chair. "He told me no such thing. The only conversation we had about you was at the river. I offered to buy you. He said the price wasn't high enough. Seeing you now, I would have to agree."

He'd lied again! Sara gritted her teeth. *Did Fargo ever tell the truth? Had his warnings about Gentleman John also been a lie?* "He probably thought he could hold out for more. I am not used to being taken from my home by a ruthless maverick who hopes to be paid for my return." She gave John a hard look. "Nor do I intend to become your mistress. You have insulted me, sir."

John laughed, thoroughly enjoying their repartee. "I assure you that, though I rob banks, I am indeed a gentleman in the purest form. I would never think to rush you.

We will take it slowly, and in time I'm quite sure you will come to see things my way. I can really be quite charming.''

"Oh?" Sara teased.

"I came to offer an invitation."

"What sort of invitation?"

He sat down and crossed his legs. "I see you have a suspicious mind. I've always enjoyed a woman who presents a challenge."

Sara remained silent.

"I've taken quite a liking to Fargo, but I'm having a considerable problem with Hector. Especially after Fargo almost killed him. He—Hector—wants to have a draw with Fargo to determine who is the fastest. An honor, so to speak, that Hector has always had. I had no choice but to allow the contest, and my men are already placing bets. I thought you might like to watch."

Sara rose from her chair. "Yes, I would." She took John's offered elbow and allowed him to lead her out of the room. "Tell me, who do you think will win?" she asked when they were outside. The sun felt good against her skin.

"Hector."

"Really?" It would serve Fargo right, Sara thought, but she knew she didn't mean it. She weighed the odds of Fargo winning. Since Will had been right about Fargo being dangerous, maybe he was also right about him being a fast gun. Even John had said the handsome man had a reputation in Texas. On the other hand, she'd never seen either Hector or Fargo draw a gun. However, there was that lethal gracefulness that Fargo possessed, while Hector was more like a thick brick.... "Would you care to make a wager?"

"Most certainly," he replied. "But what do you have to wager other than—"

"I own a substantial ranch. How does a herd of cattle sound? You could make a pretty penny off them here in Mexico? Think about it, John."

John stopped and looked at her.

"Or there's another possibility. You apparently have a nice little kingdom here. Why risk getting killed by running across the border? With a good herd, you could start your own ranch."

John laughed jubilantly. "I can see right now that you will be a delight to have around. And if I lose, what would you receive?"

"You give us horses and provisions, and let us go."

"I think not. In order for you to get the cattle, you'd have to leave anyway. I have no guarantee that you would return, or that you could or would hold up your end of the bargain. But your challenge was indeed a worthy one."

He started walking with Sara following alongside. Ahead a crowd of men blocked the road.

"Let us by, gentlemen!"

Hearing Gentleman John's voice, the crowd immediately separated to leave a clear path. Most were drunk, and Sara quickly realized she had been given her first opportunity to do something about her situation. Pretending to have tripped, she fell against one of the men. When she straightened up, she had the man's revolver. John turned and gave the drunk all kinds of hell, which gave Sara enough time to hide the gun in the folds of her skirt.

Sara smiled sweetly. "Thank you, but it was really my fault," she assured her protector. "I'm fine."

They reached the front of the saloon, where chairs had been brought out and placed on either side of the road. The chairs were all full of laughing, drinking men and women, except for the two in the center. John motioned to Sara to take one, and he took the other. Angelica had already seated herself on the other side of him. Standing in the middle of the makeshift arena were Fargo and Hector. Fargo had also been cleaned up.... Sara would have liked nothing better than to be able to reach over and snatch the hair from Angelica's head!

"All right, gentlemen," John called loudly.

A deadly, apprehensive quiet settled over the crowd.

"You will stand back to back and be given like pistols, which you will place in your holsters."

Sara would have recognized the look on Fargo's face from a mile away. That deceptively still look that meant he wasn't just angry, he was furious. Because of the darting glances he gave her, she knew that a good part of that anger had to do with her having been out of his sight for twenty-four hours. The topping on the cake was that she'd been escorted to her chair by Gentleman John. He probably thought they had been sleeping together. The possibility of his being jealous excited her. It felt so good seeing him get a taste of his own medicine.

"It will be as close to a gentleman's duel as I can manage in such surroundings," John continued, his chiseled lips spread in a wide smile. "I'll say, 'go,' then you will both step off ten long paces and turn. You will not draw until Sara says, 'Now.' If either of you draws his gun before she speaks, I'll kill him. Have I made the instructions clear?"

The two men standing in the middle of the street nodded.

"Remember, this is to determine who is the fastest draw," John added.

As Sara slowly worked the revolver up to her lap, she kept her eyes on Fargo. She was reminded of when she had first seen him, with Ocha. Her heart had ached for him then, as it did now, but she knew there was nothing she could do at this point to be of help. She was afraid the man she'd stolen the gun from would start yelling at any time. She tried to relax.

Fargo and Hector turned their backs to each other, the crowd shouting encouragement to their favorites. They were each given revolvers, which they placed in their holsters.

John immediately called, "Take your ten paces, gentlemen, and face each other." With everything ready, he looked at Sara. "Now, my dear, it's all up to you."

Sara chewed on her lower lip. John was wrong. Now it was all up to Fargo. If he didn't win the contest, she didn't know what she'd do. Neither of them could get away without the other.

Dead silence fell over the crowd. Anticipation built. Sara quietly cleared her throat so that the words would come out clearly.

"Now!"

Hector had barely gotten his gun free when Fargo pulled the trigger of his revolver. Nothing happened. The gun had no bullets. Everyone looked at Gentleman John. "Surely you didn't expect me to give him a loaded gun?"

While everyone stared in shock, Hector's thick lips spread in a confident smile. He raised his gun.

To Sara's horror, Hector pulled the trigger before she could do anything. Again, there was an empty click.

Suddenly John became furious, and he jumped to his feet. "You have insulted a gentleman's game!" he yelled. He turned to a man behind him. "Give me your gun!" he demanded. "This was a contest for the fastest draw!" As soon as the man had handed over the revolver, John turned and pulled the trigger, dropping Hector on the spot.

Fargo made a dive to the side, grabbing a rifle from a man as he went by. Everyone ran for cover as he released one bullet after another into the crowd of outlaws. From somewhere, his fire was returned. Women screamed and ran into the nearest shops and cantina. Sara didn't know who was firing at whom, but like Fargo, she saw her opportunity to do something. She stood and stuck the barrel of the revolver in Gentleman John's back.

"Don't try to move," Sara warned. "I assure you, I will not hesitate to pull the trigger. And this gun is loaded."

John laughed. "You'll never get away from here."

"If I don't, neither will you."

Sara saw Fargo virtually pick up a man and throw him out of the way. Fargo rolled on the ground, then jumped to his feet, firing the rifle. When it was empty, he grabbed another gun from a man who made the mistake of trying to get away.

Bullets continued to fly, but Fargo had made it safely across the road and was slowly working his way to Sara. Her heart sang. He *must* love her. He could have ridden away, but he was coming after her.

"Back up very slowly," Sara told Gentleman John. To her aggravation, a bullet from somewhere hit him in the leg. "Don't you dare fall down," Sara coldly demanded. Finally, they were close to the wall. "Order your men to stop firing."

"Hold your fire," John hollered out. "Hold your fire!" he yelled again. "I've got a gun in my back."

Slowly the firing ceased.

"Sara? Are you safe?" Fargo called.

"Yes."

"I'm going to get us some horses. Be ready."

As Sara waited, she saw men positioning themselves in houses and on rooftops with their guns ready, just waiting for her to make a wrong move. It would take Fargo to get John on a horse so that they could ride out of there safely. Something sharp poked her in the side.

"Let him go," Angelica warned, "or I'll cut your gizzard out and feed it to the chickens."

"You should listen to her, Sara," Gentleman John encouraged. "She is a vicious lady with a knife."

Sara moved her foot back, then brought it forward with all her might, knocking Angelica's feet out from under her. Angelica snarled and was about to do the same to Sara when an arrow hit Angelica in the chest. Suddenly there were Apache everywhere, screaming their war calls as shots again reverberated from every direction. Gentleman John limped away, and Sara didn't try to stop him. Her eyes were on the man hunched down on the horse galloping down the middle of the street. Sara ran out to meet him, and a moment later she felt herself being swooped up by a big arm, the horse never slowing down. He kept her in front of him to protect her.

Seeing eight or ten Apache slowly moving their ponies along the dusty road, Fargo yanked the horse around and took off in the opposite direction. The same thing happened. The Apache were closing in. Fargo saw one of them raise his rifle just as he sent the horse leaping over a cart to take off between two houses.

This time there was only one brave standing between him and his hope for freedom. Ocha. Fargo brought his horse to a halt. He had no weapon. The two men sat staring at each other. Ocha raised his arm, his wrist turned toward Fargo. He spoke, but Fargo didn't understand him.

"It's all right, Fargo," Sara said. "No harm will come to either of us. As your blood brother, Ocha must protect you, and I am the Apache princess Hair of Fire. Now help me down." Sara could feel nothing but an overwhelming sadness. Today, Fargo had been a magnificent warrior who cared about nothing but saving a woman's life. But the time had come for that woman to end their relationship. And it had to be done in such a way that he would truly believe she no longer wanted anything to do with him.

For two days Fargo rode with the Indians, never once being allowed near Sara. But he had no complaints. These braves had probably saved his and Sara's lives.

On the third day, the band stopped by a stream to eat. Fargo leaned against an old, overturned wagon and watched Sara silently sitting by herself. He considered going over and talking to her, but changed his mind. Hawk still stood between them. Not just Hawk, but Jude, and his father, as well. He had an obligation to fulfill.

"Take his pony away," Sara said to a brave in his native tongue.

Fargo looked questioningly at Sara as she and the other braves mounted their ponies. "Am I allowed to ask why you're taking my horse?" he angrily addressed Sara, who had moved her mount a short distance from him.

Sara looked down. He hadn't even moved from the wagon. "I told you I'd get even. Because you made me walk, I'm repaying the favor. From here on, you walk. We're past the border.

"This is the last time I will ever save your good-for-nothing hide, and the last time we will see each other," she continued. "You have lied to me and used me and my family in every way you knew how. If you ever come near my ranch again, you'll be met by a bunch of well-armed cowpokes."

As they rode off, Sara had to fight back tears. She said a silent prayer that Fargo would travel in safety, and that this would finally be the end of it. Whatever it took, Fargo had to be out of her life, once and for all.

Fargo watched Sara ride off with the Chiricahua. At least they had left him a rifle and his boots. He looked out across the land. He had a hell of a long walk ahead of him. He slung the rifle over his shoulder and headed east. If he had it figured right, it would take him a good two weeks on foot. But maybe he'd meet up with someone who would be willing to sell him a horse.

But Fargo found no horse, and he didn't see a soul. For five days he trudged on, trying to save bullets, yet having to spend one occasionally to shoot a rabbit when a trap he'd set failed to catch his day's meal. The boots he wore weren't made for walking, and his feet quickly developed blisters. Sara was definitely getting her retribution.

Fargo spent a great deal of his time thinking about Sara. Picturing her walking straight into that pond and plopping herself down still brought a smile. And what about the way she'd handled herself with Gentleman John? He was still curious about who'd shot him. All things considered, he would never have believed someone as tiny as Sara could be so capable of taking care of herself. The woman had grit.

Toward dusk on the sixth day, Fargo saw dust rising into the sky. The kind a bunch of horses would kick up. Either he was about to get himself in trouble again or help had finally arrived. He doubted that it would be an Indian party. They wouldn't leave that kind of trail for the cavalry to follow. So that left more outlaws or the cavalry.

Fargo stood waiting for some time before the riders were near enough for him to see the blue uniforms and hear the jingling noise of the horses' trappings in the still air. Unfortunately, they were going to pass by about a quarter of a mile away from him. He pointed the barrel of his rifle toward the sky and pulled the trigger twice.

Two men broke away from the long line and rode toward him. When they pulled up, Fargo gave them a welcoming smile. "Thought I'd never see you boys."

"What happened?" the private asked.

"Lost my horse. Where you headed?"

"Fort Huachuca. We been out on Indian patrol."

"How near are we?"

"We should pull in tomorrow."

Fargo hadn't realized he was that close. "How about me tagging along with you?"

The young man smiled. "Climb up behind me."

Sara sat on her horse, staring at the large adobe wall surrounding the adobe house. It was hard for her to believe she had arrived home—something she'd begun to think would never happen. A heavy sigh escaped her cracked lips as she slid from the horse's bare back. Her moccasin-clad feet felt strange on the hard earth. Not long ago she'd sworn she'd never willingly walk another inch in her entire life, yet here she was, choosing to walk to the house. Had she really been gone only three weeks? It seemed longer. She'd been with a man so set on revenge that everything else had become secondary in importance. Including her. But that was probably for the best. She loved him, and though he'd never said so, she believed he loved her. But there was no future for them, and there never had been. Soon he'd forget her, and when he finally gave up searching for Hawk, he'd return to Texas. Theirs was a love that had been doomed from the beginning. She had just been delaying the inevitable. Now the time had come to start anew, and put it all behind her.

She handed one of her Apache companions the rope that circled her Indian pony's lower lip. They bade her a brief farewell before riding off.

As Sara entered the house, Carla walked into the foyer. The chubby woman dropped the vase she was carrying and ran forward. Pottery, water and flowers went in every direction, but she didn't notice.

"Megan!" Carla yelled. "Sara is home!"

She wrapped her big arms around Sara, tears running down her broad cheeks as she spoke endearing words in her native tongue.

"I'm all right, sweet Carla," Sara told her soothingly. "I'm sorry you've worried so. He didn't hurt me."

"This is true?"

Sara nodded. "This is true."

Megan came running in, laughing, and threw her arms around both women. "I told you he wouldn't harm her," she said excitedly.

Sara pulled back. "How did the two of you know who I was with?"

Megan smiled. "I saw it in a dream. Sometimes I get good messages."

"You mean you've known all along and you weren't worried?"

"That's right, but I can't say the same for Carla and Will."

"She tells me, but I don't believe." Carla stood back and took a good look at Sara. "He did not feed you well. You are nothing but bones. I will prepare hot water for a bath. Then I will fix you a proper meal."

Sara watched Carla waddle away before looking back at Megan. "I wish you had been along to tell me I'd be all right," she said wearily as she unbuttoned her once-white

Mexican blouse. "More than once I thought I would never see the Bar C again."

"But, Sara, Fargo will always take care of you. He is your justice."

"Justice, huh? I'm afraid I look at it a bit differently. But right now all I want is to soak in a hot tub of water. Would you see that Will gets word that I'm fine?"

"You'd be proud of me, Sara."

"I'm always proud of you, Meg."

"No, you don't understand. While you were gone, I had to take over and make decisions."

Sara smiled. "After listening to all the things you told Fargo when he ate with us, I'm convinced you know almost as much as I do about this ranch." Sara started up the stairs, with Megan right behind her.

"At first, it frightened me. But, Sara, I did it. I went to Elgin and reaffirmed your price agreement, then I told Will to drive the steers there."

"Meg! You did all that? You truly have changed. I forgot all about the roundup."

"I rather liked it. I'll be able to help you more and more, Sara. It's about time. You've handled everything by yourself for too many years."

Sara stopped and looked at her sister. "To see you like this makes every moment worth it." Fighting back tears, she leaned over and kissed Megan's cheek.

"You take your bath," Megan said softly. "I'll get word to Will."

"And, Meg, make sure he'll be here for supper. I want to talk to the both of you."

At the dinner table that night, Sara briefly told Meg and Will what had happened.

"You'll be happy to know, Will, I never intend to see Fargo again." Sara didn't see the look of pleasure she'd expected. "If he comes to the house, find some excuse why he can't see me—or just lie."

"What if he returns?" Will asked.

"Then make sure there are enough available men to see that he leaves. And I mean a *lot* of men. I watched him wipe out practically an entire camp of *bandidos* all by himself." Sara smiled. "He's quite a man." Without any further explanation, she rose from the table and went to her room. Fargo had been right. What a pair they made. She brushed a tear away.

It was nightfall when Fargo returned to the lonely place he now called home. He'd been on foot for a week before he'd met up with the cavalry. At the fort, he'd been able to buy a horse from a miner. It was a hard-mouthed buzzard-bait nag. Nevertheless, it beat walking. He was dirty, tired, hungry and irritated. His disposition didn't improve when he had to settle for a cold bath in the stream and a cold meal in the chuck house. At least he got to eat before the hogs were fed.

By the time Fargo stretched out on his bed, he was already thinking about Sara. Nothing had turned out the way he'd planned it. He chuckled. At least it hadn't been dull. What was he supposed to do with a woman who saved his life? Try again. Tomorrow he'd pay Sara a visit. After all, he should make sure she'd gotten home safely, though he seriously doubted anyone would be stupid enough to try to cause trouble with a bunch of Chiricahua protecting her. Hell, no one ever bothered to tell him she was an Indian *princess!* Who ever heard of one having red hair?

Chapter Sixteen

Sara heard two male voices. Curious, she approached one of the open gun slits to listen. She recognized the voices immediately. Will and Fargo.

"So I take it nothing happened to her."

"That's right, she's fine, no thanks to you."

"Then why can't I see her?"

"Dammit, I told you she isn't here."

"Why don't you tell me where she is?"

Sara recognized Fargo's threatening tone of voice. Very quiet and deliberate. Of course, that was something Will wouldn't know. She moved to where she could look at both men without being seen.

"You don't seem to understand. Sara doesn't want to see you. Just head back to where you came from. Texas would be a good idea. You've already done enough damage around here."

"Is she in the house?"

"No. Did you hear what I said? Get off this ranch. You're damn sure not welcome."

Sara caught her breath when she saw Fargo's hand drop to his gun. Will could never outdraw him. Fargo was way too fast. Would she have to go out and face Fargo after all? She was about to run to the door when she saw him relax his hand. Sara expelled her pent-up breath. He wasn't going to draw.

"You tell Sara I'll be back at noon tomorrow. If she's not out here waiting, I'll go looking for her. I suggest you don't get in my way, 'cause next time I'll shoot you." He swung up on his horse. "Tomorrow noon," he repeated, before he turned his horse and rode off.

Sara collapsed onto a chair. She should have been the one to face him. Cowardice had never been one of her faults. But it had been hard enough when she'd left him in the middle of nowhere. She couldn't do it again. She couldn't look him in the eye and say she never wanted to see him. He'd know it was a lie, and he'd know exactly how to change her mind. Hearing footsteps, she looked to the doorway just as Will entered.

"He's coming back, Sara."

"I know. I heard the two of you talking."

"I don't believe he was bluffing when he said he wouldn't take no for an answer." Will poured himself a shot of whiskey.

"No, he wasn't bluffing. But he's not going to get his way."

"Are you asking me to stop him?"

"No, no." Sara stood. "Pour me a drink."

Will raised an eyebrow, but said nothing. He poured the drink and handed it to her.

Sara took a sip, scrunched her nose, then went to the sofa. "You wouldn't even get your gun out of the holster before he shot you."

"I doubt that he'd go that far."

Sara took another drink. "Will, I think there are some things you should know about Fargo just in case you get it in your mind to have it out with him. You know I can outdraw you. Well, Fargo's a lot faster than I am. I've never seen anything like it.'' She pictured in her mind the drawing contest between Hector and Fargo. ''But he can also be very friendly, gracious and amusing. A very likable man, one might say. And he is. What people dón't see is Fargo's deadly, cold-blooded side. He can keep it well hidden. Probably so his enemies won't suspect what he's up to or what he's capable of. I think we all have a part of that in us. I know I do. But Fargo is dangerous. Very dangerous.''

''You sound like you respect him.''

Sara smiled. ''In many ways, I do.''

Will downed his drink. ''Want some more?''

Sara held out her glass. Will walked over with the decanter and poured more whiskey. ''You're going to get drunk.''

''It would take more than this. You forget, I've worked in and been in a lot of saloons over the years. The first taste is still always the worst.''

''Next thing you'll be saying is that you can even outdrink a man.''

Sara's smile broadened. ''I can outdrink you.''

''Is that a challenge?''

''I do believe it is.''

''You're on. It's time you learned you can't best a man at everything.'' He sat beside her and filled their glasses even. ''Sara,'' he said, his tone turning serious, ''I'm glad you've finally realized you have no business around Fargo. Never did trust him.''

''Ah, but for me, Will, it's a different kind of danger. You see, I'm hopelessly in love with him.''

''Then give up being Hawk. He need never know.''

''Dear, sweet Will. Sometimes I think you're too kind for your own good. Maybe you could use some of my or

Fargo's meanness. Now drink up. We both know Hawk is alive and well.''

An hour later, Sara left Will passed out in the parlor. She had to round up her men.

At ten minutes before noon the next day, Sara saw Fargo crest the hill. He brought his horse to a halt and stared down at the scene below. Inside the wall were twelve men with rifles. Rifle barrels were also sticking out the gun slots, but she wasn't sure if he could see them. She had hoped that with a show of this many men, he wouldn't try to come down. But she didn't know. He seemed to be making his decision.

"What are you doing?" Megan demanded as she joined Sara in the doorway.

"Don't interfere, Meg. This is something I have to take care of once and for all."

"Have you gone insane? Fargo is our friend. How could you have him shot?"

"He won't come down. I know he won't."

"You're gambling he won't! What if he does? Are you going to just let the men kill him?"

Sara placed her hand on her throat. Fargo had raised his hands off the saddlehorn. He was coming down! "No!" Sara gasped.

Megan ran past Sara, across the long stretch of ground and out the opening in the wall. "No!" she screamed as she continued running. "Don't come down, Fargo! They'll kill you!" Her breathing heavy, Megan finally stopped and looked up. Fargo hadn't moved off the hill. He tipped his hat to her, and Megan waved her hand in acknowledgment.

Fargo turned his horse and disappeared.

Tears rolled down Sara's cheeks. Now Fargo would leave her alone. Megan had asked if she would have let the men kill him. She honestly didn't know. Thank God she hadn't been put to the test. She had felt Hawk was in deep danger.

Will watched Sara go into the house. He'd seen the tears. She'd had enough problems in her life without Fargo putting her through all this. Will thought about how the night before Sara had accused him of being too good. Maybe she was right. Maybe it was time he made sure Fargo left Sara alone once and for all.

Will moved over to where Sam stood. "I want you and a couple of the boys to meet me outside the wall tonight."

"Damn, Will, I thought for sure he was gonna ride down and take us all on." Sam placed the rifle butt on the ground, then rested it and himself against the adobe wall. "I said it afore, and I'll say it again. That there is one man I wouldn't care to tangle with." He scratched his stomach. "And another thing. I don't cotton to cold-bloodedly shootin' a man. Think some of the others have second thoughts, too. 'Course, if Miss Sara had asked it of us, we'd done it. Now what's this about you wantin' me and a couple of others to meet you outside?"

"We're going to pay Mr. Tanner a visit." Will rocked back and forth on his bootheels.

"What?" Sam pushed away from the wall. "You plumb loco? You saw what he did that day Miss Sara brought him here. Nearly killed the both of us, and he was out of his head!"

"We'll make sure he doesn't do any damage. It's time he learns that he can't go around walking on people. Especially Miss Sara."

"Is this her orders?"

"You don't answer to her. You answer to me. I'll expect you and several others outside come midnight."

"Don't like it," Sam said as he watched Will leave. "Don't like it one damn bit. It ain't gonna solve nothin', but it's sure as hell gonna make a bigger mess!"

The sound of heavy footsteps on the dilapidated porch woke Fargo. He was already climbing out of bed when he heard the front door squeak open. He reached out and felt for the gun belt he'd hung on the chair. Silently he pulled the revolver from the holster. With his back to the wall, he waited to see who had come to pay him a visit. A few minutes passed before he saw a man's shadowy figure standing in the bedroom doorway.

"If you don't stop right there, mister," Fargo warned, "you're a dead man!"

"Surely you wouldn't shoot an unarmed man?"

Fargo recognized Will Langdon's voice. "What are you doing here?"

"I came to tell you that if you even so much as talk to Sara again, I'll kill you. In the meantime, I intend to pay you back for what you put her through. I'm going to beat the hell out of you."

"Go home, Will. You may be big and burly, but you're the one that'll get the hell beat out of him, and you know it."

"But it will feel so good to try."

"You heard me, get out of here," Fargo snapped. "I'm in no mood to put up with another member of the Carter bunch. I've got a gun pointed at your belly, and I'd just as soon shoot you as look at you."

"Well, I'll be damned. The mighty Fargo Tanner thinks nothing of mistreating defenseless women because he knows he's bigger and stronger than they are. But he hasn't the guts to take on a real man."

"What are you trying to do, Will?" Fargo asked in a quiet voice. "You saw me fight Ocha."

"But you weren't left with a choice, were you? You knew that if you didn't go willingly, Sara's men would have delivered you there."

"It doesn't matter, does it? I fought him and I won."

"I say you're a coward."

The room became so quiet that both men could hear the other breathing.

"You don't intend to leave me a choice, do you?"

"Hell no." Will turned and walked into the adjacent room. "I'll be outside," he called over his shoulder before going out the front door.

Fargo tossed the gun onto the bed. "I haven't had a damn moment's peace since I first set eyes on Sara Carter," he grumbled angrily as he pulled on his pants. "Being around that woman is like trying to walk down a path of fresh eggs. One mishap, and the next thing you know your feet are covered with sticky yolk!" The moment he had his boots on, he made a beeline for the front door. The sooner he got this over with, the happier he'd be. The moon offered enough light for him to see Will standing in the front yard.

Fargo slowly walked down the three steps from the porch, never taking his eyes off his opponent. "Is there any reason this couldn't be done during daylight?"

Seeing something move behind him, Fargo realized his mistake too late. It was a trap. "I'm damn tired of this!" he hissed before moving forward.

A man tried to grab Fargo from the back, only to receive a hard elbow in the chest that knocked the breath out of him. Fargo didn't care about him, or the next man that tried to jump him. "If I'm going to get the hell beat out of me," he growled at Will, "I'm going to make sure you receive the same favor."

Will glanced around at the other three men, suddenly regretting the ambush. He'd never considered himself a coward, and he'd whipped more than one man. "Stay back, boys, this is my fight." He charged Fargo, hitting him in the stomach with his shoulder.

The other men gathered in a circle to watch Will's bull strength pitted against Fargo's catlike movements. The fight didn't last long. Will ended up in the dirt, facedown.

"Get him out of here," Fargo ordered angrily.

Two of the men grabbed Will under the arms and lifted him up. Will was finally able to stand with their support.

"I'm warning you, Tanner, you even get close to Sara again and so help me God I'll kill you," Will said.

"And we'll stand behind him," Sam added.

"Well, then, you boys had better get ready, 'cause I guarantee you, I'll be coming down. Now get the hell off my land."

Shortly after noon, Fargo left the chuckhouse and planted his bottom on the old wooden chair on his rickety porch. He leisurely rolled a cigarette and lit it. After a couple of puffs, he raised his feet and rested his heels on the top of the porch rail. He'd been brooding for two weeks now, and the time had come for him to make his move. His ranch was getting into fairly good shape, and his men knew what was expected of them. Now it was up to the two bulls he'd purchased from the Bar C to do the rest. Even though he didn't care about the damn ranch, he'd been a cattleman too long to let the place go to hell. And he'd be damned if he'd let the Bar C absorb everything.

The possibility of getting to Hawk through the Carters was finished. Fargo had to admit, he'd reached his wits' end. He'd even thought about giving it up, but it just wasn't in his nature to let the bastard get away. He should have thought about capturing Megan, instead of Sara. It would have forced Sara into giving him the information he wanted. Not a bad idea, but it wouldn't work now. Sara had too many men guarding the hacienda. Besides, he couldn't do that to Megan.

He had no choice but to find other avenues of information. He'd thought about following Phew everywhere he went, but he'd quickly realized it was an impossibility. The dog often took off foraging for himself, and at other times he'd just lie around the ranch, showing no apparent interest in going anywhere, or take off with some cowhand.

Before Fargo could take off in pursuit of the evasive Mr. Hawk, however, there were a few things he planned to take care of. Did Sara and Will honestly think they'd scared him off? It always came back to the same thing. An eye for an eye. Things would have been a lot simpler if Sara hadn't gathered her men. And as if that weren't enough, he'd added another problem to his list. Having the brain of a flea, he had, sometime, somehow, somewhere, made the mistake of falling hopelessly in love. And why did it have to be with Hawk's protector? Nevertheless, it had happened, and there wasn't a damn thing he could do to change it. So, he might as well get busy and do something about that too, instead of sitting around stewing.

Because the weather had become intolerably hot, he decided to attend to his problems come early morning. That would also allow him time to round up his men. Even if it meant having a shoot-out with every hand on Sara's ranch, this time he was going to see her.

* * *

The morning light still hadn't crawled from outside into the center of the barn, where Fargo stood saddling his horse. He'd decided last night that he would ask Sara Carter to marry him. Of course, she'd turn him down when she found out he still had every intention of searching out the cold-blooded killer Hawk. Maybe her refusal would be for the best. He had no business getting hooked up with a woman. On the other hand, maybe...

He hung a stirrup on the saddlehorn, then reached under the horse's belly and grabbed the girth.

He and Sara had never sat down and had a meaningful talk. They'd been too busy lying, fighting and jumping into bed. There were so many things they needed to discuss. But after their last jaunt together, it was going to be hell getting her to settle down and listen to what he had to say. Oh, she had a temper, all right, but the only time she'd shown it was when he'd pushed her to the end of her endurance. He certainly couldn't blame her for that. He'd tell her he'd come back for her when this whole business with Jude was over. Hell, who was he trying to fool? That wasn't what he needed to tell her. He needed to tell her the truth. He loved her so damn much that nothing seemed right except when she was by his side, and he wanted to spend the rest of his life taking care of and watching over her.

He slid the bit into the horse's mouth.

And although he had wanted to wring her beautiful neck more than once for keeping quiet about Hawk, her loyalty to the scavenger had drawn his admiration. It was the kind of loyalty she'd give her husband when she married.

After sliding his new Winchester repeater into the saddle scabbard and checking to make sure his revolver was loaded, Fargo mounted his horse. He gathered the reins in one hand and guided the horse out of the barn. With a wave of his hand, twenty armed and mounted men fell in behind him. Fargo headed his horse toward the Whetstone Mountains. Yep, if he didn't get killed first, he and Sara were going to have a talk.

"Wyatt," Sara called to the handsome man atop the buckskin horse. "What are you doing out this way?"

Will, who had told Sara of Wyatt's arrival, stood silently behind her.

"You must have left in the dead of night to get here so early in the morning. Get down, and I'll have Carla whip you up some breakfast."

"No, thanks, Sara."

"Well, at least come in and have a cup of coffee."

Wyatt Earp shook his head. "Why are those men standing around outside? There's at least seven of them."

"There were fifteen. Most of them are over at the bunkhouse. I've had a little trouble, but it's nothing I can't take care of. Actually, I think it's finished."

"I came to give you a message, Sara, and I figure you're going to want to take care of it as quickly as possible."

Sara's friendly smile faded. "Someone's seen Dodd?"

"He was in Big Nose Kate's saloon last night. Doc played cards with him, and managed to find out he and a couple of his boys are holed up at the old Silver Spur mine, five miles out of town."

"Will, go get my paint."

"Wyatt and I will go with you."

"No."

Wyatt shifted in his saddle. "Now, Sara, you know—"

"No one is going with me. This is something I have to do on my own. Besides, if he saw three of us, he'd suspect something right away. Go get my paint, Will, and hurry up. I'll change inside. It will save time."

"What about Megan?"

"Maybe it's time she knew the truth."

Will glanced at Wyatt before turning and leaving. He roped a horse out of the corral, jumped on his bare back, then headed him toward the foothills of the Whetstone Mountains.

Wyatt looked down at the woman still standing beside his horse. No one would ever come near suspecting what this petite woman was capable of. "You've made up your mind, huh?"

"Yes. You know I have to do this, Wyatt."

"No, I don't. You don't have to prove anything to anyone. Well, I'm going back to town and wait. You know where to find Virgil and me when you bring Dodd in."

"Thank you, Wyatt. And thank Doc for me."

"I'll do that."

As Sara watched Wyatt ride away, she was already contemplating how she wanted to handle Dodd. She didn't dare let her excitement overwhelm rational thinking. Maybe, just maybe, she would finally have Dodd Elliot at her mercy. But she'd thought that before, and everything had run foul. She turned and went into the house.

Sara took a quick peek into Megan's room as she passed by. While Sara liked to rise early, Megan, fortunately, liked to sleep late. Sara felt sure it was a throwback to when they'd been children and had to get up at the crack of dawn and tend to the chores. Satisfied that Megan wouldn't see her dressed as Hawk, Sara continued on to her own room.

Fifteen minutes later, Sara walked back out of the house, looking nothing like the fresh young lady who had entered. Armed and clad in her buckskins, she was ready to leave. A skirt and blouse lay across her left arm, ready be stuffed into her saddlebags. She glanced up at the hill, glad that Fargo had called off his sentinels.

While getting ready, she'd decided how she would corner Dodd. If she confronted him dressed as she was, he'd recognize Hawk. However, if she dressed as a lady, he wouldn't suspect a trap.

Sara whistled, and a moment later Phew came skidding around the corner of the house. She leaned down and stroked his head. "Well, big boy, this may be our last trip."

Hearing hoofbeats, she turned and watched Will ride toward her, leading her paint horse. The big gelding had already been saddled and was ready to go. Will brought the horses to a halt in front of her, then slid off his horse's bare back. He handed Sara the paint's reins without saying a word.

Sara looked at his black eyes and bruised face. He'd told her what had happened. "You're angry with me, aren't you?"

"What do you expect me to say? 'No, Sara, I think what you're doing is wonderful'? Well, it doesn't work that way. When I first came to this ranch, I felt sorry as hell for Megan for what she'd gone through at the hands of Dodd and his men. But you know what? I was wrong. You're the disaster, Sara. You're the one who has the scars that have festered and won't heal. I hope you don't find Dodd. Because when and if you kill him, you're going to learn the truth. It isn't the answer, and never has been. You've got to cure what's in your head, Sara."

"You're just like all the other men," Sara replied. "Let the sweet woman stay at home while the men go out and get the job done. Well, I have news for you, Will. What happened when all those men went out looking for Rose? They didn't find her, did they? And why hasn't the law picked up Dodd?"

"It's probably a good thing Cyrus got killed by those Indians. No telling what has happened to Rose, and Cyrus wouldn't have been able to handle it if she'd returned."

"You're right. He probably would have turned it around and put the blame all on her shoulders."

Will headed for the corral to put the horse back inside. Sara wouldn't let him help her. He wasn't sure he could handle it should anything happen to her. What he needed to do was leave and get on with his life. Sara would never turn her eyes toward him. That truth had taken him a long time to accept. And she no longer needed him on the ranch. She knew every bit as much as he did. Megan came in a close second. He'd never thought he'd see the day when Megan would go around with a smile on her face or be willing to go to town. Even that could be credited to Fargo Tanner. Yep, it was time he started a new life. Maybe he'd even go back East and join his family.

Sara let him go. She knew he was furious, but so was she. She began stuffing her blouse and skirt into the saddlebags. It suddenly occurred to her that she could probably accomplish more by taking the Mexican blouse and skirt that Penelope had given her. It had certainly worked on Fargo. Thinking about that day and how she'd been so determined to seduce Fargo made her pause a moment and smile before hurrying back into the house.

Fargo crested the hill, by the rocks, and brought his men to a halt. Seeing only a few men by the wall, he smiled. He'd been right. After two weeks of waiting, Sara had fewer men on guard. He was starting to wave his men forward when his gaze came to rest on the big paint horse standing in front of the house. Phew was lying on the ground beside him. After almost giving up hope, he was finally going to come face-to-face with Hawk.

"You boys go back to the ranch. I won't be needing you anymore."

"You sure, boss?" one of the men asked.

"I'm sure."

Fargo heard his men ride off, but his concentration was focused on the scene below. Damned if he wasn't the luckiest man on this earth. Hawk's horse stood in front of the house. After all this time, Fargo had found the man he'd been searching for. Hawk had to be either nearby or inside. Fargo pulled his rifle from the scabbard and waited.

Moments later, a man dressed in buckskins hurried out of the house. Fargo sneered as he hugged the rifle butt to his shoulder. It was too great a distance for a shot, but he could be patient. After all, he had waited a long time for this moment. He watched Hawk stuff something into his saddlebags and then mount up. He was smaller than Fargo would have imagined. A short little bastard, though from this distance it was hard to judge. Still, he figured the man to be only a little over five feet.

As Hawk put his horse into a full gallop, with Phew running alongside, Fargo took aim. A cold, one-sided grin was his only expression. "That's it, Mr. Hawk," he muttered, "just keep coming toward me." He tightened his finger on the trigger.

Hawk veered off to the left, completely changing direction and making a shot impossible. Fargo cursed under his breath. Fortunately, he knew just the spot where he could head off the bounty hunter. He was about to lower his gun when Hawk pulled his hat off and did something with his hair. Fargo stared down the sights of his rifle in total disbelief. The man had auburn hair. Then Hawk made some movement, and though Fargo would have been hard-pressed to explain what it was, the movement somehow seemed familiar. Hawk again turned his horse, this time toward the sun. It allowed Fargo to get a look at Hawk's face. In that instant, Fargo had the answer to it all. Instead of looking for a man, he should have stuck to searching for a woman. But even if he had, he would never have guessed that his quarry was Sara Carter. No wonder she'd refused to expose the bounty hunter!

Fargo had never known such wrath. Not even the death of his brother had had the effect on him that this did. For the first time in his life, he'd been suckered in by a woman who knew exactly how to use the oldest trick known to man—female wiles. She had used him, bedded him, outwitted him, and, like a dunce, he'd fallen right into her trap. Well, this time she wasn't going to get away with it. Seeing the direction she'd headed, he jammed his rifle into the scabbard and turned his horse up the mountain. He and Hawk were about to come face-to-face.

Having seen the sun flash against silver, Sara knew someone had been watching her. Fargo had probably lied again about no longer needing to keep watch on her house. Now not only did she have to use valuable time to find out if she had been followed, but she also had to face the realization that Fargo might finally find out the truth. She made a wide circle, then drove her horse to the top of a bluff, where she could look down.

Having reached her destination, Sara left her horse and Phew. Carefully she crawled onto a boulder from where she'd get a clear view below. She hoped to see Wyatt. He and Will might have made some kind of arrangement whereby Wyatt would follow her and be available should she need help. But when she lay flat on top of the rock and looked down below, it wasn't Wyatt she saw. Her heart ached painfully when she saw Fargo's profile. He had his revolver drawn, waiting for her to come up the trail. Had she not seen the sun flash against something, she would have been at his mercy. The cold, unforgiving look on his face left no doubt that he knew the truth. He'd probably watched her from the time she'd mounted the paint. Would he still be dead set on killing Hawk? Sara wanted to go to him, talk to him, make him understand that, like him, she had a commitment to her family. She slid back down the rock and remounted. Fargo would shoot her before she got a word out. But she was going to make sure she got to Dodd before he had a chance to do anything.

A good five minutes went by before Fargo realized that he'd been tricked. As he circled about, looking for Hawk's—Sara's—horse's prints, his bitterness grew. He thought of all the things that Sara had done. And even when she had known who he was, who he was after and why, she had still made love to him and acted innocent of all wrongdoing. And he had fallen for it. Damn! How big a fool could a man be?

He finally found the tracks, and he realized once again that he'd been outwitted. Somehow Sara had managed to get above him, and the footprints made it clear that she'd climbed upon the boulder. That meant she must have known she was being tracked, and now she knew her pursuer's identity. Did she expect him to be grateful that she didn't ambush him?

Following the hoofprints, Fargo took out after Sara. As he traveled, he remembered the hard blow on the head he'd received when he'd staked out Lou Duncan's cabin. Another gift from the woman he'd wanted to marry. Well, this was one time the jezebel would get a different type of reward for her trouble, and female wiles weren't going to get her out of it.

As Sara rode to the deserted mine, her emotions were at war. For some reason, Will's words were haunting her. She couldn't understand, and didn't want to understand, why. The man she'd lived to kill could be only a few miles away. But Will's words weren't the only thing haunting her. She couldn't rid her thoughts of the look on Fargo's face upon discovering she was Hawk. Pure hatred. From the time he'd arrived in Tombstone, he'd had one goal. And everything he'd done and said had been directed toward the sole purpose of killing Hawk. It was a terrible sight to behold. He had so much to live for. Was she like Fargo? Will seemed to think so. Will had said that killing Dodd wouldn't be the answer. But if she let Dodd live, would the pain finally go away? She didn't know. Yet looking back over the years, she didn't much like the direction her obsession had taken her.

About a quarter of a mile from the mine, Sara dismounted and tied her horse. She removed the clothes from the saddle bag, then quickly slipped the skirt over her buckskin pants. But she'd forgotten about the low scooped neckline of the blouse. Seeing no recourse, she pulled the buckskin tunic off and put the blouse on. A few minutes later, Sara was again going down the road, but this time she was walking. With a limp. She gave hand signals to Phew, and he took off to the side of the mine opening. Sara walked slowly until she saw Phew standing above the mine entrance, ready to attack whoever came out, if necessary. Holding the gun hidden in the folds of her skirt, and before making her limp more prominent, she began wailing. She knew someone was at the mine, because a horse was tethered outside.

Then she saw him. He had a bushy beard, his clothes were filthy and unkempt, and Sara hated his guts.

"Well, hello there, you sweet little thing," Dodd gushed.

Sara could see tobacco juice running out the side of his mouth and down his beard.

"Now, why don't you be a good little girl and come back into the mine with me? I'll fix whatever's hurting you."

Sara hadn't stopped walking. The minute she was close enough, she raised her gun and pointed it at Dodd Elliot.

"What the hell you doin' that for?" Dodd asked angrily.

"Do you know who I am?"

"Hell, no! Am I supposed to?"

"I'm the one who's been chasing you. I'm Hawk."

"Hawk, hell! Who you tryin' to fool, girl?" Dodd had already begun to back slowly toward the entrance. Once inside, he'd be safe. He had all the guns and ammunition he would need. But the low growling coming from behind and above him brought him to a sudden halt. He turned and looked up, recognizing the big dog snarling at him. He jerked his head back around to the woman.

"Do you believe me now?"

Dodd released a grunt. "A damn woman!"

"That's right."

"Just what the hell do you want with me? You've been chasing me all over the country for longer than I care to remember."

"Do you remember the Carter ranch you and three of your men raided six years ago?"

"How the hell am I supposed to remember something that long ago?"

"Let me help you. I'm the one that came out of the barn with the rifle and killed two of your men, and put a shell in your gut. But you got away." Sara watched his dull eyes light up as he remembered.

"So you're the little bitch that almost killed me. Well, if you think I'm just going to stand here and let you do it again, missy, you've got another think coming."

Though Sara had been itching to pull the trigger ever since she saw his ugly face, she'd decided to take him back to Virgil alive. Suddenly there was a gun in Dodd's hand. Too late, she realized he must have had it up the sleeve of his shirt.

A shot rang out. Dodd fell to the ground, a bullet hole between his eyes.

"No," Sara yelled in disbelief. She dropped the gun to her side and spun around. Not ten feet away, Fargo sat astride his horse, his eyes as cold as blue tombstones. His rifle now rested across his legs at the front of his saddle. His right gloved hand sat on top of the butt of his pistol.

"Stop your dog, Sara, or I'll kill him."

Sara turned and saw Phew on the move. "Down!" The dog immediately dropped to the ground. Sara turned to face Fargo again.

"How many others have there been, Sara? How many men have you killed, and how many men have you used?"

"You killed this one, not I."

"I should have let that man be done with you."

"I'm innocent of your accusations, Fargo." Though Sara's words were quiet, she was growing angrier with each passing minute. How dare he curl his lip and treat her like scum? She raised her hand, but before she had the barrel aimed at him, he whipped his revolver from its holster. Their eyes locked, and their guns pointed at each other.

"Were you going to kill me, Sara?"

"I'm not nearly as concerned about what I'm going to do as I am about what you intend to do. Are you going to shoot? Isn't that what you wanted all along? To kill Hawk and avenge your poor brother's death?" Sara tossed the gun to the ground. "Okay, here I am. Shoot me." She watched his jaw muscles twitch, saw his finger tighten on the trigger. But he didn't fire. "You can't do it, Fargo. You not only can't accept your brother being trash, you can't even kill Hawk."

"Don't push me, Sara."

Sara walked toward him, her hands on her hips. "Push you? I meant it, Fargo. I'm Hawk. I'm the reason you came to Tombstone. I'm the reason you made it to the Carter ranch. I'm the reason you bedded Sara, and I'm the reason you're here right now. As I see it, it would be a lot simpler for you to kill me than to hear the truth."

"Start walking to your horse. Just be damn glad I didn't shoot you. I'm taking you to the sheriff. I'll press charges against you for murder."

Ten minutes later, Sara and Fargo were headed back to Tombstone.

"Do me a favor, Fargo."

"Why should I?"

"I know you hate me for what I pulled, and I'm not saying I was right. But I discovered something today. You can't live with hate. It'll destroy you. And I think you're the type of man that if you don't find out the truth about Jude, it's going to haunt you for the rest of your life. My favor is real simple. Stop by Wyatt's house. He was with me the day your brother got killed. He'll tell you exactly what happened."

"I don't need anyone to tell me you shot him."

"But, you see, that's the problem. I didn't do it. The man you killed back at the mine is the man who killed your brother."

"You'd do anything to get out of it, wouldn't you? But that's a stupid question. I've already seen you in action more than once."

They rode back to town, lost in their own thoughts. Sara was bemoaning the fact that she had lost the only man she'd ever loved, and remembering Will's warning about playing with fire. Fargo had been busy calling himself just about every curse word he could think of. Even after she'd used him, made every kind of fool of him, he couldn't have killed her if he wanted to. But he'd damn sure come close

Now he'd let her talk him into something else. He would go to Wyatt Earp's house. Maybe he needed one more good stab in the gut to prove just how vicious a user Sara Carter really was.

Three hours later, Fargo Tanner rode out of Tombstone, headed east. He was on his way to Las Cruces to pick up his brother's body.

At the same time, Sara had her paint headed west toward the Bar C ranch. She kept her back straight and her head high, even though the tears continued to stream down her cheeks. Wyatt had told Fargo what had happened to Jude, and the circumstances behind it. Then he'd gone on to explain what had happened at the Carter ranch six years before, and how that had created Hawk. During the entire time, Fargo had stood looking out the window. His expression had never changed. It was almost as if he'd reconciled himself to what he was hearing.

When Wyatt was finished, Fargo had tipped his hat, said a quick thanks, and walked out of the house. Not once had he looked at Sara; nor had he looked back as he got on his horse and rode off.

As Sara neared home, she didn't feel she could carry on with her life without Fargo. But she knew she would. She'd gone through worse things and survived, and she'd do it again. The hard part was that not until today had she realized how much she loved Fargo. It had hurt her deeply to see the proud man having to hear about the things his beloved brother had done.

Sara looked at the setting sun, and at all the land stretched out between the river and the mountain range. This was her land, and if she never had another thing, she had this. Her papa would have been proud of her.

Epilogue

1882

Dressed in her usual white blouse and black riding skir
Sara Carter lowered the front of her wide-brimmed hat t
block the morning sun, then rested her hands on the sac
dlehorn. She sat silently, staring out across the land. Non
of her men were in sight. They were all busy elsewher
rounding up steers for shipment. She wouldn't be takir
part in it this year. The new cattle boss had everything we
in hand. Right now, he was back at the house, discussir
market prices with Megan. That was why Sara had lef
She wanted to be alone.

Sara gently nudged her Appaloosa forward. So mud
had changed since Fargo's departure a year ago. Will h
sold everything to her, then left, saying he had to get c
with his own life. Both she and Meg missed him.

The ranch had continued to prosper, and there had be
few problems with rustlers, though Sara had heard that I
Clanton was still up to his old tricks. The fight at the C
Corral, between the Earps and Doc Holliday and t
Clantons and McLaurys had taken care of a lot of th

Sara still found it hard to believe that thirty-five shots had been exchanged, with the men only about ten feet apart.

Since that fateful day in October, Tombstone hadn't been the same to Sara. The men she'd cared so much for, the colorful town, the excitement, had passed. The wondrous days of Tombstone were gone. Doc Holliday recovered from his shot in the hip, but left after a fight with Big Nose Kate. Virgil had been crippled and had died six months later. Morgan had also recovered from his wounds, only to be killed later in an ambush. Wyatt, who had received no injuries, had left Tombstone and never returned.

Hearing thunder in the distance, Sara looked toward the clouds lining the horizon. She could already smell the rain and feel the humidity starting to rise, but she continued to hold off heading home. Her mind was still heavy with the past.

It had taken time to get over Fargo's departure. She'd spent night after night crying and telling herself she couldn't live without him. For a long time she'd watched the hill, expecting him to bring his horse to a halt and look down on the hacienda, as he'd done so many times before. She had even tried telling herself that he'd left because he was ashamed to take an Indian home. Eventually the excuses had faded and she'd been left with the bare truth. She should have told Fargo about Hawk the first night. That was the only way there might have been a chance for them. But she couldn't even leave it at that. Even knowing why he wanted Hawk dead, she'd let him make love to her, and she'd made love to him. She had deceived him, and when she'd accepted that she'd begun to heal. With the healing had come other truths. She and Fargo had never known the true meaning of love. They hadn't been prepared for it. And when it had come, they'd

en too wrapped up in their lust, hates and vendettas.
ecause of his cattle and his ranch, Fargo would undoubtedly return someday, if only to drive the herd back
to Texas. But he wouldn't be returning to her. She probably wouldn't even know about it until after he'd left.

Sara smiled as her thoughts shifted to Rose. Her friend
had finally returned home, but she certainly wasn't of the
same disposition as when she'd left. The word *shy* no
longer had a place in Rose's vocabulary. She was vivacious and outgoing. The outlaw had taken good care of
her. Too good. She told Sara and Penelope she had never
known how wonderful bedding could be until the outlaw
showed her the wonders to be shared. Something Cyrus
had never done.

What with Cyrus being dead, Rose sold the mercantile
store and the house to Wilber Pitt, Cyrus's cousin. She left
Tombstone soon after, never to be seen or heard from
again. Sara had a strong hunch Rose had gone in search of
the man she loved.

And then there was Megan. Thanks to Fargo, she now
seemed the more normal of the two sisters. She and Sara
had practically reversed roles. It was Megan who now went
to town most of the time, attending parties and social af-
fairs. Sara preferred to stay home, attending only special
functions. She was finally content with herself.

Lightning flashed, and Sara knew she'd dallied too long.
In a few minutes, all hell would break loose. Her horse was
beginning to dance about anxiously. She spun the stallion
around and gave him his head. Heavy, rolling clouds already had turned the sky dark. Lightning danced all about,
and the thunder was deafening. She had to get to the line
shack.

Sara looked to the top of a long rising hill. There appeared to be a rider astride a black horse and wearing a

black hat and duster. The weather had to be playing tricks on her. Another bright flash of lightning lit the sky. It *was* a rider. Why did he remain sitting there? Didn't he know—

Sara pulled her horse to a halt, oblivious of everything except the man. "Fargo?" she whispered. Her clothes were already soaked from the heavy drops of rain, and her mind reminded her she was in a dry wash. She needed to get to high ground. This type of weather often brought flash floods. Still, she held her horse back. It couldn't be Fargo. He was so still. She had to be imagining it.

A loud clap of thunder directly overhead brought Sara to her senses. She let the reins go slack, and her horse skirted up the side of the hill as if one of the lightning bolts had struck him in the rear.

As she drew closer to the top, Sara's heart began pumping double-time. It hadn't been her imagination. It was Fargo!

She brought her horse up alongside his, and when he smiled she felt it all the way to her toes. "I've missed you," she said softly, finally realizing it had stopped raining.

"Have you?"

Sara nodded.

Fargo tipped his Stetson and let the collected rain roll out the back and down his duster. "I wasn't sure how you'd feel. I stopped by the house, and Meg told me you've not married."

"No one would have me," she said, half teasing. "I've watched over your ranch for you. You've acquired quite a herd in one year."

"I'm making you nervous, aren't I?"

Sara's tenseness finally gave way. "As a matter of fact, you are. I don't know what you have on your mind. Have you come to shoot me, or what?"

"No, I've come to ask you to marry me."

"What?" Sara gasped. "You can't be serious. It's been—"

"One damn long year."

"Do you love me?"

"Uh-huh."

"Well, I don't know. I should think on it." Sara looked down and cracked a smile.

Fargo pulled her from the saddle onto his lap. "Are you playing with me?"

"Uh-huh." Sara wrapped her arms around his neck. She couldn't go another moment without feeling the touch of his kiss. When his lips met hers, she knew she'd been right all along. There never could have been a man in her life to replace Fargo. But this time it was a good love. A solid one they could build on. "Oh, Fargo," she said when their lips parted, "why did you wait so long to come back?"

"It had to do with Jude and making peace with my father. I'll tell you about it later. Right now, all I want to do is hold you in my arms." He'd decided not to tell her about the time spent trying to convince himself he didn't want or need her. Or how he'd finally come to realize he'd been a damn fool to ever let her go. He'd gone through hell during a practically nonstop trip from Texas. He'd worried constantly that she had chosen someone else, or her love had died.

"Sara, I had to leave. I had to work the devils out of my head and come to grips with what was important to me."

"I did the same thing. We loved each other, darling, but it wasn't enough. We needed time to heal."

"You have no idea how I've missed you." Laughing, Fargo swung off the saddle, taking her with him.

As he leaned down, Sara rose up on tiptoes to meet him halfway. It was a glorious kiss. A kiss that Sara had waited one long year for. Never again would she allow anything to come between her and the man she loved. She suddenly wondered if they would be returning to Texas. Realizing they would actually be spending the rest of their lives together brought on a strange, playful giddiness. "You know, you couldn't even handle me back then."

Fargo leaned back and stared at her. "What are you talking about? I had you purring like a kitten," he replied in that honey-soaked voice.

"Oh? Are you sure? Or was it the other way around?"

"I'll prove it to you, my dear."

"Well, it's about time. We have a whole lifetime to talk."

"You're an ornery little minx." He molded her body against his, leaving her no doubt as to his desire.

Still laughing, Sara looked up at him. "Make me purr, Mr. Tanner."

"My pleasure."

* * * * *

TEXAS

TEXAS HEART—A young woman is forced to journey west in search of her missing father.

TEXAS HEALER—A doctor returns home to rediscover a ghost from his past, the daughter of a Comanche chief.

And now, TEXAS HERO—A gunfighter teaches the local schoolteacher that not every fight can be won with a gun.
(HH #180, available in July.)

Follow the lives of Jessie Conway and her brothers in this series from popular Harlequin Historical author Ruth Langan.

Harlequin® Historical

B E L L E   H A V E N

A colony in New England. A farming village divided by war.
A retreat for New York's elite.

Four books. Four generations. Four indomitable females....

You've met Belle Haven founder Amelia Daniels in THE TAMING OF
AMELIA, Harlequin Historical #159 (February 1993).

Now meet the revolutionary Deanna Marlowe in THE SEDUCTION
OF DEANNA, Harlequin Historical #183 (August 1993).

In early 1994, watch Julia Nash turn New York society upside down
in THE TEMPTING OF JULIA.

And in late 1994, Belle Haven comes of age in a contemporary story
for Silhouette Intimate Moments.

Available wherever Harlequin books are sold.

HBELLE-1

COMING NEXT MONTH

#183 THE SEDUCTION OF DEANNA—Maura Seger
In the next book in the *Belle Haven* series, Deanna Marlowe is
torn between family loyalty and her desire for independence when
she discovers passion in the arms of Edward Nash.

#184 KNIGHT'S HONOR—Suzanne Barclay
Sir Alexander Sommerville was determined to restore his
family's good name sullied by the treacherous Harcourt clan,
yet Lady Jesselynn Harcourt was fast becoming an obstacle to
his well-laid plans....

#185 SILENT HEART—Deborah Simmons
In a desperate attempt to survive her country's bloody revolution,
Dominique Morineau had been forced to leave the past behind,
until a silent stranger threatened to once more draw her into
the fray.

#186 AURELIA—Andrea Parnell
Aurelia Kingsley knew Chane Bellamy was her last hope. Only he
could help her find her grandfather's infamous treasure. And the
handsome sea captain was determined to show her what other
riches were within her reach.

AVAILABLE NOW: